FACTS, SMACTS!

BECCA SEYMOUR

RAINBOW TREE PUBLISHING

ALSO BY BECCA SEYMOUR

Zone Defense

No Take Backs | No More Secrets | No Wrong Moves

Fast Break

Rules, Schmules! | Facts, Smacts! | Regular Smegular

True-Blue

Let Me Show You | I've Got You | Becoming Us |
Thinking It Over | Always For You | It's Not You |
Our First & Last | Next For Us

Outback Boys

Stumble | Bounce | Wobble

Stand-Alone Contemporary

Not Used To Cute | High Alert | Realigned |
Amalgamated | Under the Blazing Stars

Urban Fantasy Romance

Thicker Than Water | Weaker Than Instinct

FACTS, SMACTS!

FAST BREAK
BOOK 2

BECCA SEYMOUR

RAINBOW TREE PUBLISHING

Donna, there's always time to spill the balls!
Just don't make it an ice cream flavor.

AUTHOR'S NOTE

Facts, Smacts! is set in Georgia and uses both fictional and real locations and references. The basketball league in both the Zone Defense and Fast Break world is called the League, not the NBA. While I loosely followed the NBA structure, I created my own league and team names, my own competition names, and took liberties to make my fun, low-angst world work.

CHAPTER 1
TYRON

"Fourteen times a day."

"No way. It's gotta be more than that."

I ruffle Brody's hair and snort when he attempts to duck away while sending me a glare. "Maybe for you, kid. You're a regular fartin' machine."

My little brother huffs and bats my hand away when I attempt to destroy his carefully styled hair. I swear, when I was fourteen, I didn't give a shit about my hair. Hell, I still don't.

Admittedly I shave most of it. Who has the time to stand in front of a mirror? Not this guy.

"I do not, asshole."

My grin stretches wide. "You let Pops hear you cuss like that, I dare you."

Once again, he narrows his gaze at me. "Shouldn't you be leaving now?"

"Aw." I clutch my chest. "You tryin' to get rid of me already?"

Brody rolls his eyes, something he's perfected a little too well since I was last home from college. "Yes," he deadpans, causing my lips to twitch. He looks far too much like me when he does that, and a bit like Pops as well. We're all grumpy shits at times.

"You about ready?" Dad steps out into the court-yard where I've been shooting some hoops with Brody before I head to the airport. His smile is soft as he takes us in, and I know he will get sappy in three, two… "I can't believe you're going to be a senior."

"Yeah, yeah. I know, Dad. I'm all grown up and remarkably handsome, considering my weird-ass genes."

Pops catches the tail end of my words when he opens the patio door. He looks between us, eyes staying a few moments longer on Dad before he huffs out a breath. He should be used to Dad getting all sentimental. This is the fourth time he's had to say goodbye at this time of year. Make that eight if we include his goodbyes to my twin sister.

Christ knows what he will be like next year when my other sister Tammy leaves, and then when Brody finally flies the coop, I imagine Pops will have to work triple time at containing Dad so he doesn't hang on to my brother's leg or something.

Preventing him from leaving… I can totally visualize that.

"He'll be fine, Jack," Pops says, moving into Dad's space and wrapping an arm around his waist. He follows up with a kiss on his cheek and whispers something in his ear. I smile over at them, relieved Pops handles Dad so well.

Don't get me wrong, my dad is hardly a shrinking violet. My height is all his, which means he's a tall guy. I also got my fair skin tone from Dad, which is shit as it means I burn quickly in the sun. But he's also got a fierce protective streak and knows how to wrangle four hyper kids while running a successful gym and keeping my much more serious and grumpy Pops in line.

Yeah, I get my outward "don't give me any shit" disposition from Pops. Funny how that works. Dad likes to tease that when they started IVF with their surrogate, their swimmers did a little meshing, blending Pops's crabby with his awesome good looks.

Pops doesn't even argue, probably because we all suspect he's right.

"I know he'll be fine, Mac," Dad agrees, albeit a little whimsically, "but that doesn't mean I'm not allowed to miss him and be sad that he's leaving."

That's my cue to sweep in and give him a tight

hug. He loves this shit—when I initiate hugs and remind him I love him. He's told me more than a million times how he was so relieved I broke out of my dickhead stage when I was fifteen and stopped being embarrassed about showing affection.

Not that I'll admit it, but I was glad too.

Being a sulky fucker is exhausting at times.

That doesn't mean I'm prepared to be all rainbows. Screw that.

Having two dads comes with a shitload of bullshit. My go-to is to defend and keep wannabe shitheads at a distance. Thank Christ, during the first week of training at college, one of my now best friends, Kieran, shared with us that he's gay. It made dropping my guard much easier, especially when our team offered unconditional support.

"You ready, Tyron?" Pops's deep voice catches my attention, and I bob my head, dragging Brody one last time into a hug that he pretends to hate.

"Yeah. Is Tammy still around?" I wonder if I can get one last hug from my kid sister.

"Nope. She's already headed out with her friends."

"Of course she has." I swear Tammy's social life is busier than all of ours combined. And since she turned seventeen, I'm relieved I'm not at home to deal with the army of douches trying to date her. Pops and Dad have it handled, though.

I hug Dad once more, reassuring him it's okay for him not to come with us to the airport—one time of him being the clingy, cringeworthy parent in public was enough—and I promise I'll make it home for Thanksgiving. It tends to be the only time I can get away between practice and games. Last year I didn't even come home for Christmas, heading to Sammy's parents' place instead, as they live just an hour away from campus rather than the long-ass flight it takes for me to come home.

Not long into the journey to the airport, I receive a text from Sammy, asking what time I'm flying in.

I shoot him the time, and he lets me know he'll collect me.

Sammy: 2nite party

Me: Sounds good. Where?

Sammy: Off-campus. Bradshaw's.

I grin. Bradshaw always throws great parties.

Me: Sounds good

"Who's blowing up your phone?"

A quick glance at Pops and he's side-eyeing me, the dark eyebrow I can see arching impressively.

"Just Sammy. Making plans for tonight."

Even though I expect it, I still sigh when he frowns and purses his lips.

"Out with it."

"It's just, it's your last year. You need to make sure you don't take too much on. That means balance and not worrying so much about letting your friends down if you can't go out or something."

"I know that." I can't hold back my second sigh. Pops is a hard-core academic. You wouldn't think it really to look at him. He's got this whole Idris Elba thing going on, and I love mocking him, saying he's too pretty to be so smart. Yeah, you can imagine the clip around the head I get when I say that sort of shit to him, but still, he's smart as hell.

On top of his crabbiness, we suspect some of his brainiac genes shimmied over to the donor's egg.

It also gifted me with a photographic memory. Tricks. There's no such thing as a photographic memory, but I'm pretty damn smart—an IQ of 185. I shit you not. Sounds like bullshit, right? Well, some of my teachers thought that over the years as well. The number of times I've been accused of cheating on a test is no joke. It wasn't until I was in fifth grade that my parents reached out for specialist support and found that my eidetic memory was just a ripple of what my brain was capable of.

"Just remember your end goal. Don't let basketball or other distractions get in the way of your upcoming application. And by that, I also mean take time to breathe."

I bite my cheek to stop the snide remark wanting to break free. He's not being an asshole. Well, not deliberately, but he knows how badly I want this. He knows how hard I've worked to juggle my accelerated program to finish this year with a B.S. and M.S. in Criminal Justice and Criminology. All while training, playing my ass off, and making sure I have time for my friends.

"I've got this," I manage, ensuring there's no bite to my voice.

He huffs out a breath and glances at me as we reach the airport drop-off. "I know you do. I've seen how hard you've worked this summer to make sure you're a step ahead for your final year."

"So I can play and not let my team down." Wanting to do it all isn't a bad thing, right?

Pops pulls up, engages the brake, and turns toward me. The struggle is clear as day on his face. He thinks I should drop out of the Bears this year so I don't screw up my chances of joining the FBI.

It's not only that.

What Pops hasn't come right out to say is he's concerned that I'll take on so much that I get lost. It all links to that balance dig he made earlier.

"You know I need this," I say. It's something I won't budge on. Sure, it means I hardly have any free time, but the camaraderie is worth it. I need the relief of being part of a team with my friends. Plus, it keeps me strong and fit. Above all else, playing with my friends keeps me grounded.

Finally, his shoulders relax, and he nods. "I know you do. Just remember to breathe, okay?"

I snort and lift both my eyebrows high. "Pot, kettle much?"

He shoves at me before tugging me into a hug. "I love you. Be sure to call if you need anything." He squeezes tightly before releasing me.

"Will do." I step out of the car and collect my two bags from the trunk. When Pops calls my name, I return to the open window. There's a new intensity in his gaze, and I immediately know what he's going to say.

"Your sister…"

"Will be fine. I've got her back."

Pops nods, a little guilt registering in his eyes that I have my work cut out for me looking out for my party-loving sister on top of everything else I manage. "Thanks, Tyron."

I smile and tap the top of the car. "You heading to the station?"

"Yeah. My shift starts in an hour. I need to get moving."

"Go fill up on donuts and shi—crappy coffee," I jest, leaning back. "Stay safe, Pops."

He nods once before he pulls away to head to work. I watch him go, dread hitting me as always. While Pops is a kick-ass detective, it doesn't stop the sliver of worry that creeps inside me whenever I leave for college.

I huff out a breath, shaking off the stink of anxiety.

Instead, I focus on this being my final year and ensuring I make the most of it. I crack my neck before heading into the airport. In a few hours, I'll be with my friends, drinking a beer and finally relaxing.

Feeling more at ease, I tug out my phone and distract myself with some more studying.

I wince when I spot Angie at the party. While we didn't start up anything last year, me ending things before they had a chance came out of left field for her. But there wasn't a connection there.

What else was I to do? She's a nice enough girl,

but she wasn't the person I thought she was. We'd been slowly building a friendship, and what I thought was a spark of attraction I was looking forward to exploring, ended up not existing.

One exchange I witnessed between her and a friend made that clear. And while I was polite, it doesn't mean I want to see her anytime soon.

I head toward Sammy and Bentley, who are in the kitchen of the sorority house we're in. Sammy's mixing liquor and pouring it into shot glasses.

"Hey," he greets. "You want one?" He already knows my answer, but he's a good guy, so he offers anyway.

"I'm good," I say with a shake of my head. "You know they use diethylene glycol in antifreeze and brake fluid, right?"

Sammy rolls his eyes before knocking back the shot. "And it tastes delicious."

I snort at his wince. "Sure it does."

He chuckles before reaching into a cupboard. "I hid this for you." In his hands is a bottle of Goza tequila. Other than beer, it's the only thing I drink. It's not full of half the shit of the crap he's mixing up.

I grin and take it from him. "Good man."

He places three plastic shot cups in front of me, and I pour. We lift the shots. "To senior year," Bentley says and knocks back the contents.

I repeat the words and do the same.

"One more." Sammy places his cup down, and I refill it.

Holding the drink up, I look at my two friends. Sammy's close to wasted, but Bentley seems to be holding his own. I won't have much more, not willing to fall on my face and end up on someone's social media. "To kicking ass," I say.

Sammy snorts before drinking up. He seems steady enough that I know I can leave him to it, plus Bentley is the only one who can keep him in line.

"I'll catch you later." I'm feeling restless tonight. Spending the whole summer at home studying, only taking breaks to hang out with my little brother to play some one-on-one will do that to a guy.

I wander around, hoping the answer will come in the form of finding someone I know well enough to have a conversation with or, hell, maybe even see a familiar face who sparks my curiosity. But after ten minutes and avoiding the conversation starters too many people attempt with me, I head outside.

The noise is getting to me, the loud voices rubbing me the wrong way. And while I appreciate so many students telling me they're excited about this year's basketball season, it's hard to give a shit when I want to relax.

Once in the darkness, I step farther away from

the house. Despite the number of residences dotted around the area, it's a big yard. I walk away from the twinkle lights haphazardly tied up at the back of the building and make my way toward where I can just make out some sort of seating in the blackness. It's a rickety wooden bench, and I test it with a shove of my foot, checking it won't collapse on me. When it doesn't wobble, I sit, relaxing in the quiet.

While it's not silent, because of the music and noise from the party, it's much more peaceful here. As I stare at the sky, it's hard to spot any stars; there's too much light pollution around. But the half-moon is bright.

The "Fuck" snaps my attention to the shadows surrounding the house. A grunt follows along with a thud. Alert, I jump up and head toward the sound, my steps quiet, my movement cautious.

I don't call out as I follow the shuffling. There's no one I can see milling around, but I know what I heard.

Once around the corner of the building, my eyes take a second to adjust to the slip of light seeping out of the side window. A quick scan of the area shows me a couple of trash cans and mountain bikes. There's a shift of movement, and my gaze drops to a sneakered foot.

I react immediately, my pulse picking up speed. "Hey, you okay?" Two steps forward, and I crouch.

"Fuck." A groan. "Yeah."

From the gruffness and strain in the voice, it doesn't sound like the guy's okay. "You need a hand? What happened?" My gut tightens.

A grunt escapes him as he pushes himself to sit, revealing his face. Even in the shadows I see the scrape on the side of his temple, and it looks like he has a bruised eye too. "I can manage," he says gruffly, and I ease back, taking in his face entirely.

Surprise flickers through me. "Logan?" As soon as his name escapes, the feeling in my gut pulls taut. A pulse of vibrating energy fills my muscles, making my limbs shake.

I know this guy.

Logan's gaze connects with mine. His wince is immediate; whether from the movement or the fact it's me, I have no idea. "*Fuck*. Tyron."

Well, that clears that up. His reaction doesn't do a thing to release the tightness in my limbs. It does the opposite.

My feet propel me forward, and for the first time, I'm touching him. Logan. I carefully tug him up, but rather than stepping away, I palm his cheek, tilting his head, forcing him to look at me. "Who did this to you?"

You hear that deep-ass grumble in my voice? Yeah, it kind of surprises me too. While I don't like seeing anyone hurt, my reaction to Logan is over the top. But between you and me, I'll be honest here and let you know there's no reining it in.

And why's that exactly?

Here's the thing. Logan Bryce is fucking beautiful.

It's something I thought for the first time last semester, after listening to him interact with the class and the professor in one of our shared subjects. He's eloquent and funny. Smart too.

There's also this embarrassed smile that quirks his lips just so when he realizes he has the room's attention. There's usually a slight flush of his cheeks as well.

That I felt all this had taken me by surprise, for sure. But one thing I've learned from growing up in such an open family is you follow your gut and what feels right.

Last year that meant me staring a hell of a lot.

But now…

After searching my gaze and swallowing, he closes his eyes. "No one. I'm honestly fine."

I should let go of him. The warmth of his skin is pretty damn addictive, though, and honestly, I'm struggling to pull away and release him. It's only when he bites his bottom lip and his eyes flutter open, our stares connecting, that I know me being up all in his space will make no sense to him.

How can it when we've barely made eye contact over the past three years? Not for lack of trying on my part, though. Some of those blushes I just mentioned? Yeah, they may have been reacting to my full-on stares.

Forcing a step back, I scan what I can see of his body, giving him a quick check. His clothes aren't torn or soiled, and there's no fresh blood on his face that I can see either.

With a sigh, he wobbles. Instinctively, I reach for him, holding his arms carefully.

He looks a mess. From the stink of alcohol, he's been drinking a fair bit too.

"What happened?"

"Nothing. I'm fine."

I don't let go, partially because he may fall on his ass if I do, but he's so *not* "fine." The swelling on the corner of his eye is fresh, and the graze on his temple isn't deep. It does trail to a small cut, though. I examine it a little more closely, getting into his space once again. Since he doesn't push me back or try to get out of my grasp, I can get close enough to see it's not deep and won't need stitches.

And I totally don't inhale. Do I want to? Maybe a

little. But I imagine all I'll smell is liquor rather than his enticing scent. *His enticing scent?!* The fuck.

Apparently, I'm more fascinated by Logan Bryce than I realized.

Not that I usually go around sniffing people, but I'm curious about Logan.

"Can you see out of your eye?" I ask, ducking down a couple of inches to see the damage better.

"I see four of everything," he murmurs, his limbs trembling under my hold.

"That the beer, or do you have a concussion?"

He sniffs, a wince quickly following. "Shots." His words don't sound super slurred, so that's something.

"Perhaps we need to get you checked out."

A soft chuckle escapes him, and he wobbles. "You wanna check me out? All you have to do is ask once, Tyron."

Alrighty then. I hold back my smirk, even as Logan's eyes widen. It's as if he can hardly believe those words spilled out of his mouth. This is not the time to be amused by his half-assed flirting, faux pas, mistake… whatever it was. Sober, Logan Bryce is pretty quiet—not to be confused with dull or even an introvert.

Last year he became the treasurer of the

LGBTQIA+ club, and as I mentioned earlier, he's witty. I witnessed his humor many times in class.

As far as I'm aware, other than being the club treasurer and part of the social club, he keeps to himself. Hell, I've never even seen him at a party before. What's brought him here tonight? Did he arrive like this, or has someone done this to him since being here?

Whatever, the answer is one I won't like. Him or anyone being hurt like this is not okay, and fuck if my protective instincts don't rush to the surface.

"Come on. Let's get you inside." I shift to move him. When I do, he stiffens, shaking his head, wincing just once before he stills. "What's wrong?"

"I just need to head home." More certainty and a little clarity enter his tone. His attention drifts to my hands. "You can let me go. I'm not going to fall."

I'm not convinced, but when his gaze jerks to mine, I can see he's on the edge of freaking out or snapping or something. "Okay." Releasing him, I shuffle back a little. "Do you have any friends inside? You need me to call anyone?" The question of who did this and what happened burns on my tongue.

"Uhm, yeah. My friend Michelle's inside. That's who I'm here to meet."

"Michelle Carter?"

"How did you…? Never mind. I'll text her again."

I stay alert as he texts his friend, scanning the area to look for signs of… something, a scuffle maybe. One of the bins is tipped over. There's a gate from the front leading to this side alley. It's a small gate, and it's latched, but there's no lock. To get to the side of the house, I passed a small shed. Angling toward it, I see the door's slightly ajar, and there's no light.

Before I can ask if he came from there, Logan's name is called from the front of the house. It's Michelle. She appears before the small gate, her gaze widening when she sees me before it narrows when Logan turns in her direction.

"What the hell?" She shoves through the gate, only stopping when she's holding Logan's face. "Logan." Clear exasperation colors her voice. "You need to be—"

"I'm fine." Logan cuts her off, and her gaze flicks back to me.

"I've got him," she says, her words a little uneasy. "Thanks for helping him."

I stare at her, gaze unwavering. She doesn't seem overly surprised by his condition. That she just assumes I have nothing to do with this is… I don't know… odd. It's strange, right? Well, obviously I don't go around beating the shit out of people. But it's not like I don't have a reputation for being a cranky motherfucker. People tend to stay out of my way.

I've heard the rumors about me, though. Some are accurate, and most simply hilarious. All I stay clear of and don't bother confirming or denying.

"You need a hand getting him home?"

Immediately she shakes her head. "I've got him. Thanks." She loops her arm through his and leads him away. I watch their slow progress, uncertainty and curiosity vying for the top spot.

If I'm sensible, I should forget this ever happened.

You're smirking, right? Maybe shaking your head a little while scoffing, "Sensible?!"

Yeah, me too.

CHAPTER 2
LOGAN

"Ouch, fuckshitass… motherf…" I end with a pained grunt and pause. Damn, I look like Herman Munster mounted me and held on for the ride. If you have no idea who that is, you didn't spend two precious years with your grandpa, who took delight in introducing you to black-and-white TV shows.

My pause is futile, though. A break isn't going to stop this hurting.

Heaving a breath, I prepare myself for the bite, wondering whether a scorpion's sting would be worse. Hopefully I'll never find out, but the anti-septic makes me wince, grit my teeth, and wonder not for the first time why I do this to myself.

My hazel eyes peer back at me through the mirror. My bruised eye is not as bad as it has been in the past. Yeah, it's already black with traces of purple, but at least I can see through it.

And honestly, it's more on the edge of my eye socket than my eye itself.

I turn my head and examine my jaw. There's a bruise there. This one's not too bad. It'll be easy enough to cover it up. While I don't usually use powder or foundation in the light of day, sometimes embracing cosmetics comes in handy. The good thing is I've got a couple of days' worth of healing before classes start. It should mean there's barely any bruising left on my jaw. My eye, not so much.

Thank Christ for the clumsy persona I don when needed and my "inability" to hold liquor. Who'd have thought silly gossip had its uses. But in these instances, confirming I'm a lightweight who struggles to walk in a straight line without tripping when sober gives me the perfect excuse for the scrapes I get myself into.

Knowing my face is as good as I'm going to get it, I throw the sullied cotton pads in the trash. I need a shower. It'll help with my sore muscles. The energy it'll take to strip down and step inside the cubicle is more than I can fathom, though.

I need a coffee, and probably something to eat.

Despite the stink of alcohol, I'm not actually drunk. Even though my hands are steadier than they were a half hour ago when I legit stumbled at the side of the house, trying to remain inconspicuous while I waited for my friend—yes, we all know how *that* turned out—there's no way I can cook.

I simply don't have it in me.

That means I'm going to have to seek out food elsewhere.

Tugging a hoodie on and making sure the hood is pulled up, I grab my phone and keys. It's only ten thirty, so there will be plenty of places open close by. My college town may not be huge, but it caters well to weekend crowds of college students needing late-night food and snacks.

Once I'm outside, I head toward a small diner that's open 24/7. It's closer to the outskirts of town, but it's worth the long walk as they have the best coffee available at this time of night. The cherry pie is also the bomb.

With each step, I welcome the fresh night air, inhaling it and allowing it to clear my head. Heading out earlier tonight to meet Michelle probably wasn't the best decision I ever made. That it led me to Tyron Channing is mind-boggling.

And then, when he touched me, getting all concerned and growly while being in my space, breathing became difficult. The man is next-level sexy. He's also intimidating as hell, and outside of his basketball player friends, I've never seen him engage with anyone.

Okay, maybe that's a bit of an exaggeration. He shares and asks questions in class, but there's never anything exactly friendly about the exchanges I've witnessed. But then he held my face, practically cradled it, and holy hell, how could I not physically react to that sort of protective care?

A fresh wave of goose bumps trails my skin at the thought, but they quickly disappear when embarrassment floods my system. Jesus, if someone like Tyron found out how I damaged my face and sported enough achy muscles to rival a stint at a demonic boot camp, my humiliation would know no bounds.

I should have just gone straight home.

Feeling defeated and pointedly trying to ignore just how much I want to analyze Tyron's reaction to me, I walk in silence, not even bothering to pull out my phone to watch TikTok. It doesn't take long to reach the diner, a relief since I seriously built up an appetite earlier. You know, from getting my ass handed to me.

I step inside the diner, enjoying the familiar warmth and smells. The summer was a long and lonely one, and being back at college, as well as the familiar diner, goes a long way toward relaxing my shoulders.

Darlene's gaze flicks to mine from where she's standing behind the counter. "Look what the cat dragged in." She makes her way toward me and wraps me up in a hug. Okay, so you're probably wondering why it is I'm getting such a greeting from Darlene, one of the amazing servers here. I don't usually go around cuddling up to people this way.

Long story short, last year she caught me staring at a poster on the notice board here. Maybe she saw me hesitating. Maybe she saw me alternating between nausea and excitement. Whatever it was, she'd all but scooped me up and told me her brother was responsible for the poster. Within fifteen minutes, she armed me with delicious coffee and introduced me to Luce, her brother, who last year became my mentor of sorts.

I'm pretty gutted that he moved out to Atlanta over the summer.

"Hey, Darlene. Good to see you." I happily embrace her, having missed such easy touches over the break.

Darlene steps back and winces when she takes a good look at my face. "That from tonight?"

I bob my head, finding it impossible to hold back my embarrassment. "Yeah," I say, pulling my hood back. There's no point trying to hide. "I'm a little out of practice."

She snorts, despite the concern in her gaze. "Well, you came to the right place. Let me get you a plate of joy to help ease away those sores, okay?"

Warmth heats my chest, and I follow her over to a tall stool at the counter. Sitting here means we can catch up. "Sounds good. Thanks."

A cup appears before me as I sit, and the goddess that Darlene absolutely is pours me a coffee. "Fresh pot." She winks. "I had a sixth sense that someone I adore would need it."

I chuckle and watch as she busies herself, cutting me a slice of pie. "How have things been this summer?"

"Quiet and glorious."

"I don't know whether or not to be offended by that."

She smirks as she places a plate before me, along with a fork. "I've missed you the most, but a quieter town for a couple months is something my feet appreciate."

"Fair enough," I say before I shove a piece of cherry pie in my mouth. I close my eyes and moan at the burst of flavors. This is seriously the tastiest pie ever. The pastry is just the right side of buttery. The cherries the perfect balance of sweet and tart. I moan in appreciation.

"Damn, I'll have what Logan's having."

I snap my eyes open and swivel in the direction of the voice, nearly launching myself off the stool in the process. A large hand reaches out and steadies me. Not for the first time tonight either.

"What are you doing here?" My words are at least three octaves higher than usual, but fuck, Tyron is here. Now. His hand still on me. His gaze focused and unwavering.

He doesn't smile. Nor does he release me.

My traitorous heart picks up speed, pumping fast, my pulse going crazy.

"Are you going to fall if I let go?"

"No." I shake my head, a little dazed by our second run-in. When his gaze flicks to my bruised eye, it's enough to get me pulling myself together. My limbs lock up as I give him a small nod and turn back to face my pie. I'm hoping it's enough to have him walking away or ordering, but his presence at my side remains.

Fighting my desire to take a peek, I instead focus on my coffee and concentrate on taking a sip. Darlene's disappeared into the kitchen, so she isn't a help. Easing out a breath, I take a second sip and notice the sound of voices that hadn't registered earlier.

When I arrived, there were other people around, but my attention had been on Darlene and my thoughts on pie and coffee. I peer over my left shoulder—the opposite of where I know Tyron is still standing. My gaze falls on a full booth of Bears basketball players. I know at least a couple are Tyron's housemates. Only because it's public knowledge rather than me being stalkery or anything.

I turn back to my food, hesitant to take another bite with Tyron standing so close.

"Is the pie that good?"

Surprise has me flinching at the sound of Tyron's hard voice. It's not that he's being aggressive or a dick. It's just unbelievably deep and rumbly. One that speaks of taking no shit.

"Uhm…" I side-eye him when he leans an arm on the counter at my side, his chest and face filling my periphery. "It's okay."

He's silent for a beat. "That moan sounded like it's more than okay."

Heat slams into my cheeks.

"Foodgasms are about sensory pleasure, so I expect your moan reflected that."

Wide-eyed, I'm now openly staring at Tyron. I have no idea how to respond or even if he expects me to.

"It's also a big link to porn, with this thing about women moaning so men know how good they are in bed and that they know how to satisfy their partner."

"Uhm…" It's all I can manage. I seriously have no clue what to do here. But that doesn't stop Tyron, as he appears to be on a roll.

"The thing is, humans aren't the only primates who vocalize pleasure. Baboons and macaque monkeys do."

"Macaque monkeys?" The question is out there before I can stop it. I've never heard of them before.

Tyron nods. "Yeah, macaque monkeys. There's like twenty-three species of them, but it's only the females that do the whole verbalizing thing. They shout to get the dude to come."

He stops speaking and simply looks at me. I now know shit about monkeys and moaning that I never needed to know in this or any lifetime, but Tyron's still staring at me.

"Okay…" Shell-shocked by the random information, I drag the word out.

"So," he finally says, "the cherry pie. Is it just okay, and you were making the noise to make the server feel good, or was it amazing and sent you to a happy place?"

"I—" I close my mouth and squint a little, peering more closely at Tyron. Is he winding me up? Looking for some sort of rise or reaction.

His brows lift in expectation, the first glimmer of some sort of emotion—ignore his whole who-did-this-to-you moment, which I'm sure will make its way into a couple of my fantasies—I've witnessed from him. "It's my favorite pie." I offer a careless shrug and wince at the movement. It pulls one of my achy muscles just a little too much.

"Where else do you hurt?"

I freeze in the cyclone Tyron has caught me in.

When I don't respond, the skin around his eyes tightens. Peripherally, I see his hand twitch, and I have no idea what that's a precursor to.

"Yo, Ty. Come on, man."

I look in the direction of the voice. It's Sammy. One of the basketball players. He's practically being propped up by Bentley. Tyron doesn't look at them, though. His attention remains on me. And holy shit, it's a whole heap of smoldering delicious attention, and from the whirlwind of the last few minutes, I have no idea what to do with that.

"Your friends look ready to leave." Proud as hell that my voice remains steady, I release a breath. "Maybe you'll need to wait another time to try the pie." I sit a little straighter, remembering I have a backbone and also appreciating the reminder that at the table, his team captain, Kieran Kendall, is sitting with his boyfriend. It was a pretty pleasant surprise when a clip of them at a baseball game this summer went viral.

Held hostage in Tyron's intense gaze, I don't even notice until it's too late. But at some point, Tyron took hold of my fork and scooped a piece of my pie. He holds it before him, his stare unyielding, before he opens his mouth, lips closing around the fork.

He pulls it out clean as I swallow hard, my attention fully on his mouth as he chews.

"Delicious."

The one word has me jerking my gaze to his, and then he's gone, moving back to his friends as they gather their things, placing cash on the table before leaving. The whole time, I can't look away. I watch until the group leaves. Focus on them as they walk past the window. It's not until the last second, just before he disappears from view, that Tyron stares straight at me.

"Holy shit." I all but collapse on my stool, managing to grab the counter before I fall.

"I was thinking the same thing."

I lift my head. Darlene's standing to the side, her brows high, and she's fanning herself. "And now you're here!" There's absolutely a whine in my voice.

Darlene's smirk is fast and wide. "I think you did just fine without any help."

I snort, not at all sure about that.

"You want a new fork or…?"

I snatch hold of the damn thing, not even caring

that there's enough heat pouring off me to warm the whole diner in the thick of winter. "I can manage with this one."

"You sure can, honey."

She sets about clearing up the empty table while I fork another piece of pie. This mouthful tastes extra confusing and delicious.

CHAPTER 3

TYRON

THERE'S PROBABLY SOMETHING YOU SHOULD KNOW about me. Hell, maybe you've already figured it out, but I'll spell it out just in case.

I have a tendency to fixate on details or information that I find interesting. Shocking, right? This is the first time since high school that the usually abstract "thing" of focus has taken the form of a very live, very real, and admittedly sexy person.

You've already figured out I'm referring to Logan, right?

Last week all my previous observations and interest slammed forth, smacking me in the face with how intrigued I am.

Hell… I even took a bite of his pie. Who the fuck does that? Me, apparently. But in my defense… Okay, so there is no defense. I acted on instinct. And from the way his lips parted and pupils dilated, I don't think he minded one bit.

Lucky for sure.

But back to my intrigue. That part of my brain won't switch off.

That wouldn't be an issue, but I don't have time for stalking. Okay, not stalking per se, though I have checked out his limited socials, but I don't plan to be a creeper.

Not that it will be possible since everything's locked down tight. Smart and sexy.

What I don't have an issue with is running into him a time or two or giving Brandon Sampson a death stare if he even thinks about taking the empty seat next to Logan.

Fortunately for him, he looks away and heads to another row.

Maybe I shouldn't use such intimidation tactics, but Logan is taking up so much of my thinking time that if I don't get to know him and figure him out, then I will drive myself to distraction.

In silence, I take the seat next to Logan, my gaze on him as he rifles through his bag. I haven't even got my ass comfortable before he's looking at me and doing a double take.

"Logan," I say, dipping my head in acknowledgment.

There's a widening of his eyes followed by his gaze darting left and right. The need to flee is clear on his face, and when his fingers squeeze the handles on his bag, I work hard at relaxing my muscles, hating the idea of him running.

"Hey."

Surprise rushes through me that he hasn't bolted. It's enough to make me relax a little more and actually smile. His brows shoot high, and he swallows hard. From the widening of his eyes before his focus drops to my mouth, I don't think he's intimidated any longer.

Hey, I can be charming when I want or need to be. It just so happens I tend to keep my smiles for people who matter. There's no need to worry about me keeping my ego in check, though. My friends do a good enough job at making sure I keep my head out of my ass.

But still, Logan reacting to my smile is pretty awesome.

That he's not unaffected gives me hope.

"I thought we could partner up in this class. Share notes. Bounce ideas around when working on our assignment." My words hang between us while the class continues to fill up. Confusion bleeds into his features, which I kind of expected. I much prefer when he looks at me with a slightly unfocused expression, as though he's in a Ty haze. "How about I just add you to this doc where I'm going to take notes? You can then add your observations and thoughts if you want to?"

While I phrase it like a question, I'm not really asking. Sure, he doesn't even have to open the document, but I'm still going to add him and give him editing rights.

I quickly go about getting that all sorted, side-eyeing Logan as I do so. He remains staring at me for a few good seconds until noise at the front lets us know Professor Lester is about to start.

I fire off the invite to Logan's email, which I didn't have to go all stealth to find. Our college emails are not hidden away.

When I see him open the doc, a full grin stretches over my lips. I like that he's curious. I also like that it doesn't take long for him to be typing away in the online doc I've created, adding in his observations along with questions he has.

Two things are clear after an additional ten minutes. One, Logan is legit smart and reflective. His notes are clear and concise. The second is this elective is going to be so fucking tedious. Causal Inference for Microeconometrics doesn't scream riveting, I know. But data analysis can be a handy-dandy skill set when joining the FBI. Not that I want to specialize in data. Fuck no. But still, if someone's talking numbers and economic behavior, I want to understand what the hell they're talking about.

Considering the snooze factor, I'm wondering why Logan's taking this course and what his end goal is.

I open the chat on the screen, typing out to Logan:

WHAT TUTORIAL CLASSES ARE YOU IN
FOR COMPUTER LABS?

Logan's typing pauses, and he glances my way. I angle slightly and enjoy trailing my gaze over his face. I enjoy the slight blush even more.

THURSDAYS @11 AND FRIDAYS @9

My smile is immediate. *Same*, I type out. There's a slight tilting of his lips that I savor, and I want to pull more from him.

MY THURSDAY WORKOUTS ARE OVER
BY 10. WANT TO MEET FOR A COFFEE
BEFORE CLASS?

His reaction is less subtle. Logan whips his head in my direction. I look at him full-on and raise a brow in question. His blush is back, and to add extra kindling to the heat forming in my gut, he gnaws on his bottom lip. That I like this look on him is an understatement.

For a moment, he stares at me. It's actually quite impressive he keeps his attention on me for so long. Just when I think he's going to glance away, perhaps type, or simply ignore me, once again he surprises me with a subtle nod. I grin, perhaps a little maniacally, since it's only coffee, but I don't feel like keeping this smile to myself.

How can I when he's just agreed on a coffee date?

I turn back to my laptop and quickly throw down some notes that I half listened to before flicking off another message to Logan. This time with my cell number and the time and place to meet.

When I receive his number right back, I pull out my phone and add his digits, smiling the whole time. Jesus, if any of my friends could see my reaction, they'd be cornering me for an intervention.

The rest of the class goes by with brain-numbing details that, while I'll retain them, do nothing to spark my interest. By the end, I'm ready to stretch and flex my glutes.

"Have you got another class now?"

Logan pulls his focus away from packing up his laptop. "Uhm… yeah. Brain and Behavior."

"Fuck, you're full of surprises. I took that class last year."

"You did?" He tilts his head and studies me.

"Yeah. It was a good class. You have Norris?"

He bobs his head. "Yeah. Is she any good?"

"She knows her shit."

He smiles at my words. "That's always useful." A chuckle follows.

"It is that."

"What about you? Do you have a class?"

"Shit." His question reminds me I need to haul ass. "I have to meet my sister. If I'm late, she'll turn into a drama llama and make me buy lunch."

"Drama llama?"

"Absolutely. No chance I'm calling her a queen. And hell, who has the time for drama and all of the associated bullshit?"

Logan's expression twitches when I speak. It's subtle, but I saw the wince.

My frown is immediate, but before I have the chance to respond, he's backing away. "I'll see you Thursday, I guess." Uncertainty fills his gaze. "If you need to cancel or whatever, just let me know."

"Why would I—" But he's already gone, caught up in a group of moving students exiting the room. Alone, I focus on collecting my things and getting my ass to my sister. While I don't understand Logan's reaction, it won't stay that way for long. Today we've shared a few more words, and we have a coffee date. Something I've never had before.

The date, that is. Coffee I can guzzle by the gallon.

But a date… nope. My time isn't something I give easily to people.

A flurry of excitement bubbles in my gut at the thought of our first date and having some time outside of class to get to know him.

Focusing on that feeling, I make my way to Book Grind to meet Lexi.

My sister isn't here yet, so I order us drinks and savory muffins, surprised to see Tiller here, who I met at the same party that Logan was at. He seems like a good guy, and I'm happy he's joining some of the practices in a pseudo-coach role. We spent time chatting, especially last week. I'm keen to get to know him better, but the coffee place that doubles as a bookstore is busy, and I need to snag a table.

I'm not joking about the drama llama comment. If there's nowhere to sit and eat, my sister will get hangry. She's a mean fucker when she wants to be. Multiply that level of meanness by a hundred when she's hungry.

Fortunately, she has some of my traits that make her personality redeemable, and she can be good fun to hang out with. When she's not being a pain in my ass, of course.

"Please tell me you've ordered." Lexi expels a dramatic sigh as she sits across from me a couple minutes later. "My last lecture went on forever."

"Yes, I've ordered. What did you have?"

"Architectural History and Theory." She rolls her eyes and drops her head back. "It's tedious."

"You've had what, two classes for it?"

"Plenty enough time to tell me I'm going to be bored silly." Lexi pouts, her pink-stained lips sticking out.

"Just make sure you focus and don't skip out."

A second eye roll follows.

"I mean it, Lexi. Pops will blow a gasket if you fail a class on the grounds of you being bored." There were two close calls last year where she barely scraped by with a pass. Pops wasn't happy.

"I won't. Don't go saying shit to him." There's a slight whine in her tone that's wasted on me. Not once have I ever snitched on Lexi.

"When have I ever said shit to Pops or Dad about you?" I narrow my gaze at her.

She scrunches her nose. "Fair point, but I'm sure you've been given orders since it's our final year. Something akin to not letting me screw up."

I snort humorlessly. "One, I'm not your keeper. If you fuck up, Lex, that's on you. And you know Pops only worries."

"I know." She sounds defeated, making alarm bells ring.

"What's got into you? We're only a few days in,

and you're being…." I search for the word, trying to pinpoint what's going on with Lexi. "Fuck." I wipe a hand over my face. "Please tell me this isn't about a douchebag."

While I do get super protective over my twin, I let her live her life. That includes dating whoever she wants, and however often she wants. Within reason. The only time I get pissed off is when she slacks off due to either being caught up in a "relationship" or partying too hard.

Or if the guy is a complete waste of space.

Despondent, she says, "Nathan started dating over the summer."

"Ah." I nod in understanding. Nathan is a genuine douchebag, so I'm not cut up by this information, but Lexi apparently is. I try for brotherly wisdom. "Since only 28 percent of relationships last after college, it makes sense, so you shouldn't be too surprised." I frown when she shoots daggers at me. "What? You weren't even technically in a relationship, right?"

"God, you're an asshole." She scrunches up a paper napkin and throws it at me. I catch it with ease, taking delight in knowing it'll make her pissy. Her narrowed gaze is right on cue.

"Maybe," I say. "But that percentage is accurate. Hell, it's even lower than that, really, since the higher end of that percentage is linked to colleges with religious affiliations."

Our drinks and food arrive, which tears Lexi's gaze from me. She almost inhales the food like a woman possessed. Sensibly, I don't comment as I grab one of my supplements, pick up my coffee, and take a sip. I sigh at the taste, enjoying the rich flavor. Between the caffeine and the guarana, it'll give me the boost of energy needed to get everything done.

"Why do you even know that statistic anyway?" Lexi asks after swallowing a mouthful of pumpkin muffin.

"Rabbit hole."

She nods in understanding.

That's the thing with research. Sometimes I'm centered and focused, so there's no chance of me drifting off into nonessential information. Other times, I'll grab onto one detail, and a brief check on the life cycle of a star will lead me to college relationships and the history of fertilization—the composting variety. Those are the times I follow the maze of the burrow and see where I end up.

"Are you really put out by Nathan?" While I love riling her up, I don't want her to be sad.

She shrugs. "Maybe a little. I thought about him over the summer and considered whether this year we'd finally get serious. We weren't together or anything, so it's not like he cheated." She picks at another crumb of muffin.

"Perhaps just focus on graduating and getting a killer internship."

"You're probably right."

I freeze before slowly placing my coffee on the table. "I'm what now?"

She flips me off.

"I'm serious. Are you feeling unwell? Been possessed by a demon, maybe?"

"Fuck off, Ty." A smile follows her words, taking away any sting. "I'm just saying, if I really want to make it as an architect, I need to get serious."

I shit you not. My sister has rendered me speechless.

The number of times I've had to find and ferry her home since being at college has been exhausting and frustrating. Plus, it hasn't been easy when I've been on the road so much at away games.

"This is going to make me sound selfish as hell," I say, not willing to hold back since I never do with Lexi, "but thank fuck. Another year of pouring you into bed on top of all my other shit—" I shake my head in genuine relief. "—will make my life a whole lot less stressful."

Lexi winces. "I'm sorry. Has it really been that bad?"

Shit, she looks stricken. That's not my aim here. If I'd been truly over watching out for her, I would have said something. "It's not been great," I settle on, "but you've been having fun, and you've been safe. I didn't want to stand in the way of that."

"Jesus." Lexi fans her face with her hand. "I wanted coffee, food, and for us to talk crap, not whatever this is. What the hell, Ty!" She's back to throwing scrunched-up paper my way, cutting through the unusual tension and this impromptu heart-to-heart we're having.

"Okay, okay." I throw a napkin back at her, chuckling when it hits her on the nose. "Serious talk over."

Seeming as relieved as I am, Lexi leans forward, resting her elbows on the table. "So, what are you going to do with all this spare time of not stressing over me?"

Thoughts of Logan pop into my mind. We've already established he's caught my interest, but it's my sister's term of "do" that makes my heart stutter. Do I want to "do" Logan? He's certainly captured my interest enough to get my dick's attention and my brain working overtime. Something that's never really happened before—the combination of both.

"Holy shit, what or rather *who* are you thinking about right now?" Lexi grabs my forearm and squeezes.

"What do you mean?"

"Don't you pretend you're dim and don't understand what I'm asking. Spill, brother."

My gaze connects with Lexi's. There's very little we don't share. Obviously, we don't generally talk about our hookups, but it doesn't feel like Logan would be just a hookup.

Not only that, I don't do hookups. Ever. Kind of impossible to do when I'm a brilliant mash-up of demi- and sapiosexual. Something I finally made peace with a couple of years back after talking to my dads and figuring out why, then at twenty years old, I'd had one sexual relationship. And attraction tended to take a long time to form.

Intelligence is hot as hell. Am I right?

"I have a date."

"You have? Oh my God, with who? Do I know them?" Bright eyes peer back at me. The interest in her gaze that of excitement. And I get it. I've never technically been on a date. My one sexual experience was with one of my high school best friends. Even at prom, I went as a group with my teammates.

"Not sure. Maybe."

When I don't say anything more, she huffs and pushes at my arm. "You have to give me more than that."

"Maybe after my date. If there's a second."

"You suck," she grumbles, not wasting her time pushing. She knows better. "Fine, but let me know how it goes, okay?"

"Okay."

My "okay" is as good as a promise, so she lets it be, focusing instead on inhaling her coffee and talking about what internships she's going to look into.

I make a mental note to do my own research too. It's best she has all the information. Compiling the pros and cons is a given, which will inevitably help here. As soon as I get back to my house, I'll see where I can fit the time in on my planner.

CHAPTER 4

LOGAN

This week's been weird.

Everywhere I turn, I see Tyron. Yesterday I saw him three times. Twice he was with his teammates. They were talking and laughing about something. Thankfully his focus was elsewhere, as I swear every time we make eye contact, I can barely concentrate on anything else but him.

And we make eye contact a lot. Like *a lot*, a lot.

The man is temptation personified. Not only does he have the most piercing, intense gray eyes I've ever seen, but I've seen enough of his body to know that every muscle appears as if sculpted from marble. And hot damn, he's built, as in seriously *GQ*-model built.

Wrap all that together, and I'm confused as fuck. Adding to my "weird week" observation.

Everyone on campus knows Tyron Channing is smoking-hot or unbelievably fit, depending on which way they swing. This isn't new information, but what is new is his attention on me.

Well, sort of. There were a few times last year when I turned crimson when I realized he was listening to me in class, but there were no "moments" (if that's what they are) outside of class.

Then.

Now is a whole other story.

At first, I thought I was imagining it. Thought maybe it's just since the party incident, I was simply noticing more. But that eye-contact thing I just mentioned… yeah, there's been a lot of that. It sounds ridiculous, but when Tyron sets you in his sights, I swear the world around you stops existing. He has this way of capturing every particle of your attention.

Add in the smiles.

Holy-fuck-me smiles. Like, I've seen him smile before. I think. Maybe. Probably when with his friends. I'm pretty sure when the Bears won the play-offs last season, he would have smiled, but honestly, prior to these past two weeks, the name Tyron Channing was synonymous with intimidating, intense, and maybe even straight-faced smoldering? I have no idea if that's even a thing, but he pulls off serious so well, it's impressive.

But back to the smiling.

Every single day when I've seen him, and we've made eye contact, his smiles are immediate, and I swear they're just for me. You may be thinking I have a screw loose or am going completely OTT here, but his smile catches my breath every time. It's beautiful.

He's beautiful.

And now, and more specifically since that first night at the diner when I was embarrassingly banged up, I'm no longer certain he's completely straight.

"Has a straight guy ever flirted with you?" The question spills out of my mouth, but since Tyron has been at the center of so many of my thoughts, I can't hold it in anymore.

Bradley stops what he's doing and stares at me, his surprise evident. Rather than questioning me, he draws his brows together, clearly thinking through his response. "The only ones who have weren't as straight as they thought or at least made out to be."

That's kind of what I figured.

I bob my head, trying to ignore the flutter of wings in my stomach.

"Have you ever hooked up with someone who said they were straight?" Heat hits my cheeks, but I know Bradley won't call me out on it. Bradley's my closest friend. When we met in the LGBTQIA+ social club in orientation week, we easily clicked, so much so, we've been housemates for the past two years.

"There was Rob, who you know about," he says, closing out the admin email. As the club's social rep, he's thick in the middle of pretty much everything. "There's been a few others, which you don't know about for obvious reasons." He studies me, concern etched in his gaze. "You want to talk about something? No names necessary."

I save the Excel doc I've been working on for the last thirty minutes, trying to work out this year's club budget. It's almost done. There are just a few questions I need to ask Jodie, the president. "Maybe." My hesitation is clear.

"No pressure, but if you do want to talk 'straight' boys, you know I'm here for you."

"Go on," I prod, seeing he has more to say.

Bradley pulls his dark-rimmed reading glasses off and smiles. "Just be careful. Closeted guys can be complicated. Men who are 'experimenting' even more so. You know I'm all for hookups, the more regular, the better." He bounces his brows, and I snicker. Bradley is not exaggerating, and more power to him. Hell, I've been a little envious of his ability to score and chase fun and the D, even though it's not my style. "That doesn't mean you need to avoid said individuals, but I also know you don't do casual."

"I don't do anything, more like." I sigh, frustrated that I don't like the idea of random hookups and one-night stands. I've tried. Even got close a time or two, but I prefer dating and long-term relationships.

Not that my total of one boyfriend gives me much experience, but still, it's who I am.

"Hey. None of that. We're all different, and you know how freakin' awesome our differences are."

I nod, trying to absorb his words.

"Speaking of," he says, glancing around the otherwise empty room, "how're things going at The Court?" He doesn't lower his voice since we're the only ones here in the club's meeting space.

I shrug, a little frustrated. "It's *going*, I suppose."

"You still pissed off by your fall?"

I groan and rub my hand over my face. "Well, that didn't help. But the summer and lack of practice really messed things up." I shrug. "I don't know, before I headed home for the break, I finally felt like I was making decent progress. But at this rate, there's no chance I'll be ready for the fall showcase."

"Does it matter if you're not? Can't you be in the one after?"

A huff of breath escapes me. "That means re-enrolling, which I don't want to do. School's going to get more intense, and I can't let my grades slip, not so close to the end. Plus, interviews will start in the new year. Maybe I shouldn't have started to begin with. It's ridiculous."

"No." Bradley shakes his head and squeezes my forearm, offering comfort. "You worked so hard for this, and why you signed up was important to you. To your grandfather."

Emotion swells my throat, thinking about my estranged grandpa, someone who I managed to track down and reconnect with three years ago. It's actually the reason why I came to Georgia for college. Not that I'd ever tell my parents that. Especially my dad.

"I know." I clear my throat, thinking about the promise I made before my grandpa passed last year.

"Plus, it's been so good for you."

"Yeah, all the bruises and twisted ankles have been awesome." I chuckle, trying to find amusement in the situation.

"You know that's not what I mean." He quirks his brow and smiles. "You've changed. *It's* changed you. For the better, I will add. Not that you weren't fabulous before."

I snort at "fabulous." No one else, barring my fellow students at The Court, would ever use that word in a sentence describing me. Just so you know,

I'm not secretly seeking compliments by saying that. But "fabulous" screams so many wonderful and flamboyant connotations.

Logan Bryce is not that.

"I'm serious," he pushes, giving me his "don't you dare argue with me" look. "You hold yourself differently."

"That's because I'm usually limping. Heels fucking hurt, man."

He chuckles. "You're more confident. Hell, I'd even say you've got swag."

"Jesus," I say with an abrupt laugh. "Cool it, yeah."

He tuts. "Fine, but I want a ticket."

"I know. I haven't forgotten." Since Bradley is one of only two of my friends who know what I've, for better or worse, gotten involved in, I've already promised him a ticket to the showcase. He and Michelle. Even though I'm already nervous and constantly have doubts, I appreciate their support. "And on that note, I have to run."

Bradley glances at his phone. "You don't have class yet, right?"

"Not till eleven." Stealthy, I am not. I jerk my attention away so damn fast, trying to avoid eye contact, that I'm less than subtle.

"Huh."

That one response has me glancing at him. He's staring at me intently, a small smirk playing on his lips.

"There's no *huh*. I'm just going for a coffee."

"With Michelle?"

"No." My skin heats again. Since Bradley and Michelle are the only two people I really spend one-on-one time with, it's no wonder he's sus. When he doesn't say anything else, I relent a little. "I'm meeting with someone from class. We've agreed to be study partners."

Immediately his brows shoot so high, I'm worried they're going to keep going and get lost in his hair. "But you hate studying with others."

"That's because I'm the one usually carrying paired or group work," I mumble, shoving my laptop into my backpack.

He nods, knowing this about me. "Which means what exactly about this maybe-not-so-straight boy that you're meeting with?"

"Fuck, really?" I hang my head and scrunch my face before glancing at him. "How do you do that?"

"It's a gift."

"A fucking annoying gift," I mutter.

Bradley shrugs. "Probably to others. But still, what is it about this guy that's made you agree to buddy up?" While there's a hint of teasing in his tone, he's curious and interested in my response.

"I don't know."

His pointed look tells me he knows I'm full of shit. "So he's hot?"

"Well, yes, but that's not why." His lips twitch, but I ignore him, saying, "The guy's smart. Like really fucking smart." Three years back, when I first shared a class with Tyron, I'd practically done a double take. It had taken just three weeks for the rumors to fly about his smarts and another week for those rumors to have absolutely been proven accurate.

"More-than-you smart?"

"Yes."

"Wow."

"Right?"

"And what else? No offense, but there are plenty of other people smarter than you."

I laugh, not even bothering to flip him off since he speaks the truth. I'm not a genius. Rather, I'm dedicated and work hard to get high grades.

"He's… interesting. Confusing but interesting." Which I know is as clear as mud. But you've been there some of the times I've spoken to Tyron, so you understand. He's a walking, talking, basketball-playing, genius conundrum who's also the hottest man I've spoken to (and jerked off over).

"Okay." Bradley claps his hands together, a new eagerness in his expression that's a little disconcerting. "In that case, throw some deodorant on." He shoves a canister he tugs from a drawer at me.

"Nice," I deadpan. "Way to be subtle saying I stink."

"You don't stink, but I know you're going to get all hot and sweaty over this guy. You're so damn thirsty, you're drooling." He stands back as I go ahead and give myself a fresh spray, just in case. "Excellent. Here's a mint."

"I'm not going there to make out. We're drinking coffee and studying."

"Uh-huh."

I'm sure he's going to start tapping his foot or possibly shove the mint in my mouth if I don't hurry up. With a sigh, I pop the mint past my lips, my eyes watering immediately. A second later, I sneeze.

"Do you need me to check for boogers?"

"Fuck off." I grab my bag and flip him off, all while the asshole is snickering. "I'll see you back at the house later."

"Yes, and I'll be happy to hear all the details you're willing to share." He winks. "Have a good time."

My stomach flips over. The silliness has been a great distraction, but it's time to meet up with Tyron.

Here goes nothing.

The first few minutes are awkward.

We did this whole skit about who was paying for the coffee, which Tyron won. Then I was taken aback when he held the chair out for me as I sat. I shit you not. He legit held the back of the chair as I sat and did this whole scooting-it-forward maneuver before he sat opposite me, a small smile on his face and a little pink in his cheeks.

But thank God he can hold a conversation. After all that, I had no idea what to say or do. We're here to discuss the course and how this whole buddying-up thing will work, but I've never done that before, so I have no idea how to ask without sounding like a prize doofus.

With that in mind, I let him lead, and since this is the second time he's made me chuckle, I ease back a little more, my shoulders not as tight.

"That's what I said," he says, a look of approval in his gaze. While his eye contact is still intense, I've decided I like it. It's as though I'm his sole focus. "The guide didn't appreciate it."

I smile around my sip of creamy coffee. "How old were you?"

"Twelve. I was on a trip with my dads. They did the whole warning about not dropping a penny from the top and didn't appreciate me explaining that a penny wouldn't kill someone."

I chuckle, my brain snagging on the "dads," as in plural, but I work at pushing it aside. "Did your precocious twelve-year-old self give them a lesson in velocity?" I can just imagine a younger version of him. He was probably already six feet by that age. I can visualize him schooling the guides and their reaction.

"I may have." He smirks and stretches his one leg out, his foot brushing against my calf. I jolt at the contact, my heart speeding up, but I don't move it away. Neither does he. "Dad was convinced they were going to kick us out as I may have taken over the guide's job at one point."

Laughing, I shake my head. "Do you do that a lot?"

"What, take over tours?"

"Not that exactly, but, I mean, you don't seem to mind being the center of attention and, uhm… imparting your knowledge." Realizing how that might sound, I add, "Not that I have an issue with it.

I think it's good to share knowledge, especially when you're correcting misinformation."

For a beat, he studies me, and it's impossible not to react to his scrutiny. Once again, my pulse speeds up. This time, it's the worry that I might have offended him somehow. I don't think I have, and Tyron seems like the kind of man who doesn't offend easily.

"I've been known to stop a conversation in its tracks a time or two. I also have no issues with being the center of attention, as long as it's for the right reason. Have I been called a smart-ass?" A one-shoulder shrug punctuates his question. "Too many times to count."

"Does that bother you?"

"Heck no." Tyron shakes his head. "I rarely make people come across as dicks."

"Rarely?" I quirk my brow.

"Well, some people deserve it, and really, they're the ones making themselves look like ignorant assholes. I may just be good at shining a light on it. It's also rare as I don't tend to give my attention to people who don't matter."

I part and close my lips, looking super attractive, I imagine, because that sounds all levels of self-involved. It kind of gels with the perception of Tyron I had two weeks ago.

"You think I sound like an arrogant dick, right?"

I snort. "Well, there's no arguing about how perceptive you are." He smiles and waits for me to respond. "I suppose it comes across as arrogant," I admit, getting the feeling Tyron will appreciate the truth. "As though you don't speak to anyone who's beneath you." I half expect him to cut in, but instead, he watches me, curiosity sparking in his gaze. "But I don't think that's accurate."

"No?"

I shake my head. "No."

"So what do you think it is, then?"

I hesitate for the briefest of moments, taking in the brightness of his gray eyes and the way he's angling slightly toward me. "I think you're good at reading people, maybe. I also think that you've learned not to give a shit about what people say or think about you." I lean forward a little, unable to resist searching his perfect features. "But I've never heard or seen you being an outward asshole. You've never been… mean."

His brow quirks at my word choice, and my cheeks warm. I wave his reaction away. "I couldn't think of a better word."

"Mean's a good word." He arches a brow at me, and I swallow hard since we're still leaning close. "I think I'm not the only one here who's perceptive. It's an attractive quality."

His words have me jolting back in surprise. As soon as I do so, embarrassment floods me. Jesus, what a way to make an impression. There's nothing like a whole-body jerk to let a guy know you're awkward as fuck.

Thankfully, he doesn't call me out on it. He doesn't laugh or even widen his eyes.

I clear my throat. "So, you didn't get kicked out?" I need a safer topic. Then there's the whole study talk that needs to go ahead. You know, the whole point of this meeting.

"Nah. Pops flashed his badge even though we were out of his jurisdiction when the guide started grumbling and edging on being ridiculous."

"Your dad's a cop?"

"My pops is. He's a detective. My dad co-owns a gym. He runs the place."

The information takes a moment to percolate. Two dads. Fuck. Is it bad that I'm envious?

It takes me a beat to realize we're sitting in silence, and Tyron is witnessing, no doubt, multiple emotions flicker across my face. There's no judgment I can see or even feel coming from him. He seems to be letting me take my time.

Rather than firing the hundreds of questions I

really want to at him, I settle on: "You have siblings other than Lexi?"

"Yeah. Two. Another sister who's a high school senior, and a pain-in-the-ass brother who's just turning fifteen." There's a gentleness in his tone I haven't heard before. "How about you? Siblings?"

"No. I always wished for one, though. I wouldn't have even minded a sister." I don't elaborate that my parents wished for a "decent" child, too, one that hadn't destroyed my mom's womb or decided to embarrass the family by "choosing" to be gay.

Those weren't quite their words. Mine are certainly more palatable.

I pick my coffee up and drain the cup, not wanting to think about my parents.

"So," I say, wanting to get back on track. Sure, it's been nice getting to know Tyron better, but we're here to work, and Tyron is far too distracting. "Us studying together, it's not something I've done before." I wait for my earlier embarrassment to hit, but it doesn't arrive. Tyron's put me at ease, making me feel more secure that he's not the type of dick-head jock you watch in college movies. Thank Christ. "I'm not sure how you want it to work or what you want to achieve," I admit.

I've spent time looking over our shared notes. Tyron even went through and responded to my observations and questions. What he thinks I can offer him boggles my mind. It's abundantly clear that I'll be the only one getting anything out of this partnership.

Tyron is back to studying me for a beat. "Data interpretation isn't the most fascinating of tasks," he says. "I thought working with you would make it more interesting."

His tone is so casual and matter-of-fact that I find myself nodding and saying, "Okay. I can understand why most people don't find it that interesting." Somehow I ignore how his words affect me. How I'm the one who'll make things interesting.

"Which is why I'm wondering why it's one of your electives." He eases forward, arms on the table, his hands super close to mine that are clutching my coffee cup.

"Oh." My brows dart high. "I uhm… actually find it super fascinating," I say, almost sheepishly.

"In that case, I definitely made the right decision asking to partner. Maybe I can feed off your passion."

Holy shitballs. Is it me, or did it get hot in here? Speechless, I fumble my grip on my cup. While it's not deliberate, it gives me a reason to look away. I go to take a sip but remember it's empty.

"You want another coffee?" His hand lands on my

cup, ready to take it off me, his fingers making contact with my skin.

Honestly, that's not me releasing an undignified squeak, because that would just be embarrassing and unnecessary. Jesus, I have no idea what's wrong with me.

Trying to calm down, I clear my throat. "No, thanks. It's probably almost time for class." I have no idea if it is or not. Not once have I reached for my phone to check the time. I've been too focused on the man before me.

He pulls his gaze away and glances at his cell. "Shit, you're right. We need to go if we're going to make sure we get a workspace next to each other."

I swallow back my surprise that his concern lies in us sitting next to each other rather than us being late.

Tyron stands, his large palm clasping my backpack, which he heaves on his shoulder. I have no idea what the hell is happening here.

"I can take that." I reach for it but stop midway at the shake of his head.

"I've got it." And then he's practically herding me out, opening the door, and letting me step through. Meanwhile, my head is spinning, and I have no choice but to let him take the lead. My head's too foggy to do anything other than follow.

"Thanks," I mumble as he releases the door behind him.

Once we're out in the fresh air, I inhale deeply, trying to get my head together. Heck, who am I kidding? My emotions are all over the place. Tyron is pushing so many buttons I didn't even know I had. The crush forming is so fast, so ridiculously big, I'm relieved he's not a mind reader.

Having the hots for Tyron is unexpected, and I'm not quite sure how sensible it is. I have enough going on in my life. Which immediately makes me think of my extracurricular project.

I have no idea what Tyron will think if he finds out, and honestly, I'm not comfortable sharing this with anyone new just yet.

CHAPTER 5
TYRON

Workouts are grueling. By the time our strength coach is done with us, I have enough sweat pouring off me, no one in this room will need to visit Niagara Falls any time soon.

"Get your ass up off the tiles, man." I wedge my foot in Leon's side, nudging him. He's a hyperventilating puddle, but the locker room floor is gross. Just the thought of a black light in here makes me shudder and nudge harder. "Seriously, you only have to look at these tiles and you can catch MRSA."

"Fuck, Ty. I'm dying here," Leon grumbles, but he starts to peel himself from the floor.

"There are better things to die from, and you don't want pus-filled bumps on your ass."

That gets him moving more swiftly. "Jesus, I wish you didn't know so much shit."

I snort. "Your pus-free ass thanks me for it, though." I grin at him as I head for the shower, needing to get the sweat and stink off me.

We're just three weeks into the school year, and the schedule Coach has got us on is fierce. While technically it's not more time-consuming than last year, our win put a shitload more focus on us. We've still got time before the season starts, but that doesn't stop Coach from thirsting for the title.

Hell, nor the rest of the team, including the new blood that's joined us this year.

"Are you meeting with Tiller later?" I call out. There's no point in making it clear who I'm speaking to. Every bit of free time my housemate has these days is spent "training" with Tiller. Yeah, I totally air quoted that word.

"We've got some plays to go over." Leon's voice is steady, but if I could see his face, I can guarantee there'd be a trail of pink blazing up his neck and across his cheeks.

I won't be an asshole and call out that I can imagine what type of "plays" he's going over with Tiller. At the moment, the rest of our friends are completely oblivious to Leon and his intense after-hours coaching. There's no chance I'm rocking that boat. Hell, I'm more than happy to take the heat off my friend when and if he needs it. We all have our quirks and discoveries to make.

Take me, for example. My sexuality is somewhat of a gray area in the team. They know I don't date, but only a couple have a firmer handle on what that means. The interest I have in guys—admittedly, one guy with the exception of one subscription service I'm a member of—is not common knowledge.

It's not about hiding it. Nor is there going to be a big coming-out statement. Why would there be when I'm unapologetically me?

"So you're not coming out for pizza?" I call out to a chorus of groans.

"No pizza," Kieran shouts. "Once a week, Ty. That's the agreement."

I scrunch my face, washing the suds off under the spray. Fucking Kieran is a hell of a captain and friend, but he's an asshole. I hate it more that he's calling me out on a half-assed promise I made to reduce my pizza intake to once a week. Apparently, pepperoni pizza, even if I add a few veggies, doesn't fill my healthy-eating quota.

It's a fact I've spent the last few years ignoring until the stupid promise I made under duress.

"Fucker," I grumble, making sure the word isn't hidden under the sound of water hitting my skin.

Hearing some of the guys snicker, I roll my eyes.

Maybe I should make it a mission to find out their vices—though most I obviously already know—then dangle said vices in front of them only to snatch them away.

Finishing off, I head out of the shower, get dressed, and check the time. It's coming up to 9:00 a.m., which means I need to get my ass into gear. I have class over in the Thomas building, right next to Tantor House, which happens to be where Logan has class at nine.

If I get a move on, I should be able to catch him. He's usually five minutes early.

I quickly grab one of my guarana tablets and wash it down with a swig of water. I'm going to need the energy boost to get through the day after this morning's session.

"Right, I'm out. Text me if anyone's around for lunch." I make a hasty exit, taking advantage of my long legs and powerful stride to cut through the foyer, then the courtyard. I feel eyes on me most places I go, which isn't meant to be as conceited as it sounds. It's just the way it is. But I ignore the looks, the second glances. The only people I have time for are my friends, my sister, and most recently, Logan Bryce.

It's the latter that's causing a few second glances. Not so much with my friends, as they haven't witnessed my hyper attention, nor do they actually know I've started dating the guy. Not that they'd give a shit either way. I'm just not ready to share this with anyone. Not officially, anyway.

If anyone asks, I'm not going to conceal it, but it's no one's business what Logan and I are to each other.

I pull out my phone, smiling at Logan's response to the text I sent him this morning. It's something we do all the time now—exchange texts. At first, his responses were short and a little delayed, but not so much anymore. It's a relief since life's so busy. We've only managed a couple more coffee dates and a picnic-style lunch. But with Coach telling us tonight's practice is now running this afternoon instead, it means I finally have a night not stuffed with commitments.

And I know just the person I want to spend it with.

Checking the time, I smile. With a few extra minutes to spare, I'm able to grab Logan a coffee. I've done it a few times now, handed him a fresh coffee as I'm passing him by. The blushes and sweet smiles are totally worth the effort.

Hell, I can't wait till we're finally alone so I can kiss that sweetness out of him. While we haven't discussed it, we're taking this slow. And I'm more than okay with that. Since I've never kissed a dude before, the build-up is all levels of sexy, the anticipation riding me perfectly.

And while it doesn't happen often, I like kissing. It's warm and comforting and sends my body into sensory overload. It also helps me get out of my own head. Which, come to think of it, is a bit of shit since I'm not up for kissing any random.

Once I have his takeout coffee, I head toward the building where I hope he'll still be. If he's not there, I have no issues going into his class. I don't want him to be uncaffeinated. The man's love for coffee rivals my own.

When I spot him leaning against the wall, my chest tightens. I didn't think that would ever be a good feeling, but I swear it's the best. Spending time with Logan, talking to him, and even texting so often has become one of my new favorite things. Just the thought of him takes me to my happy place. I like the sensation a lot.

Logan laughs as he reaches out and flicks Bradley's ear.

I'm not worried about their interaction. Knowing Bradley is Logan's housemate and best friend, I'm happy he has someone he can hang out with. Someone who makes him so at ease that he's able to smile and laugh.

I know, I know, I sound like the biggest pussy ever, but I don't give a shit.

Bradley spots me first, his eyes widening when my trajectory is clear. He stands a bit straighter, confusion bleeding into his gaze. I offer an up-nod, never having actually spoken to the guy before.

At my silent greeting, color floods his cheeks. It's enough to get Logan frowning and following his line of sight. Our gazes connect, pink flushing his skin, and how I freakin' love the heavy swallow that has his Adam's apple bobbing.

"Tyron." Did you hear how breathy he made my name? Fuck yes. Hottest sound ever.

My smile is instant and just for him. I pass him the coffee. "For you."

He takes it, the pink turning to a bright red even as his lips curve. "Thanks. You didn't need to do that."

"Didn't need to but wanted to."

"Tyron Channing." Bradley saying my name draws my attention to him. My smile disappears as I take him in. He may be important to Logan, but I don't know the guy.

"Bradley Hoffman," I say in response.

His mouth hangs open before he seems to recover, his attention flicking to Logan. "You know Tyron Channing?"

Huh. Refocusing on Logan, I tilt my head as I take in his reaction. It seems like he hasn't told his friends about us either. That's more than okay and something that we'll need to talk about. If he had spoken to his friend about me, I wouldn't have minded. It's not like I asked him or technically need to keep us a secret.

Logan's gaze flashes to me before moving to his friend. "Uhm… yes, we have a class together." It's clear Bradley has more to say or ask, but Logan continues, "And I best get into my class now."

"Can you give me a moment with Logan? I need to talk to him alone." I glance briefly at Bradley, happy that he nods immediately.

"Sure. I'll catch up with *you* later," he says pointedly to Logan before leaving.

"You okay?" I ask as soon as we're alone, stepping a little closer. I'm officially in his small bubble, liking being near enough to catch the scent of his minty shower gel.

"Yeah." He peers up at me. "And seriously, thanks for the coffee."

"You tend to function better with two coffees in the morning." When surprise flickers in his eyes, I smile, saying, "I pay attention."

"That you do."

"So," I start, nerves fluttering in my gut, "training's now this afternoon, not tonight. Freeing me up."

"O-kay...," he says slowly.

"I thought we could grab a pizza tonight." I just won't tell my friends that's my plan. You saw how they reacted earlier. I'm usually more disciplined, but sharing my favorite food with Logan is something I don't want to miss. "I should be ready by six."

When Logan doesn't respond straightaway, I wonder if he's already got plans.

Before I get the chance to ask, he says, "Yeah, sure. We've got that pop quiz coming up." He nods.

"On Monday, yeah." We have. No idea why he's mentioning it, though. We've already started prepping. Maybe he's struggling with a concept. "We can go over extra revision if you need to. I've got a pretty good handle on it."

When he smiles, my shoulders relax, relieved that seems to be what he's worried about. "Of course you do," he says. "You have a handle on everything."

I chuckle. "Well, not quite everything, but I study hard to make sure I give it a good go."

His gaze softens, a look I like on him. "You work your ass off. I have no idea how you stay so dedicated or how you find the time."

A little embarrassed at his compliment, I shrug self-consciously. "If you looked at my planner, you'd see where I build in times to take a breath," I joke. Well, sort of.

My planner is an elaborate combination of colors and tasks. Life's busy, which means I have to build in time when to call home, let alone when to take some free time. The only thing that hasn't made it on there yet is Logan. Which, honestly, is freaking me the fuck out a little.

It seems I'm willing to grab any moment I can with the guy. Scheduled in or not.

A rush of students starts to sweep past us, making their way into class.

"I best go. Just text me the details, and I'll meet you there."

"I'll text you, but I'll come to your place so we can walk together," I counter.

A small smile appears on his lips. "Okay. I'll send you my address."

I watch him leave, openly ogling his ass. This isn't anything new—my focus on nice asses. What is new is the stir in my pants when I wonder what it'll be like if I slide my dick between his ass cheeks.

Once he's out of sight, I pull my mind out of the gutter and haul ass to make it to class on time and without a minute to spare. Jesus, there's nothing like cutting it close. I need to keep a better eye on the time. It's not Logan's fault he's so distracting.

Trying to push my excitement for our dinner date aside, I tug out my laptop and focus on my class. This is one I need to be acing. Sure, I'm on top of the reading material. Ahead, in fact. But the whole point of a lecture is to provide additional information and thoughts.

I make copious notes through the lecture and even work out what the focus of my assignment is going to be. It puts me in an even better mood that gets me through practice with a smile on my face. Okay, I'm smiling inside. I don't want to give Coach any reason to ride my ass.

I push hard and run drills, making sure to practice the plays I'm instructed to. It's a relief when the clock stops, and we're not given extra runs as everyone's been making time.

Still, after two and a half hours, I'm exhausted. And hungry.

It's only the thought of seeing Logan that keeps my eyes from drooping. Usually, with nights off like these, I'd study and have an early night—meaning by eleven thirty—try to catch up on sleep. The sometimes 4:30 a.m. alarms take their toll.

But I have a date to get to.

"Hold on. I'll come with you," Kieran calls.

I pause at the locker room door and peer over at

him. When he reaches my side, I step out with him, saying, "Actually, I'm heading out."

"You are?"

"Yeah. Got a date."

"What?" His hand snaps out, resting on my forearm, stopping me in my tracks. While he's smiling at me, his surprise is comical.

I roll my eyes. "It's not that big of a deal." Okay, it so is a big deal. I really like Logan. Since I'm not ready to share just how much I'm into him yet, I tamp down my eagerness, ensuring my expression remains neutral.

Narrowing his gaze at me, Kieran squeezes my arm lightly, the gesture friendly. "Don't do that."

I won't insult him by firing back "what?" Instead, I crack my neck, letting some of my guard slither away. It's shit of me to try that on Kieran since he's one of my best friends.

"Talk to me." There's a widening of his eyes when I feel heat travel up my neck. "Holy shit." He tugs me away from the door when we hear movement coming from the other side. Once there's distance between us and the building, he finally lets go and turns to face me. "You really have a date."

"We've already established that." I quirk my brow at him.

"No shit, wiseass. This is the first time I've known

you to go out on an actual date. You must really like this girl."

And there it is.

The assumption, which I totally get and am not at all pissed off about—that it's a girl who's finally caught my attention. How can I be annoyed since it's not something I've ever shared?

Having gay parents meant I grew up thinking long and hard about my sexuality. It's how I eventually opened up to them about where I thought I sat on the awesome rainbow spectrum.

Since getting to know Logan, my interest's soared, and my cock's constantly rock-hard with possibility. Apparently, it has a few years to make up for.

"How serious is it?" he continues, curiosity lifting his brows when I don't respond immediately.

"This isn't our first date," I settle on.

"No?"

"We're dating." I shrug a little too casually, unable to hold back my smile when I think about Logan. "I'm dating. Shit." I chuckle. "Never thought I'd say that for a while or like the sound of it so much."

Kieran clasps my shoulder and squeezes. "I'm happy for you, man."

"Thanks. We haven't talked labels or anything. I haven't done the whole: Will you be my boyfriend thing," I say, rubbing the back of my neck in embarrassment. "Honestly, it sounds lame in my head, so I know for a fact I'll feel like a dick saying it aloud."

Kieran's practically bug-eyed. "Boyfriend?" He's staring at me like I'm an alien species. "Boyfriend? You meant to say that, right? It's a guy? You're dating a guy?"

He looks so flummoxed I can't hold back my laugh. "Jesus. Do you need a paper bag or something? Since you have your very own boyfriend, I know I don't need to explain the basic principles to you." While I'm teasing, I'm not so much of a dick to recognize this is a shock to him. It will be for all my friends. Hell, even my family is going to do a double take.

Not that I'm not going to enjoy getting a rise out of them all. Just a little.

People are so easy to screw with. It's one of life's small pleasures.

"But—" He cuts himself off with a shake of his head. His reaction plays out like a movie. I see the moment he pulls himself together. Recognize when he balances his kick-ass captaincy skills with that of a newly out-and-proud gay man.

One who's also a good friend.

"Okay." A nod joins the word, the movement resolute. "I can't wait to meet him when you're ready.

And I can absolutely recommend the boyfriend gig. It's pretty fucking awesome." Warmth fills his tone, no doubt thinking of Dean, who these days tends to be attached to his hip. I'm actually kind of surprised he's not here waiting for him after training.

Their being loved up is weirdly cute. But I'm especially happy that Kieran came out publicly over the summer. No longer hiding away, he's less tense. I can't begin to imagine what that was like for him. It's a shit of a thing, and I'm grateful I've always felt safe enough to be unapologetically me.

My parents have done a pretty great job.

"Thanks, Key." I clap him on the shoulder. "I need to get going. I don't want to be late."

"Okay. See you later." He bounces his brows. "Or not."

I snort as I walk away, mulling over my decision not to share Logan's name.

Considering the time I've been spending with him, it's not a difficult task for my friends, or anyone really, to work out who I'm dating if they pay atten-tion. Me shifting gears from barely acknowledging Logan to hanging off his every word is a giant neon sign letting people know something's changed and that Logan has snagged my attention.

I shove my hands in my pockets as I walk the

couple of blocks to Logan's house, quietly calling bullshit at me "mulling things over."

One of the reasons I'm being obvious as fuck by being glued to his side while not yet fully committing to saying his name to my friends is those bruises.

It's so unlike me not to push and prod until I get answers. Not to come right out and ask. That I haven't done so sits heavily in my chest, and I'm not a fan of the feeling.

If I wasn't attracted to Logan and definitely not racing toward boyfriend territory with him, I have no doubt I'd already have the answers. Shit, just after the holidays, I'll be filing my application for the FBI's Collegiate Hiring Initiative.

And that right there is at the heart of everything.

I like Logan a lot. More than I've ever liked anyone. Sure, it's only been three weeks, but my attraction and interest grow every text exchange and second we spend together.

What if I don't like what I discover? What if his injuries are something I'm best off not knowing? What if it's something illegal? Which then causes a gigantic fucking problem considering the stringent FBI background investigation.

While I can't ignore getting answers forever, I want to enjoy our first dinner date. Savor spending time with him. And hopefully get the chance to finally kiss him.

With renewed resolve, I loosen the tension in my shoulders, and a short walk later, finally reach his house. A quick knock on the door and I'm not left waiting long.

Logan's before me, his hair swept back and styled, a light blue shirt with the top two buttons open, and dark jeans that I'm eager to check out his ass in.

"Hey," he says, just as I say, "You look good."

Flushing, he stares at me a little wide-eyed.

"Told you, you looked good" is hollered from somewhere behind him.

Logan's blush deepens, and he waves a hand dismissively in front of him. "Ignore Bradley. He doesn't know when to keep quiet."

"You want me to ignore him even though he's right?" I lean against the doorframe, raking my gaze over him.

"Uhm…" He clears his throat. "Thank you?"

My smile is instant. "No problem. Just speaking the truth. You ready to go?"

Logan wipes his palms on his jeans. He's trying to be subtle, so I glance away from the action. "Yeah, sure. Let me grab my laptop."

Frowning, I ask, "Why? I thought we were going for dinner."

"Well, yeah, but then there's the pop quiz we talked about."

"Right, yeah." I nod. "Well, we can do that after. Maybe come back here and spend a bit of time going over any questions you may have."

There's a slight hesitation as he drags out the word "Sure?" But there's a lilt to his tone that sounds very much like a confused question.

"It's fine. I can make the time. I have a late start tomorrow." I step back so he can come outside.

"You do?" he asks as we make our way down the street. The pizza place I like is only three blocks away. The evening so far barely has a chill, so it'll be a pleasant walk. "What time's late for you?"

"Seven."

Logan snorts. "That's the crack of dawn territory."

I smile. "True, but it beats having to get up even earlier when I have to be in the weight room at five or something."

"Jesus. More power to you." We cross the street. "When's your first game this season?"

"November seventh against Carolina."

"Are they a good team?"

"They can hold their own. We haven't lost a game

to them in five years, though." I indicate up ahead to the pizza place. "This okay if we eat here?"

"Definitely." He shoots me a small smile. "I love this place."

"Yeah? Me too. Pizza is life."

Logan chuckles. "I'm a pizza fan. Not as much as you, maybe?"

"Was it the drool that gave it away?" I arch a brow as I hold the door open for him. Immediately, the blush I've come to expect touches his cheeks.

"Thanks," he says, briefly making eye contact before peering ahead.

What I like about this joint is there's a more casual section at the front of the restaurant that's set up with easy-to-wipe tables for fast food and pizza-by-the-slice purchases. At the back is a cozy area with checkered linen. While not fancy, it's quaint and romantic. I've never eaten in this section before. Tonight, I'll be changing that.

"You want to sit anywhere in particular?" Logan's eyeing the available tables.

"I've booked a table in the restaurant." I watch his expression, hoping he'll be pleased.

"You have?" His brows arch.

"Yeah. Have you eaten in the back before?" When he shakes his head, a tingle of warmth washes over me, happy we can check out the restaurant together. "Perfect. I've never eaten out back either."

I indicate he should step forward, and we head down the short corridor. When I spot Luca, the owner's son, I return his smile.

"Tyron, your table's ready for you." His attention travels to Logan. The look of appreciation settling in his gaze is immediate.

While I'm friendly with Luca, since he works at my favorite place to eat, that look right there is not one I like. I step closer to Logan's side, my smile dropping and my palm moving to the arch of Logan's back. The catch of Logan's breath is quiet, but standing so close to him, I hear it clearly. And fuck if I don't like his reaction.

Luca sees my move, which was the point. The asshole's lips twitch, but he sensibly stays quiet as he leads us to our table.

There's candles and soft music, and holy shit, this place is romance personified.

The bubbles of nerves popping in my stomach take me by surprise, but my steps don't falter as we continue to our table, my hand not straying from Logan's back.

By the time we're sitting down and have ordered drinks and food, I'm feeling more at ease. That's mainly because of the soft smiles Logan sends my way. Sure, he's a little wide-eyed and startled, but that's okay.

"So you have a couple of months before the season starts for you," he says. "How do you manage to balance all that on top of your degree and your master's? 'Cause you play regularly, right? It's not just a once-a-week thing?"

I like that he's not a hard-core basketball fan. Not that I won't be talking him into attending as many home games as possible. But with basketball taking up so much of my time, being with Logan is a welcome relief I didn't realize I've been craving.

"I'm not going to lie. As soon as the season begins, every aspect of my life becomes even more intense. Sometimes we'll have back-to-back away games, which means I can miss a whole week of classes. We have a guaranteed twenty-five games this season. More if we reach the tournament."

His brows lift, and he takes a swig of his beer. "And that's on top of your, what did you say, about twenty hours of training a week?"

I nod. "It's not necessarily on-the-court training, yeah. But that's how much time we spend on average doing strength training, running drills, and watching tape."

"So, how *do* you balance it?"

"The summer vacation, I researched and got on

top of all the reading I need to do to carry me through till January. Every chance I get, I work on my assignments and do additional studying for exams." When I see his frown and worry appear in his gaze, I'm quick to add, "But I'm on top of it all, so it means I'll always make sure I have time for you."

Rather than ease his frown, his brows scrunch up further. He shakes his head. "Don't worry about me. I'll get through everything just fine. Not that I don't like hanging out with you." At his admission, he smiles almost shyly. "From November, I'll have more free time anyway, making it easier."

Almost immediately, he clamps his mouth shut before glancing away and taking an extra-long gulp of beer.

"Why November? What's happening then to free you up?"

"Oh, just a project's coming to an end. It's not a big deal. So, do your dads manage to watch many games?"

The switch in topic is as obvious as a neon flashing sign. Rather than push, I answer, "Only a couple of times a year, if I'm lucky. It's a long flight, and getting time off can be difficult. They were there for the championship game last season, though." They were proud as hell too.

"That's great and understandable, considering the

distance." He places his beer down and gnaws on his bottom lip.

"What is it?"

"I've only been to one game, which was when Michelle had a spare ticket. Maybe I'll make a bigger effort this season."

"Yeah?" My smile is immediate, as is the stumble of my heartbeat. "You just let me know, as I have access to four tickets a game. I usually give them all to Lexi and her friends."

"Oh, I wouldn't want to take one if her friends usually go."

I shake my head. "One will definitely have your name on it. Whenever you want. Every game, even. Two if you want to bring a friend." From the way he shuffles in his seat, I probably need to tone down how intently I'm focused on him. It's hard with the flickering candlelight and the way shadows dance over his features, highlighting his strong nose and cut jaw.

It's taking everything in me to keep pulling my stare away from his lips as it is.

"Well, thanks. That's really generous of you." He tilts his head and studies me back, and I'm more than happy to have his attention on me.

"No problem. You coming and cheering me on is hardly a hardship," I tease.

He chuckles. "Is that what I'll be doing?"

"Damn straight. Fuck, I may even have to get you a Bears jersey with my number on it."

Even in the dim lighting, I see a blush spread across his cheeks. His lips part just so, and I wonder what it'll be like to kiss him and trace my tongue over his bottom lip.

My dick nudges against my zipper, encouraging me to make that happen as soon as possible.

Our server arrives, drawing my attention away from Logan's mouth. Probably not a moment too soon, as I'm on the edge of dragging him out of here and finding a dark corner to finally sweep him up in a kiss.

"Thanks," we both say, and we chuckle before we dig in, enjoying the fresh dough and the tangy spice of the pepperoni.

CHAPTER 6
LOGAN

From the candlelit restaurant to how he met me at my door, everything so far about this night screams date. The thought makes me giddy.

To have an actual date with Tyron, especially if this is what a pre-study session dinner looks like, would no doubt blow my mind. I can only imagine how much more gone for the guy I'd get if that ever happened. Because, yeah, he's ridiculously charming and irresistible. How could I not be wishing for the impossible?

The impossible in this situation is my mouth on his… well, anything he's willing to let me touch or lick or suck.

Just three weeks since I entered the Tyron Channing Twilight Zone, and my crush is so intense, warning bells are my constant companion.

Despite the loud alarms trying valiantly to protect my heart, the "what if he *is* interested" keeps growing louder. Foolish of me or not, I'm not willing to silence hope just yet.

It's dark by the time we step outside.

For over two hours we've talked about everything and nothing. I've learned even more about his family, his team, and his plans for the FBI. The latter still blows my mind while also seeming somehow to make perfect sense.

Never have two hours sped by so quickly. Certainly I've never spent so long in a restaurant simply enjoying someone's company.

"You really didn't need to pay." I glance up at Tyron, secretly delighted by his offer.

I don't date often. Not that that's what this is. The one relationship I've had was with a guy who was super amicable and split the bill exactly fifty-fifty. Right down to the exact penny, which is all fine, but being spoiled every once in a while is something I'm not used to. It feels good.

The attention from Tyron is sweet. It should be unnerving considering the way he's making my fantasy date plans run away with me, but him paying like that... I'm going to sound like a dipshit here, but it feels special.

He makes me feel special.

"But I really appreciate it," I add on, my gratitude earnest.

He peers over at me as we walk side by side on the street in the direction of my place. We're so close, our shoulders are brushing. The touch makes the sensation in my belly heat warmer. Not quite as much as the inferno earlier when he'd guided me into the restaurant with his palm just above my ass. This touch is more subtle and comfortable.

"No problem. The food was good. The company even better." He adds on a wink that has me tripping over my feet. Immediately, he snags my arm.

"You okay there?"

"Uh-huh." I nod, feeling a little breathless.

Tyron Channing *winked*… at me.

Before you go rolling your eyes, think back to everything you know about this guy. Sure, he's funny, and I know he can be loud with his friends. But flirting and full-on teasing, and a sweet wink… It's all making my axis super wobbly.

He's not at all what I expected, which I'm sure I've said before. But it's absolutely worth mentioning again, as the conundrum Tyron is proving to be has firmly planted himself into my heart.

I focus on not falling on my face while every cell in my body sparks to life.

Tyron's still holding my arm.

And holy shit…

Once again, my breath catches. This time it has everything to do with how he trails his palm down my arm and loops his fingers with mine.

Jesus. I feel like I'm in high school all over again with the way my heart and stomach are flipping out at such an innocent gesture.

But this is *huge*.

Tyron Channing is holding my hand, and it feels… right.

We walk in silence. Not passing anyone along the way. Our college town can be sleepy. It makes the moment feel even more intimate.

"Do you still want to do some extra studying for Monday?" The gravel of his voice sends a fresh ripple of awareness along my skin. It's a slow caress that I cling to.

A little confused by his question, since that's the purpose of our getting together in the first place, I simply nod.

"Cool." He squeezes my hand a little, pulling a fresh smile to my mouth.

In what seems like the longest and most intense walk in history, we finally make it to my house. By the time I open the door, after reluctantly releasing Tyron's hand, the wings in my stomach are fluttering so fast, it's likely my feet are going to leave the ground.

There's music coming from Bradley's room. Thank God. His witnessing it isn't something I want, and I don't want him to scrutinize me about this. Honestly, at this point I wouldn't even know how to begin to explain what's going on between Tyron and me. All I'm sure of is that I seriously need to get control of myself.

I lead Tyron inside, heading toward my room.

With every step, I remind myself that I'm not a virgin. Nor is this the first time I've studied with someone in my space. It hasn't passed my notice that thinking of Tyron in my sanctuary, I immediately thought about sex. I'm not even apologetic.

He's incredible in so many ways. Just thinking about his dick and what beautiful damage he could do with it sends a fresh buzz of awareness through me. And there I go again. Getting so way ahead of myself.

That need to get back under control is right there in my head. I just need to grab on to it.

Once we're in my room, I turn at the sound of the door closing behind us.

Tyron's before the door, a muscular, powerful presence that sucks the air out of my lungs. No smile lifts his mouth, but his eyes, those crazy intense grays that captivate me, hold me hostage.

I need to speak.

I need to get a grasp of this situation.

"I didn't think… didn't know… are you…?" With too many thoughts buzzing about my brain, I slam my mouth shut, since I can't seem to form or finish a full sentence.

Studying me intently, Tyron eases away from the door, moving toward me. It's predatory, and hell if I don't feel like even if I ran, there'd be no escaping. And holy shit, I like the feeling a lot. Heat blooms in my gut as he draws closer.

"Am I what?" The grumble of his voice makes me swallow. He's about a foot away when he says, "You can ask me anything."

A whoosh of relief joins my shaky breath. "I thought you were straight." I can't *not* put that out there.

He stays silent, still studying me. When I raise my brows, silently indicating it's his turn to speak, his lips twitch. "That's not a question."

His words do the job of cutting through the thread of tension pulled taut between us. I snort. "Fine." I smile despite my nerves. Direct it is. "Are you gay, bi, or something else?"

A crackle of energy forms and seems amplified as I hold my breath. I want him so fucking badly that his answer could quite possibly slay me. Isn't that a fucking riot?

"I'm definitely not straight."

Is it hot in here? I swear an inferno has ignited somewhere deep in my chest.

"You're not?" A wide grin that I have no chance of holding back forms.

"Definitely not."

There's still space between us that I'm desperate to erase, but the tightening of his eyes tells me he has more to say. When pink crawls up his neck, I follow the journey in wonder.

"I'm usually better at being super clear and transparent," he says, rubbing his hand over his shaved head. There's a coyness I've never seen from him before in that one move. "Sorry we haven't talked this through, and I haven't been clear."

My wonder turns to full-on surprise. That Tyron can be so endearing is not the revelation it would have been a month ago. "It's okay, but you don't have to come out to anyone. That always has to be done in your own time and when you're ready."

"It's not that," he says. "Honestly, I'm not a big-announcement kinda guy. I suppose that's where I went wrong, and I should know better. Hell, I do know better."

Now I'm just confused.

"So, full disclosure. Demi- and sapiosexual… I'm a happy balance between the two. Add bi in there, too, for good measure."

Surprise jolts through me. While I'd wondered if he was gay or bi, maybe even pan, demi never crossed my mind. Making the assumption he was a bit of a sexual animal was pretty lame of me, and I wince internally. Just because he's on the basketball team doesn't mean he's constantly putting out. Logically I know this, but yeah, back to those cringy assumptions I had.

Aware my brain is buzzing over this information, I pull myself together and smile. "Thanks for telling me." My head does keep snapping on sapiosexual. That he finds my intellect hot is a big turn-on.

"I've been curious about girls mainly. Even had sex once with a friend."

"O-kay." I drag the word out, still not accustomed to this level of honesty and oversharing. It's refreshing and notches up my respect for Tyron even more.

"A lot of people think you have to be in love to screw around, but that's total bullshit. It's all about the connection. And when I feel it, my dick doesn't have an issue one bit." The slow gaze of my body follows. It's a long sweep down and up before his gaze meets mine. Heat licks along my skin at the invisible caress, along with the knowledge of what he's telling me.

We have a connection.

The temptation to look at his groin to see if he's hard for me pulses in my veins, but I hold back, refusing to look away from his penetrating stare.

"There's actually one porn star who I get off to as well."

There's no holding back how my jaw drops nor the flush traveling up my neck. The visual of him jacking off dries my mouth. I lick my bottom lip and swallow hard, liking how his attention drops to the movement. "Yeah?" The question is a croak.

He nods, gaze latching back on to mine. A smile plays on his lips. "Oh yeah. Only the guy's solo scenes, and only since I discovered his interviews and audience chats. He's smart and funny."

That it's a guy he gets off on hardens my cock. I like solo scenes, too, and have spent many hours getting off to my favorite subscribers.

"But you're the first guy in real life who's got my dick genuinely hard."

Fire pulses in my veins at his admission. "I…" I swallow hard. "I get your dick hard?" Holy fuck. The confirmation punches my cock against my pants.

He chuckles, the laugh transforming his usually serious expression to a thing of beauty. "It's always hard. I can be reading a text from you, and bam… stiffy. Hear you laugh, and I'm close to jizzing."

Ho-ly shit. What the hell am I meant to say to that? Thank you? Thank fuck? Maybe I don't say anything at all and simply pounce on him.

"My experience is nonexistent in this situation," he continues. I nod in understanding since, based on what he's said, I'm the first guy he's wanted to explore with. At least, I hope that's what he means. I'm more than up for exploring with Tyron.

Whatever I said in the past about baby-bis—about me staying away—let's just ignore that. Fickle is my middle name, apparently, but I like to think I wouldn't give it up so easily for just anyone. The past few weeks, I like to think Tyron and I have become friends. If not friends, friendlier.

Him buying me coffee and tracking me down makes me think the former for sure. This chemistry between us is something I'm unwilling to ignore.

I release a shuddery breath, wanting to step up and make this easy on both of us. "You can kiss me if you want."

The flash of heat in Tyron's gaze is immediate. It's also the only warning I get before he steps into my space, loops one arm around my back, cups my cheek with the other hand, and finally presses his lips to mine.

The tenderness isn't totally unexpected. How can it be when Tyron has obliterated any preconceived notions I had about him?

A ghosting of his lips and the sweeping of his tongue are all it takes to have my breath hitching. When I do, he shifts the hand palming my cheek to my nape, and lightly squeezes. It's the precursor to Tyron kissing me senseless.

Our mouths move with an ease I've never experienced before. Every touch ratchets up my pulse, every lick threatening to short-circuit my brain.

I'm absolutely in this.

Tyron tastes of spice and certainty. I drink down the flavor of his kisses, desire rippling across my skin.

The way his larger body and thick muscles wrap around me hitches my breath. I press my body against him, chasing contact. Responding immediately, his large hand clamps my ass, tugging me in.

With our jean-clad groins touching, I no longer need to wonder if Tyron's hard. His length is thick steel as it pushes against my pulsing cock. I shift, seeking friction. At the movement, we groan, capturing the sounds as we continue to kiss and grind.

"Fuck." The word tears out of Tyron, and our mouths part. "You're so hot."

Taking in his flushed skin and blown pupils, I grin. "I think it's safe to say you're hotter."

He quirks his brow and dots a kiss to my mouth. Before I can capture his lips, he eases back. "It's not a competition, but if it was, this is one I'd happily lose." Tyron searches my gaze. "Do you still need help with the pop quiz?"

The question takes me a moment to catch up, my brain hazy and my needy cock drawing my attention. "Uhm… I suppose we can study."

"You mentioned it earlier. Did you not need help?"

I give a slow shake of my head. "Not really." When he remains silent, as if waiting for clarification, I add, "I assumed that's why we were meeting today. Dinner and studying."

Two lines appear between his eyebrows. "Just dinner and spending time with you. That was my plan anyway."

Happiness sparks in my chest. "Yeah? You just wanted to hang out?"

Tyron assesses me a beat, a tinge of pink appearing on the apples of his cheeks. "I told you earlier that I've had sex before, but it was with a friend I cared a lot about and I found attractive. We dated for a short time before college."

I nod.

"So you know I've read a shit-ton of books and observe the hell out of people."

I did know this. Even having his genius IQ confirmed hadn't come as that much of a surprise. There'd been rumors about him around campus.

"But dating isn't so—"

A hard knock on the door cuts Tyron off. Bradley's "You decent?" follows. The asshole only pauses for a second, not giving me time to answer before he opens the door.

"Shit, sorry, I didn't—"

Instinctively, I jerk out of Tyron's arms, my wide eyes on Bradley before my gaze narrows. "When you knock, you wait for an invite," I grouse, the interruption making me genuinely pissy.

Red hits Bradley's cheeks. "I know. Shit, you shouldn't have to remind me. You know I'm used to a house with open doors." He scrunches his face and shoots a glance at Tyron. "I have seven siblings," he explains with an apologetic shrug.

I look at Tyron, who doesn't say anything. The tendons in his jaw seem tight, as though he's clamping his teeth down. A glance back at Bradley, and it's no wonder it seems like he's close to shitting himself. "Did you need something?" I ask, wanting to get him out of here and rid the room of the tension.

"Yeah. Your dad and mom have called on the house phone." Sympathy fills his gaze when I wince. "They expect a call by nine. Your cell's off."

I bob my head. I turned off my cell deliberately, knowing it would be worse if I'd just silenced it and let any calls ring out.

"You were at the library for a study session." With that, he casts another tentative look at Tyron before edging out of my room. "I'll speak to you later."

When the door closes, I angle toward Tyron. The apology on my lips is cut off by the hard flint in his gaze.

"Is there an issue with me being here?"

Startled, I shake my head. "No, of course not. Why would—"

"It seemed like you couldn't get enough distance between us when Bradley entered the room."

Understanding slams into me, and I'm quick to say, "That's not what I was… well, I was, but that was about protecting you. It's not my place to out you. I didn't know if you wanted to share this part of yourself with anyone."

Tyron Channing does silent stares far too well. Each second feels like an eternity as the intensity of his gray eyes holds me captive.

"Thank you." Air rushes out of me at his words. "That was thoughtful of you but unnecessary."

His response has me asking, "So, do your friends know? Are you going to be publicly out?" With the news of Kieran, the Bears' captain, coming out as gay over the summer, I know that it can be a big deal in the world of college and pro basketball. Sure, it's ridiculous, and I'm sure every LGBTQIA+ person in the world dreams of a day when coming out isn't an actual thing anymore, but this is the shit we have to deal with. Day in and day out sometimes.

"Kieran knows there's a guy, but not your name yet. But I don't plan on a public announcement." There's a minuscule shake of his head as his words penetrate, and a sinking feeling settles in my gut.

I like Tyron a lot. The kiss was phenomenal, and I absolutely want to get up close and personal with his cock. But hooking up with someone in the closet fills me with dread. That's what he means, right, about not going public? While he said my moving away was unnecessary, maybe that was just about Bradley and assuming he could trust him.

Which he can.

"That's your call for sure," I say, offering a supportive smile despite the disappointment tightening my chest.

Before I can say anything else, the sound of the house phone my parents insisted on having installed starts ringing. The dread in my stomach renews. "I have to take this call."

"Okay. Do you want me to go?"

"Not want," I admit, even though it would be more sensible to nip this in the bud now, "but my parents are difficult, so it's probably best." I hold back my grimace, wondering what Tyron will think about my dad's attempted hold on me and my life.

I wish I was exaggerating.

When I told my parents Brixham U was my school of choice, Dad was pissed. He then went on to ensure his company became a generous donor to the school. That should give you an inkling about the type of person my dad is.

The phone stops, which means I really have to go, as Bradley will have answered it.

Curiosity burns in Tyron's gaze, but rather than pushing, he steps into my space and peers down at me. "I'll see you tomorrow."

"You will?" My voice is quiet.

He gifts me a smile, one that makes my belly flip, and I'm sure I've discovered my kryptonite. "You definitely will." He punctuates his words with a gentle press of his lips against mine. His fingers ghost over my cheek in a sweet caress. Pulling away, Tyron captures my gaze before heading for the door.

When he's gone, I find myself rooted to the spot,

only getting my ass into gear when Bradley appears and passes me the phone.

"Good luck," he mouths. A step back, and he leaves me alone, closing the door behind him.

I take a deep breath and hit Hold on the phone.

"Sorry for keeping you waiting. I was just drying off from a shower." I force a smile, hoping the action will prevent my anxiety and frustration from traveling down the line.

"Your father wanted to speak to you earlier, but he's now attending a meeting." The only emotion evident in Mom's voice is disappointment that she's been forced to make this call. "Your father wants you home over the Christmas holidays."

Shock has me holding my breath, but panic notches up my pulse. No way am I heading to my parents'. College offers me a sanctuary, the only place that helps to keep me sane and away from them. When I said goodbye at the end of the summer break, I intended it to be the last time I'd be home, unless a miracle of some sort stopped my parents from being controlling, homophobic assholes. That and Dad had a change of heart about me eventually joining the company he's the vice chairman of.

"You know how important the holiday period is for me to get ahead of my studying without distractions," I remind her, my tone calm and even.

"Without that time, I wouldn't be able to maintain my GPA." My high GPA and my subject choices are the only reason they tend to stay off my back.

"Your father insists. He's invited the O'Connells."

Alarm pulses in my head. No chance in hell I'm going. Mr. O'Connell is a bigger prick than my dad. He's also the CEO of FSB Yellen, specifically for wealth management. Not only do I have no plans to ever work for a bank or for FSB Yellen, but using my degree or skills to work for anyone linked to my parents is not going to happen in this lifetime.

"I'm sure Mr. O'Connell will be the first to understand my need to maintain my GPA," I say calmly, ignoring the sweat beading my brow as I try to figure out how to get out of this. I rack my brains, inspiration forming when I think about Tyron and our studying together. "I've actually already organized study sessions and a small research project with a classmate."

The sigh that reaches my ears is not happy.

"While I don't want to disappoint Dad, the sessions were approved by one of my professors," I lie. At this point, I'm willing to forge a transcript if necessary.

"The research project is for one of your professors?"

"Of course." I scrunch my nose, hoping she buys my bullshit. "I can hardly back out now."

"I see. I'll speak to your father, and I'm sure he'll be in touch."

Silence follows, and I don't have to check to know she's put the phone down. I do, anyway, just to be sure. I toss the phone to my bed, relieved the call's over and thankful it was Mom I spoke to. Dad would have given me a lot more shit.

While I expect I will be hearing from him and his complaints, the time it will take to come up with a nonexistent project to tell him about will be worth it.

I need to get through a few more months, and I'll be home free. College will be paid for, I'll be qualified, and hopefully, I'll have been successful with my Financial Crimes Enforcement Network application in their graduate program.

These are the plans that keep me going and why I don't tell my parents to go fuck themselves. Not yet, anyway.

While being beholden to my parents is a stress that never fades, I can't wait for the time I can let them know I'm working for the government in FinCEN. I may even do a video call so I can see my dad blow a gasket. Working for the government will get a worse reaction than when I told them I was gay.

I'm banking on it.

I shake my head and focus on anything but the call with Mom.

Tyron.

Just the thought of his name makes me smile and my heart flutter.

That kiss.

I touch my lips, recalling with ease how he chased my tongue and captured my breath. The knowledge of him not coming out creeps into my mind, a black shadow of disappointment. It's a feeling I'm used to, so it shouldn't surprise me, but the hollowing in my gut makes itself known.

Am I a fool for wanting to see where this connection with Tyron leads? At this point, I'm not interested in what's rational, nor how it's important I protect my heart. How can I when I remember his taste with such vividness?

Tomorrow. That's when he said I'll see him again. Not even a stern talking to could keep me away.

CHAPTER 7
TYRON

I MAY HAVE FORGOTTEN TO TELL LOGAN ABOUT THE fundraiser taking place today, but between our dinner date, our first kiss, and then his obvious stress about the call with his parents, it slipped my mind to let him know.

I did send him a text this morning saying I'd collect him at one forty-five and for him to wear clothes he could get wet and dirty.

Yeah, I may have added a devil emoji and had all sorts of delicious thoughts about Logan being both of those things since then. It's been years since I've wanted to get hot and heavy with anyone, and after that kiss, I'm on board for so much more.

There's a chemistry between us that gets me cranked up. Blowing my load while jacking off to thoughts of him is my new favorite thing. I'm eager to switch it up and put coming *with* him at the top of my list, though. If he's down with it.

"Whose car's this?" Logan asks as I open the door for him. From the shy smile he tips my way, he appreciates the gesture, so I'm pleased I followed Pops's lead on this one. It's something he always does with my dad.

"Sammy's," I say before I capture his mouth. A surprised squeak follows as he leans into the kiss and opens for me. Tightening my hand on his waist, I allow myself one more sweep of my tongue against his, then I pull away.

Eyes closed and mouth slightly parted, Logan appears blissed out. The look is one I store away, liking it a lot.

He peers back at me and smiles. "Be careful, greetings like that will stick, and I'll be expecting them all the time."

I grin at his teasing tone. "It's a hardship I think I'll manage."

"Is that right?" Bright-eyed, his stare is questioning and open.

"Absolutely. Maybe we need to agree to say goodbye the same way." I quirk my brow at him and step fully away, indicating for him to get in the car. He studies me for a beat, his face flushed before he shakes his head a little and sits down.

After closing the door behind him, I make my way around, aware his gaze follows my movement. I'm used to being openly watched. It usually pisses me off, but I like Logan's attention.

Once settled and pulling away from the curb, I say, "We're heading straight to Sudscape."

"The car wash, right?"

"Yep. Car handwash fundraiser is about to start. We do a few small events over the year, and usually one bigger, more formal one. Some we join with other school teams for, but this one is all Bears."

"So you've dragged me out to put me to work, huh?"

Grinning, I cast a quick glance at him before turning my attention back to the road. His smile is big, and hell if he doesn't look delicious in the sports shorts he's wearing today. That tee has to go, though.

"You know it. But this one's worth it. The cash goes to the local immigration center, helping people get back on their feet, providing kids with school supplies and stuff too."

"That's great. It's good to give back."

"It sure is. Speaking of," I say, peering over at him and letting my gaze trail over the monstrosity of a T-shirt he's wearing. I don't even have to finish before he shoots me a cocky grin.

"There a problem?" The asshole's lips twitch.

"There will be if any of my friends see you wearing that."

His laughter fills the car. It's deep and happy, and it's impossible not to grin at him.

"You don't like the Mountain Lions?"

"Wearing a football shirt to a Bears gathering is going to get your ass handed to you."

"It's a good thing you're a black belt in Muay Thai, then."

An indignant snort spills out of me. "We don't grade in Muay Thai." When he laughs, I know he's doubling down on his teasing since I've already explained this to him.

"Your fighting experience speaks for itself and is your only grading system, right?" he sasses.

"That's right, wiseass."

"So, will that be enough to defend me from getting my ass kicked?"

I put the blinker on to turn onto the main street and snort. "I said 'handed to you,' not kicked. I think you can handle the ribbing and the extra water bombs, so I can't imagine you needing a defender."

"So you're saying I'm going to be a target."

"A very sexy target, but yeah." I glance his way when I speak, liking the soft smile at my words.

"In that case, I can turn it inside out."

"Or just take it off." I bounce my brows up and down. "I have the best ideas."

"You're so magnanimous."

I laugh. "Thanks. I've always thought so."

"Maybe you should take your shirt off, and I can wear yours. You guys have enough hard pecs and bulging muscles between you to make all the queer guys swoon."

Up ahead, I spot the car wash. My friends and teammates are all set up, something we did earlier, and there's already a line of cars ready for some sudsy action. I use the moment to talk my dick down. The thought of Logan dressed in my clothes has me rock-hard. "Holy shit."

"What?"

I shake my head, thinking back to something I talked about with Leon at training and the way my dick is eager for attention. "I'm a total alpha."

There's a beat of silence before Logan snorts so hard and loud that I jolt in surprise. He tries to speak, but breathing and laughing together appear to be something he has difficulty with.

I roll my eyes as I stop the car and switch off the engine. That his laughter is out of control should offend me. Since I know I sounded like a douche, offended is the last thing I am. "You don't agree," I say, my grin stretching wide as I unbuckle my seat belt and look at him.

"I…" He shakes his head. Tears fill his eyes, and I swear, Logan takes sexy and obliterates that word. Logan out of control is fucking glorious. "Sorry…" He wipes his eyes. "You are, yes…." He gasps and tilts his head back. Any calm he's searching for isn't in the ceiling, though.

"How about I show you how alpha I am when you wear my jersey?" A tendril of humor laces my words, but desire chases it down, vying for attention.

My words have him snapping his gaze to me. Wide-eyed, Logan stares at me, his laughter gone, though amusement is still evident in the flush of his cheeks.

"I'm not sure if that was a question or a directive there." A sultry tone weaves through his voice. While it's the first time I've heard it, I think it may be my favorite.

Not taking my focus from him, I lean over the back of my seat. The movement gets me in his space, and I don't miss the hitch of his breath or the way he catches his bottom lip with his top teeth.

It takes me a moment to rummage around the bag I stashed earlier. Feeling the familiar lightweight material, I take hold and pull it before me.

Logan eyes the fabric in my grip and angles his

head. "What have you got there?" There's more than mild curiosity in his question.

"Strip your shirt." The request is low and gruff, recapturing Logan's attention.

With his gaze on me, he quirks a brow. "Jumping to second base already, huh? In broad daylight and with witnesses. I'm not sure anyone's ready to see that." A twitch of his lips follows.

"As much as I'm up for discovering all the bases with you, not a chance we'll be having an audience. Now quit stalling. Shirt off and put this on." A holler from the guys catches my attention, and I'm super aware that time is ticking.

The noise grabs his focus too, and Logan jolts into action. He strips off the offending shirt, and I get a glimpse of flat pink nipples. They're larger than mine, a little darker too. Zeroed in on them, I'm tempted to reach out, but this is so not the time. Heck, I'm kind of surprised he's even switching shirts without a fuss. I was only half kidding about him getting a ribbing. If he had, I would have made sure the guys didn't push too far.

When Logan's head pops out of the neck hole, his hair a little messy, I smile, taking him in and marveling at how ridiculously sexy he looks wearing my training shirt.

"This is clean, right?" He takes a big, over-the-top sniff.

I snort. "There's not a chance in hell you would have yanked that over your head if it hadn't been. Trust me."

"I'll take your word for it."

There's another rowdy holler from outside, and it's time to leave. I allow myself a beat to take Logan in. Yesterday I told him I had no plans to ever make a coming-out statement.

Which is absolutely true.

As far as I'm concerned, Logan and I are dating, and hopefully soon we'll reach the point of being boyfriends, after we've got to know each other better and I also ask him the questions refusing to disappear. That need to seek the truth hasn't changed, but it's no longer going to hold me back. Not after yesterday, and especially seeing him now, hot, bothered, and teasing me mercilessly.

Our dating is a fact, one I don't need to explain to anyone.

"You ready?"

He bobs his head and smiles, though it's not enough to disguise the appearance of his nerves. "Yep, sure. Put me to work."

I squeeze his leg. "If any of my friends are assholes, it's because of me, not you," I say quickly, trying to chase away the trace of anxiety evident in his gaze. When he frowns, I add, "By that, they're likely going to tease the shit out of me."

When he nods, I step out of the car, throwing over my shoulder, "You're the first date I'll have ever introduced them to, so they're not going to hold back," before I close the door.

Before I can reach Logan's side, he's jumping out of the car. His cheeks are redder than a moment ago, and there's startled confusion etched on his face. I don't have time to ask him if he's okay before five separate shouts for me to get my ass moving greet me.

Snatching Logan's hand, I give a light squeeze and tug him over.

Kieran's smiling, taking in the man at my side, while Dean, his boyfriend, is staring wide-eyed at us. Leon does a double take before his expression settles into one of understanding. It's Sammy who clamps on to Bentley's arm, his gaping mouth wide enough to have me shaking my head.

"It's no wonder you were all so desperate for me to get here. Just look at the dirt left behind on the rims." I shake my head, eyeing the missed smears of dirt on the car they're apparently half-assed washing. "Never fear, the mighty Ty is here."

"Mighty pain in the ass, more like," Sammy

sasses, having finally closed his mouth. His gaze travels to Logan and our clasped hands.

"This is Logan," I introduce. "I've already warned him you can be assholes, but beneath all that, you're good guys." I peer at Logan, who's focusing on me, a nervous smile playing on his lips. "Logan, my housemates." I point toward my other teammates working on a different vehicle, letting Logan know who they are.

"Hey," Logan says. "You need me working on this car too?" Confidence radiates through his voice even though he's gripping my hand too tightly to be as calm as he seems.

Kieran answers, "There's spare sponges and rags over by Dean. Help yourself. The sooner we get this car finished, the quicker we can move to the next and start raising some funds."

"Sounds good." Logan makes to release my hand, but I'm not ready to let go yet. When he looks at me, I aim to give him my best puppy-dog eyes. His snort is low, as is his "Alpha, huh?" before he tugs me over to the supplies.

And then we're washing the cars, getting ridiculously soaked, and joking around. There are a few glances and quirked brows, but my friends are going with it. The simmer of acceptance and gratitude for my housemates and team threads through me. This here is exactly why I joined the Bears. I wanted this bond, needed a group who I can rely on, no matter what.

I only hope I find the same team and connection when I join the FBI next year.

"I'm just saying it's not great for the environment." A wet sponge hits me square in the face. I grunt at the hit and narrow my gaze at Sammy, who's not hiding that he's responsible for the throw.

"Seriously, we know hand washes use more water, but it's for charity. It means we can make the exception for the good of the immigration center."

I part my lips to question his words but am stopped by Logan's laughter. In the past hour we've been working, there's been a noticeable shift in Logan's body language. He's constantly chuckling and chatting animatedly to Dean and has even pulled Bentley into some sort of conversation that has him smirking.

Impressive since Bentley's super quiet and doesn't easily warm up to people. Not that I do either. A frown and a hard stare is my go-to to get people out of my space. Bentley's different, though. Taller and wider set, he should be intimidating. Maybe he can be for all of a couple of seconds before he usually smiles gently and speaks so softly that it doesn't take but a beat to reassess your opinion of him.

Basically, he's the gentlest guy I know. Probably the kindest too. Hell, I don't know how he deals with Sammy's loud sass, but they've been best friends since day one and are rarely separated for any length of time.

"What are you grinning at?"

I switch my attention to Sammy. From the way his brow's cocked, he knows exactly who's the reason behind my smile, and it's not his best friend.

"You're saying that as though it's unusual to see this reaction from me." I bite back my smirk.

Snorting hard, Sammy shakes his head, glancing over at Logan, who's still chuckling at whatever Dean's saying. "Not sure about unusual. An indicator that the apocalypse is looming, maybe."

"Just because I've made a conquest, doesn't mean I have plans for war, hunger, and death, so I think we're safe." Confusion crosses Sammy's features, so I clarify, "You know, the four horsemen of the apocalypse."

Holding up his hand to indicate I should pause, Sammy's eyes widen. "Hold on there. You're freaking me out. I thought you only dealt in facts."

I chuckle. "I can guarantee that's not the case if

I'm talking about the horsemen and the fiction it came from."

"Thank fuck for that. But let's also get back to the 'conquest' statement." He side-eyes Logan before dropping his voice. "Is that what this is? A conquest with Logan?" He shakes his head. "I don't know, man. It seems like you're pretty tight. Other than that brief interest you showed in Angie last year, I can't imagine you inviting just a hookup into our fold." He squints. "And the whole demi thing means nothing casual, right?" It seems to register that he's answered his own question. "Shit, is he super smart too? You're into that as well, right?"

While it's entertaining, witnessing his verbal processing, I nod. "He's smart."

And fuck if I don't have kickass friends. Just last night I opened up a little with them, dropping terms like demi- and sapiosexual with them like it was no big deal. The thing is it wasn't. A couple scratched their heads thinking I was talking Latin to them or some shit.

But I caught them up to speed.

"Damn, Ty. The whole package, huh. Good job."

"You're right about that. I was being facetious with the whole 'conquest' thing."

"So you're dating?"

Before I can respond, a new voice cuts through the air. "Logan, hey."

The voice snatches my attention immediately, and all joking around with Sammy disappears in a blink.

It's a face I recognize. Danny Lloyd.

My hackles go up, and in my periphery, I see movement from Kieran. He's moving closer to Dean. Understandable since last semester the guy was a prick to Dean while attempting to hit on him. Although I've never spoken to the guy, his actions tell me all I need to know.

"Danny, hi." Logan angles toward Danny with a cautious smile that doesn't reach his eyes.

It helps to cool the blast of tension racing through me that not only is Danny approaching us, knowing full well we all think he's an asshole, but he's seeking out my guy.

Being levelheaded is part of my genetic makeup. Shit, it has to be considering my plan to join the FBI, but from the way my gut tightens, I don't like Logan uncomfortable, especially when that discomfort is caused by a prick.

With Logan being the treasurer for the social group, I expect that's how they know each other. The knowledge settles in me, and I relax my shoulders, but there's nothing I can do about my hard stare.

"Have you gone and joined the basketball team?"

Danny chuckles. With the way his gaze is fixed on Logan and not straying around our group, I don't doubt he's not as at ease as he's pretending to be.

"No. My skill set doesn't reach that far." Despite the tightness of his smile, Logan's attempting to be friendly.

"I don't know. I imagine you've got plenty of skills, all of which would be wasted on this group."

Logan's brows jump in surprise. Danny's smile and light tone didn't do a thing to hide his bitchiness.

"Uhm… I'm not sure about that." With Logan's attention on me, his cheeks heat before he says to Danny, "Are you in the line for a car wash?"

Danny's gaze zips to me, and I relish the moment his stare connects with mine. The widening of his eyes is immediate, and he glances away quickly. "I wasn't going to, but if you're free, you can absolutely show some TLC to my dirty rims."

The fucker has a death wish. It's the only explanation. Fuck, maybe I'm losing my touch if my hard stare didn't stop him from saying such stupid shit.

"Oh fuck." The words come from Kieran, who tugs Dean back a step or two. It's enough to get Logan's and Danny's attention. The former's looking confused, while Danny's sneer is back.

A few strides later and I'm at Logan's side, my palm immediately clasping his waist. I'm totally getting this possessive alpha gig locked in. Danny's just lucky I refuse to let my more negative reactions rule me. No way is a dickhead like him going to be the reason I destroy my future.

Not that he knows that.

"Are you seriously standing here, being a sleaze, and hitting on Logan?" Quiet and deadly, each word is razor sharp.

"I'm here about a car wash, which is what you're doing here, right?" The stupidity just keeps on rolling from him. "I think that Logan's more than capable of answering for himself. Though what the fuck he's doing here is beyond me."

"Whoa, let's tone it all down," Logan says at my side. That he leans into my touch unravels a thread of my tension. "If you want a car wash, you'll need to join the line, and we'll happily service you—" My squeeze of his waist at his word choice has him cutting off and grunting. He picks up quickly, though. "Wash… hand wash your car. I'm helping out Tyron and his team."

An ugly confusion swirls across Danny's features. "So you're what, together?"

I'm about to tell him to fuck off and that it's none of his business, but Logan's "No" stops me short.

With my arm still wrapped around Logan, I peer down at him, my frown directed his way. I clutch his chin with my thumb and pointer, angling it up to me. By the time our gazes connect, his eyes are as wide as saucers. "Yes. We're dating."

I feel him jolt in my arms like a zap of electricity arced through him. "We are?"

"You are?" Danny asks, which I ignore.

Aware my friends are surrounding us and will no doubt be wondering what the hell is going on, I make sure every word is deliberate, clear, and precise. I don't want them, Danny, and especially Logan, to misunderstand anything. "We are dating. Exclusively," I tag on. I'll willingly open it up for discussion, but since Logan knows I don't make a habit of dating, I hope he's on board with it. "We have been for almost a month."

"We have?" Logan's dropped his voice to a whisper.

"Our first coffee date…." I let the words hang.

"Not a study meeting?" A twinkle appears in his eyes. There's a softening in his gaze, too, and he angles toward me more fully, an ease in his shoulders that makes me happy we're talking this out. It doesn't stop me from being pissed off at myself for missing his cues and him missing mine.

Something I clearly need to be working on during training next year, and definitely a failing I won't talk about in my interview.

"Not *just* a study meeting."

At the bob of his head and his soft "Okay," I capture his mouth for a brief kiss, savoring his taste and how he leans into me. As I pull away, I hear my friends chuckling and Danny grumbling something about "fucking basketball players."

Since he's walking away, I don't give a shit.

CHAPTER 8

LOGAN

W ITH THE SUN SPILLING OUT ONTO T YRON'S BARE CHEST and warmth wrapping itself around my heart, I'm finding it hard to feel embarrassed about the car wash scene. Before Tyron's "we're dating" revelation, I never considered myself to be dense. In fairness, Tyron, for whatever un-Tyron-like reason, hadn't exactly been clear either.

Dimness aside, I really don't care about the misunderstanding. At all, in fact.

Right now, I'm all about savoring the way Tyron's skin tastes as I trace my tongue over his nipples. His shuddery groans are doing wonderful things to my dick. It's his eagerness that's urging me on. While his vocal pleas and demands aren't exactly surprising, now that I know him better, I can barely believe being with him this way is real.

"That feels so damn good. Do the other one," he instructs, his tone breathy and pupils blown as he angles to look at me.

"Like giving orders, huh?" Something I'm not complaining about. On Tyron, it's hot. And since he's so new to everything—sex and men—it's a relief that he's a hundred percent in this.

"It's that alpha in me. Now it's made itself known, it's demanding as hell."

I snort as I worry at his nipple, earning a fresh moan. After laving the tender flesh with small licks to ease the sting, my fingers take over so I can speak. "I'm not sure how I feel that you're referring to this 'alpha' element as a separate entity." In truth, it's adorable. Not only that he thinks of such things, but he says them too.

It would be easy to believe he has no filter. I know that's not the case, though. He's comfortable speaking his mind with his trusted few. That I'm snuggled deep in with that small group is a feeling I really like.

I'm also quickly learning that the hard-ass persona—the grumbly, standoffish one—is a far cry from the real Tyron. Admittedly, I love this side of him.

"Sometimes there's a personality trait so big that it deserves it," he teases. "Possessive looks hot on me, right?" He bounces his brows up and down.

It's no good. He totally deserves the swift thump of a pillow in his face. I'm laughing hard as I pull the cushion away, revealing his grin.

We've been making out since the moment we came to his place and Tyron shuffled me none too subtly into his room. We've barely come up for air since. Well, beyond me checking out his room and marveling at how eerily tidy and organized it is, as well as engaging in these ridiculous conversations that keep popping up.

"You know, kissing daily can keep your teeth healthy."

"Is that right?" I arch a brow as he hooks his arm around my waist.

"Absolutely. Saliva has antibacterial properties. So the more we kiss, the better our teeth. We've no time to waste. I have a dentist appointment coming up."

Amusement flickers to life in my chest. "I'm mildly grossed out by that."

"It's also great for your mental health," he continues, ignoring my "grossed out" statement. "Honestly, if I wasn't so self-aware, I'd be concerned that I've kissed so few people."

The thought is sobering, which I don't think is his

intent. I should be jesting at his arrogance, yet he's legit speaking the truth. "Does it bother you?" I ask. When his brows furrow, I clarify, "Having people think of you in one way when you're something totally different?"

A soft smile lifts his lips, and he sits up, studying me intently. He has my complete attention. Our knees brush, and his hand settles in mine. "My sexuality is something I've chosen never to make a big deal about since it's part of my genetic makeup. That there's never been a rainbow arrow hovering over my head is neither this nor that. I'm not naïve. Now that we're dating, I'm preparing myself for some disbelief and challenge."

"Because you play basketball or that you're attracted to men and women?"

"I'm attracted to you."

The distinction slams into me, fizzing in my stomach with the ferocity of a Mentos in a bottle of Coke. "I'm attracted to you too." A grin punctuates my words. I'm unable to hold back just how awesome his assertion makes me feel.

"I suppose I'm preparing for people pulling apart labels, challenging whether I fit the mold, whether I tick all the boxes of what it means to be demi- or sapiosexual. Not that they're super common terms to most people. I expect most will see me with you and assume I'm gay or bi."

Sympathy calms my heart, and I squeeze his fingers. "I'm sure you don't need me to tell you about not fitting into a box, not even needing to take on a label."

Tyron lifts my hand and kisses my palm, and just like that, another Mentos has been added to the mix. "I had a super similar conversation with a friend recently, but thanks for reminding me. I own my sexuality and feel good about using a mesh of three terms as my positioning on the rainbow spectrum. No doubt those who identify as demi or even sapio-sexual have different experiences than mine, and that's the point, too, right? That we're all different and on our own journey. Honestly, no one has the right to tell me if I do or don't tick all the boxes. I also have no hardship with telling anyone who's a dick-head or a homophobic prick to go fuck themselves."

I laugh and fall into him. Grabbing hold of me, he tugs me down.

"Make sure it's not on camera." I'm more than aware that there will be media attention when the basketball season starts. Tyron's made it known that while he has a reputation and a voice, he stays well away from the media, both social and with team coverage.

Well, as much as possible for a championship player.

Since I only have a private TikTok and Insta account where I've posted a grand total of zero videos and photos, I can relate. Working for the government and having aspirations that I hope will be challenging and rewarding, I have no desire for anything to bite me in the ass.

My project flashes in my brain, but I refuse to wince about it. It's one thing I refuse to negotiate on. I can't break my promise to my grandpa. It's also the reason why I'm super careful, and only two of my friends know.

I have no idea where Tyron and I are heading, but I'm not ready to share this piece of myself yet.

"Shit. What's the time?" I jolt out of Tyron's arms and seek out my phone. A quick look tells me I'm late. "I'm so sorry, but I have to go."

"O-kay." He drags out the word, confusion pitching his voice. "You have an appointment or something?"

He sits up as I grab my tennis shoes and shove them on. A quick glance in his direction, and I see his concern. Of course he's wondering where I'm going. While I won't lie to him, I'm wondering how flexible and vague I can be without him outright pushing.

Inquisitive is part of Tyron's genetic makeup. Me

evading him is going to be like waving catnip under a cat's nose.

"I have a meeting about the project I'm doing."

"The one you won't tell me anything about?"

I snort, completely expecting this. Pausing from tying my laces, I smile at him. "If I tell you it's not a big deal and it's something to do with my grandpa, will that be enough?"

"But if it's not a big deal, why can't you just tell me?"

"You don't like me being a man of mystery, huh?" The teasing words are out there. They're a mistake for all the obvious reasons, but Tyron is so easy to banter and flirt with. I sober when his gaze becomes laser focused. "Can you just wait until I'm ready to tell you?"

After a beat, he scoots forward so we're touching. "You think you will?"

The pause highlights my hesitation. "I hope so. I want to." Truthfully, shitty of me or not, I'm a little embarrassed about the whole thing. A performer, I am not. Beyond my two friends, who I've spent three years getting to know and trusting, the thought of letting anyone else in and sharing my project with anyone makes me uncomfortable.

If I was passionate about it, it would no doubt be different. But I'm not.

Me attending drag queen school and working toward the fall performance is all about honoring my promise to my estranged grandpa, who I discovered was a drag performer. In the couple of years I spent with him, he shared enough stories to make me wish I'd been able to see him on stage, completely in his element, working a crowd.

While our time together was limited, I loved him and respected him. Sure, we didn't have long to get to know each other, but he showed me more understanding and compassion than my parents ever have.

"Okay." A warm hand squeezes mine, pulling me out of my thoughts.

At the touch, I realize my gaze is wavering with unshed emotion. Fuck. I clear my throat and smile at Tyron. While his intensity remains, there's a softness in his expression that has me breathing easier.

"When you're ready is fine."

"Thanks." I lean over and kiss him, reveling in how freeing and right it feels to take kisses whenever I want them. "Here's some more good health care for you." I pull away, grinning, enjoying the smile aimed my way.

"Will you text me later when you're home?"

I don't ask why he assumes I won't be home to work on my project. He's right, obviously. "Yeah, I can do that. I really do have to go."

He releases my hand and watches me leave, and I do so with a flutter of emotion and a little bit of dread. I've had a physical day already. Throwing on a pair of four-inch heels and working on my routine is going to destroy me.

My biggest mission tonight is to not fall on my ass—or my face—like I did that night I first caught Tyron's attention while getting the group performance locked in.

While I'm reluctant to train, I don't want to make a complete fool of myself in November. Not when the fall graduation showcase is close to being sold out.

***

"ONE AND TWO AND THREE AND FOUR— LOULOU, YOU missed a step." Dixie looks to the ceiling before recentering their gaze on LouLou.

I hold back my cringe, knowing exactly what it's like to be under Dixie's scrutiny and the harsh end of their tongue.

"Six weeks. That's all you have before your final performance. At the moment, it looks like four star divas and one weak-ankled link. You look lost. Your moves aren't sharp." Manicured fingernails dance through the air as Dixie continues to express their frustration.

LouLou folds their arms but listens intently. We all know better than to interrupt Dixie when they're on a roll.

"Let's go again. From the beginning."

I hold back my groan. We've been at this for forty-five minutes. Before that, I spent half an hour working on my individual performance. At least I practiced in bare feet during the first thirty minutes. This group rehearsal, Dixie demanded we practice with our heels and long trains.

It's close to eight, so we'll be finishing anytime now. The club's doors open at 8:30 p.m., so already bar staff are stocking up and setting out tables. Fresh balloons are being arranged overhead for Annie Rection's performance later tonight. While it's good practice to have people around, as I hope it helps me get used to having an audience, I'm not convinced I'll be ready.

"Drink afterward, darling?" Dolly whispers next to me as we head back to our starting point.

I glance over at Dolly. With her blonde wig in place, something she always practices in, she gets into position. She's fabulous as Dolly, and when out of drag, Donnie is a pretty cool guy. "Best not. I didn't study today, and I have a heap to get through," I mumble, relieved Dixie is distracted by something so hasn't cued the music yet.

I cant my hip, position my hand just so, and wait to begin.

"Please tell me you've been gallivanting and getting up to delicious mischief." Next to the sparkly purple backdrop, even without full makeup, Dolly looks like she belongs here.

"Charity car wash."

"With the sexy Bears?" Her tone sounds so impressed, it's impossible not to grin.

"I suppose there are a couple who may fit into that category," I admit, trying hard to drop my smile and form my fierce face. It's something I'm not great at and have been schooled on a million times. Both Dixie and I have figured there's no hope for me nailing that look.

Heck, last week I even tried to mirror Tyron's intensity, since he's the star of so much inspiration in my life, but with no success.

"Ooh." Dolly flicks me a look when Dixie turns their back. "Maybe just one sexy player in particular? You've never mentioned a player before. Oh my," she gasps, daring to move her hand and press it against her chest. "Please tell me it's that delicious Kieran Kendall. Did you see that smoking-hot kiss?" She fans herself.

I snort as loud as I dare. "Since he kissed his

boyfriend, and they're very much an item, that'll be a no."

"A pity."

"I saw that kiss. Kiss-cam, right?" Mia Harddick whispers from behind me. "Closeted jocks…" A whimsical sigh follows. "…coming out for sexy twinks and love. It's what keeps my queer heart pumping and wishing for."

"Do you have a thing for athletes, Mia?" Dolly asks, her focus following Dixie's movements as they stop heading our way and talk to a man I don't recognize.

"I have a pretty big *thing* for athletes if I can snag myself one." She chuckles, and I bite down on my cheeks to stop myself from joining in. "How is it you managed to get all sudsy with the basketball team, Dewanna?"

Dewanna Boner. A name I settled on when I joined this motley crew of hilarious, bitchy divas.

Heat fills my cheeks.

"Ooh… you dirty, wonderful whore. Please tell me you've hooked a basketball player." Dolly's so excited, she breaks her stance and faces me.

Happiness bubbles into my gut when I think about Tyron. "I may be dating a pretty incredible power forward." The words sound as alien as they do wonderful.

"Girl." Dolly flutters her hand dramatically over her face. "Please spill the balls and tell me everything."

"Dolly, why are you flapping at imaginary dicks swinging in your face when you should be preparing to start?"

Dixie's words have Dolly moving her ass, but not without her mouthing, "Everything" to me before she repositions at my side.

"We're going to start again, and this time, strut like you have money to earn, and don't miss a step."

A moment later, Britney's "Toxic" pumps through the speakers.

Counting the beats, I focus on where to step, when to lift my fabric train so I don't trip, and wait for my verse. Who knew group choreography while lip-synching could be so damn hard. Probably thousands of performers, I expect, but still, give me an Excel document and mathematical equations any day of the week.

Powering on through, I form the words, exaggerating my mouth with the lyrics and shimmying on down to the floor, gyrating the fuck out of it.

And this, ladies and gentlemen, gays and theys, is a moment I am distinctly proud of while being resolutely mortified.

More power to the amazing performers who nail

the hell out of this and find the absolute buzz. Oh, how I wish it was me.

That doesn't mean I'm not embracing it and even having a little bit of fun.

Come November, after my performance, the only gyrating plans I have will be with Tyron. All being well.

CHAPTER 9

TYRON

"Maybe." Focusing on Logan is a pretty clear sign that I'm talking about him, but I can't resist looking. He's draped across my bed, jean-clad ass on display, half focusing on me while attempting to study.

This setup is almost identical to how we've hung out over the past three weeks.

Studying together tends to be the only time we manage to steal away for the two of us. Between practice and training, classes, Logan's commitment to the social group, as well as his project, which he disappears to twice a week, studying is officially combining dating with making our brains work overtime.

It's working, though—stealing kisses between discussions and turning the pages of our textbooks. And Logan on my dark gray cotton bedspread simply fits. He makes my room feel more welcoming. Even his scattered books and the way he kicks off his tennis shoes haphazardly don't piss me off.

Hell, he even survived meeting my sister last week and handled her nosiness like a well-seasoned pro. After that meeting, I reassured Coach that once the media got wind of my same-sex relationship, Logan would have no problem with "no comment" responses.

Coach had extended the training clock by fifteen minutes because I overshared.

"Are you listening, Ty? Oh…" Dad falters a little. "He's there, isn't he? You never get distracted, beyond you following the disturbing fact trails. You're not naked, are you? Please, tell me you're not in a post-coital haze talking to me? I don't think my brain can handle it."

"Dad, do you really think I'd be functioning if I'd had sex with Logan?"

Logan jerks so hard, he falls off the bed, landing with a heavy thud and a grunt.

I snort loudly, peering over the side.

"What was that noi— Nope. No, don't tell me if it's sex noises." Dad's practically hyperventilating. Sure, it would be easy to nip this in the bud now and end the call, but I take too much pleasure in winding my old man up.

"It's not sex noises. I do think Logan may have a sore ass, though."

"Ty," Logan snaps, horror bleaching his features.

Shrugging, I offer him a wink and reach out, tugging him up. He falls onto me with another grunt and cusses me out, not quite quiet enough that my dad can't hear.

"Is that…? I think I need vodka. Maybe whiskey."

I snort. "He fell off the bed, Dad, horrified I'm talking to you about sex," I clarify, dotting a kiss on Logan's head, effectively stopping him from pushing out of my hold.

"Right, well, it's important we can talk about sex. You're both consenting adults. You're no longer a child."

"Twenty-two, Dad." I hold back my eye roll and pull Logan closer, so he's sitting between my legs.

"A grown man who'll still be coming home for Thanksgiving and maybe even bringing his boyfriend?"

Since I told my dads two weeks ago about Logan, they've reacted exactly as I expected—with understanding and complete acceptance. I think Pops must have had a chat with Dad afterward, though, as I'd felt the unasked questions down the line during that first call. But since then, there's been no undercurrent of why I waited till now to disclose my interest in men, or if I didn't feel able to share.

If I'm right about Pops's interference, I'm grateful.

Sometimes there's no big secret. No fear. There's simply the right time, and since getting to know Logan, it's become mine.

"Well, Logan's not technically my boyfriend." Logan freezes in my arms. "Yet," I tack on. The sound of Logan's gulp hits me in the chest, and I squeeze him tighter.

I want that—to do the whole asking him officially —but I'm committed to knowing what he's holding back from me first.

When he told me his project was about his grandad, my burning need to know settled into a low simmer. For now. He's shared the story about his grandpa's estrangement with me. It's sad as heck, but I'm glad he had the chance to get to know him. Even if it was for a short while.

"Dating or official title, or whatever it is you kids are calling the whole mating ritual these days, he's still invited. Use the credit card for his ticket too."

Familiar warmth laps at my skin. Dad's legit one of the kindest people I know.

"Thanks, Dad. I'll ask him later, but no pressure, okay?"

"When have I ever put you under pres— Don't

answer that." The swiftness with which he changes the subject is hilarious. We're both thinking about the musical number he guilted my siblings and me to do when I was ten.

"Uh-huh. That's fine as long as those recordings stay deleted."

They so weren't deleted, and Dad's lack of response confirms it.

"I best get going. I need to pick your brother up from training. Stay safe. Love you."

"Love you, Dad. Tell the rest of the Brady Bunch I love them too."

"Will do, son."

The call ends, and I place my cell on the bedside table, refusing to let go of Logan as I do so. Once I'm phone free, I encourage him to turn around and face me. The dopey, almost coy smile on his lips is enough to have my dick twitching and my pulse picking up.

"I love that you're so close to your family."

"I'm lucky." Gushing doesn't seem right, not when, from the trickles of information Logan's shared with me about his upbringing, he doesn't have the best relationship with his parents.

A soft hum presses against me when he leans into me. Following up with a gentle kiss against my skin, he murmurs, "So what video footage do I need to track down?"

Immediately, my fingers settle on his ribs, and I dig in, tickling the crap out of him. He squeals, the sound so high I expect the whole house heard. "It's best you erase that detail from your memory."

Wriggling around in my arms, Logan tries his best to escape. Laughter fills the room as he attempts to tug my hands away.

"Uh-huh." I'm relentless and loving every loud chuckle that's verging on hysteria.

"Uncle, uncle!" he cries.

I pause my tickling but don't release him. Instead, I tug him fully onto my lap and capture his still-smiling mouth in a kiss.

He presses into me, his mouth moving, his laughter dying away as he rocks on my lap. Urging him on, I grip his glutes, loving the strength under my fingertips. The friction of our rubbing dicks is pretty great, but I have a better idea.

"Pull your cock out," I instruct.

I love that he doesn't question me and ask if I'm sure. He's jacked me off once, and I happily returned the favor. Both times were awesome. But getting us both off with my hand, at the same time, hell yes.

He's already on display by the time I shuck my shorts down my ass and tug myself out. The whole time my focus is on his uncut cock. I can't look away.

He's long and hard. There's a sexy vein that runs to the left and a pearl of cum that I can't resist.

So I don't.

I scoop it up and place the tip of my finger in my mouth.

"Holy shit, that's hot," he says breathily. "Does it taste like you thought?" Logan stares at my mouth and dips his tongue out, sweeping it over his bottom lip.

"Salty and bitter. It's not the best taste in the world. I wouldn't want an ice cream flavor made out of it, but it's not bad."

Logan grins, swipes the drop of precum off my cock, and sucks it into his mouth. I groan when he opens his eyes, and our gazes connect.

"Salty and bitter. And given a chance, I'd suck you dry and drink you down every single day."

"Fuck." I haul him close and, once again, capture his mouth.

Our kiss is messy and dirty as I suck his tongue and kiss the hell out of him. Fire shoots up my spine, need punching into my gut, and spreading to my groin. My cock pulses, and I jerk forward. Rubbing dicks is the best thing ever. But I can make it so much hotter.

I force my hand between us, not willing to break our kiss. Logan gives me more room. Wrapping my hand around him, I practically growl at the heat and steel in my palm.

"Jesus," Logan gasps, breaking the kiss and peering down.

Space appears between us so I can see what I'm doing. Snatching up my cock, I press us together, our dicks so close that I feel every pulsing vein and stiffening jerk. I rub us together in a long, slow motion. It's dry, my hand rough. Swiping my thumbs over the gathering beads, I smooth it down his length, enraptured by Logan's shuddery breaths.

Like me, he's struggling to know where to look. Our gazes are everywhere—focusing on our mouths, our eyes, our cocks, and my hand. They dance between all four, never settling for long.

"You need lube, or are you okay?" The last thing I want to do is stop, but I don't want to rub his dick raw.

"Keep going." His words shudder out of him, his hips still rocking. "It'll be fine. You feel so incredible."

Desire threatens to take my senses, but I manage a smile. "I love you telling me what you want and what feels good."

"This—" He cuts off when I increase the speed of my hand. "Feels better than good." Half-lidded eyes peer back at me. A small smile tugs at the corners of his mouth. "Next time, I want to suck you off."

The visual slams into me so fast my vision blurs and my balls tingle. "Will you take all of me?" I say with a wispy breath. I'm so close to coming.

"Every last inch. All the way to the back of my throat so I can swallow around you."

My orgasm slams into me so fast, there's no chance of me holding back. "Fuck, holy shit. Nngh." I paint our stomachs, my hand sliding over us even as I become overly sensitive. I work fast, gripping hard, barely seeing straight. Desperate for Logan to come.

"Fuck, fuck, fuck…." Logan spills over my hand, one shot spurting high and landing on my chest.

I watch every drop as I slow down, mesmerized by the movement. Acting on instinct, I ease Logan away from my lap and lean over him.

"What are you—"

My tongue on his dick shuts him up.

"Ty, fuck me."

"Soon," I say with a hum and a raised brow before mouthing over his cock, getting a real taste of his cum. While still bitter, it's a flavor I could become addicted to. It's more than that, though. It's Logan. It's how I make him feel when I lick a long line down his cock. It's his shuddery breaths, his blown pupils, the absolute desire and blissed-out adoration on his face.

This right here is what gets me off and feels so fucking right.

Once he's clean, I glance down at the remaining mess on my hand, my dick, and stomach. "If we're quiet, we should be able to sneak into the shower together."

Logan gazes up at me, his smile so tender, my heart lurches. "A shower with you sounds perfect."

We manage to shower without any interruptions from my housemates. But it's getting late, and my alarm's set for 4:30 a.m. Logan and I stand in the front doorway, saying goodbye. Each time he tries to leave, I snag another kiss, not quite ready to end our night.

Every evening we get to see each other is like this, and I'm not even embarrassed.

"Ty, seriously, man. You're letting the cold in," Sammy grouches from the kitchen.

Since he's right, I can't debate it. Instead, I flip him off—even though he can't see—and make to tug Logan back inside so I can close the door and have more kisses. His palm on my chest stops me, though.

"You need to sleep. I'll see you tomorrow."

A dramatic sigh spills past my lips, but it earns

me a smile. "Fine. Promise you'll think about Thanksgiving, though."

Pink flushes his cheeks, and he nods. "I promise."

That's good enough for me. Sure, he seemed a little overwhelmed and maybe a bit flummoxed at the invite, but I hope he does take the trip with me. Yes, it's still a month away, but I'm not worried about making plans.

Not with Logan.

"Perfect." After one last kiss, he pulls away, nudges me inside, and tugs the door closed behind him.

Once alone, I head to the kitchen where Sammy and Bentley are. When I enter, Bentley's smiling and shaking his head as Sammy's speaking quietly, close to his ear. I take them in, holding back my smirk.

All the guys have teased me mercilessly at my dumbass move with Logan. You know, the one where I thought we were dating while Logan remained oblivious? Not that I didn't deserve the ribbing. I swear I'm usually a hell of a lot more clued in than that. Just ask Leon.

With Logan, the only explanation is I wore blinkers. Since the moment I gripped his chin before the school year started, something clicked in me. An inability to properly communicate my thoughts and feelings was switched on in the process, apparently.

But Sammy and Bentley… there's going to be a major wake-up call pretty damn soon. Though, I really hope the brewing explosion doesn't happen till the end of the basketball season.

Only time will tell.

"I'm heading to bed." My smirk threatens to break free when Sammy jumps. He doesn't pull far back from Bentley, though.

"Finally pried yourself away from lover boy, huh? Good job, man. Any longer and I was sure we'd be dealing with your grouchy ass in the morning from not having enough sleep." Sammy folds his arms and leans back against the kitchen counter, the space behind them a mess.

"You know," I start, ignoring his description of me being a grump, since he's not wrong, "there's a direct link between a person's favorite sleeping position and their personalities."

"There is?" Bentley asks. "What does it say about a person who sleeps on their side with an arm outstretched, you know, like taking up all the room and smacking people in the face?"

At his side, Sammy's eye twitches, but he remains mute.

"They're friendly and open-natured," I say, as Sammy grins and angles to look at Bentley. "They're also not great at trusting and can be stubborn." Sammy's grin turns into a frown.

Bentley huffs out a laugh. While amusement carries the sound, the rigid set of his shoulders screams frustration. "Sounds about right."

This right here is something I'm not getting into. I will if I'm asked or if there's a clear need, but until that point, my plan is to focus on juggling my workload and time with Logan. "I'll see you in the morning." I give them a two-finger wave and back out of the kitchen, shaking my head when I hear Sammy grumbling.

Undressing, I eye my bed, scanning for cum stains. Seeing none, I give myself a mental pat on the back and slip under my sheets. As soon as my head hits my pillow, I draw in the scent of Logan's bodywash. It's minty with the hint of tea tree.

I shuffle around, sighing contently. That he'll be going home smelling of my bodywash from our joint shower shouldn't make me as happy as it does. But I'm struggling not to get giddy when it comes to thoughts of Logan.

I'm in deep.

But I refuse to balk or worry too much about just how invested I am. Not yet anyway.

CHAPTER 10
LOGAN

THE STIFFNESS IN MY MUSCLES REFUSES TO LOOSEN. Tyron's shot me a few worried glances, but I pointedly ignore each one and keep taking deep breaths and releasing them as quietly as I can.

I can't help it.

This is too surreal. Precarious even.

I'm just waiting to hear something derogatory, which is unfair of me, considering not a single person in Tyron's friendship circle has given me a reason to believe they're prejudiced or assholes.

Maybe after this, I'll feel reassured and finally get over myself enough and share the truth with Tyron.

I hate that I've made this a big secret. It's blown out of proportion. I know that. But feelings and personalities are unique, fickle things, so it is what it is.

"She looks ridiculous."

I swallow hard.

"Shut your lying mouth." Sammy throws a hard candy at Dean, which Kieran swipes out of the air before it can smack his boyfriend in the face. "She's amazing. Is totally going to win the challenge. A Tim Burton theme is genius."

Dean grunts in response, and I side-eye him.

"No chance Molly Goldmuff is going to let that happen. The skills in her *Corpse Bride* makeup are on point. Just look at it."

Dean tuts and shakes his head. "You're blind. A baboon could do better."

"You know," Tyron starts, and despite my rigid shoulders, I smirk at the chorus of groans, "baboons can decipher language and even word sequences. They're also empathetic as fuck."

Kieran snorts loudly at Tyron's description. "Those the actual words from an article?"

"I may have paraphrased." Tyron shrugs and eats a handful of popcorn.

I lean over and kiss his shoulder, unable to resist. The gesture earns me a soft smile and a kiss on my lips.

"You okay?" he whispers, just for me. When I nod, he doesn't break eye contact. I'm not surprised he doesn't believe me.

Most of the time, he's observant to a fault. That knowledge has my gut churning. I don't want him to call me out or put pressure on me. My brain and emotions will share when they're ready. Illogical or not.

"No way!" Sammy's gasp drags our attention away and back to *RuPaul's Drag Race*. "This show's fixed."

A ripple of laughter goes around the group at just how invested Sammy is in the show. Over the past few weeks, I've heard the occasional conversation, but this is the first night I've hung out and watched the TV program with them.

It stands to reason that I'm anxious, but that doesn't stop my curiosity.

The group of friends is fascinating to watch. There are more than the housemates here too. There are four other guys from the team. There's beer, candy, and popcorn being shared around, and mind-boggling, if not hilarious, banter as everyone seems to have a favorite contestant.

"We should head back to The Court soon." Dean's suggestion has me whipping my head in his direction so fast, there's a painful crunch in my neck.

"Hell yes." Sammy nods enthusiastically. "Last year was a blast. I like it when there's a special event the best, rather than just their standard shows."

"Damn. Just how often do you go to this place?" Banks, one of the freshman players, asks. "That's the drag club, right?" Curiosity fills his tone.

"Yeah. It's a cool place. Entertaining as hell. I've got a cousin who used to work there." Sammy tugs out his phone.

Shock slams into me. "You do?"

"Yeah. Sal. I grew up just a few towns over. Most of my family are still there, and Sal headed out this way a couple of years before I started Brixham U. He's not there anymore, but he can usually hook us up with discounted tickets."

I stare wide-eyed at Sammy, my brain short-circuiting.

"What's wrong?" Tyron's stare is concerned.

"I just…" I shake my head and look around at the group. "I suppose I'm struggling to meld together everything I thought I knew about the team with the reality." I swear, every week I have to do a double take when I see how down-to-earth, friendly, or simply cool and normal they are. That's on top of the number of times I see how open they are to, well, everyone.

Dean snorts. "So much this. I felt the same way last year. They're a mind fuck, right?"

Kieran shakes his head and tugs Dean close. "We're not that bad."

"Well, not all of you." Dean sends a withering gaze at Tyron. "Some of you play the asshole card with spectacular ease."

"Thank you." Tyron beams. "It's a skill set I've perfected over the years."

"If we do go, it needs to be before the season starts." Sammy's typing on his cell. "Come three weeks, we're not going to have enough time to rub one out, let alone have a night out with all of us."

Bentley's snort drags Sammy's attention to him. He narrows his gaze at Bentley's smirk.

A text alert sounds, and from Sammy's smile, it's obvious it's his phone. "He's on the case. If he can get tickets, it'll be fifteen bucks each. November fifth. Add it to your planner, assholes. There's a showcase or something going on."

Ice freezes my chest, making it difficult to breathe.

November the fifth is a day locked into my memory.

It's *my* showcase. The drag school's end-of-season hoorah, as it were. No way these guys can attend that event.

"Isn't that a bit... uhm... close to your first game?" My question gets everyone's attention. Heat rushes to my cheeks, but I need to push on. "Won't you have like back-to-back practices or something?"

"The weekend before our first game is always

free." Tyron's quizzical voice destroys all hope of me pushing. I can't go on without making this a huge deal. Obviously I'll be there so won't need a ticket, but I can't say that now.

It's something I'll have to figure out later.

Pressing my lips together, I offer a tight smile and nod, not trusting my voice.

I need to warn Tyron. I know this, but I don't know if I can without being mortified or without it changing things. I should be able to handle any teasing, especially the friendly kind. But before joining the drag school, I wasn't half as confident as I am now.

That quieter, shyer part is still frustratingly close to the surface.

A flash of heat presses heavily on my chest. It blurs my vision, and sweat breaks out on my back. I need to get out of here.

"I need to go." I stand abruptly. I'm aware I have everyone's attention, but all I can think about is getting fresh air and hiding away. "I'll call you later."

I don't give Tyron or anyone time to react. A few steps get me to my coat, and I tug it on as I leave the house and race down the street.

By the time I round the corner, I pull in air, letting it expand my lungs and clear my head. "Fuck." I latch on to the wall and hold myself steady.

This is fucking ridiculous.

I hate my reaction. Hate the drama I've created, even if it's in my own head at this point.

Feeling so knotted up and unable to escape from this ridiculous weave I've created, I blink back frustrated tears. Vibration from my pocket has me swallowing hard. But I can't look. Won't.

How can I explain to Tyron that I've snowballed something that shouldn't be a big deal into a giant tangle of drama? Hell, he told me with stark clarity when we first met that he abhorred drama and stayed away from it.

I ignore the call and force my legs to move.

It's late, and the temperature has dropped. I tug my jacket and do up the zip as I trudge down the street. I'm not ready to go home. Not yet. Talking this out with Bradley would probably be the sensible thing to do, but I'm not sure I can handle his sympathy right now.

Discussing this will inevitably bring up my parents and their disappointment in me. Their uncensored threats about staying under the radar. Bradley's one of the only people I've shared the reality of my upbringing with. He's also not great at holding on to his thoughts or his venom whenever we discuss them.

I can't deal with that, not when my own brain is

buzzing and raw disappointment sits so heavily on my chest.

There's only one other place to hang out. That's my favorite diner. Cherry pie and coffee will help calm me. Hopefully I can then apologize to Tyron and find the courage to share with him just what he can expect in a couple of weeks.

One thing's for sure, I won't let my grandpa or myself down. Sure, my emotions are conflicted, but beneath the tangle, I'm proud of how far I've come.

I'M CAFFEINATED AND FULL, BUT I DON'T FEEL MUCH better. The annoying ring of my phone sounds again. I made the mistake of turning it off silent when I got home, losing myself in "I kissed a boy and I liked it" TikToks. Sure, they're gushy and make my heart ache for Tyron, but they ease something inside me too.

Seeing Dad's name on the caller ID always punches dread into my gut. But it's not a call I can ignore. Not yet.

"Dad." My tone's without inflection. I can't muster anything more.

"I'll be in town tomorrow."

Moving fast, I sit bolt upright, feeling the color drain from my cheeks. "What? Why?" Even as I say the words, understanding settles over me. In the past three years, he's never attended a donor appreciation dinner. Not once, and I like it that way.

"You'll meet me outside the hotel at six thirty sharp."

Well, there goes rehearsals and my sanity. I should have expected him to do something like this, since I've managed to dodge any conversation about the holidays. My father is nothing if not the master at having the last word.

"I want to hear all about this project that will keep you from coming home at Christmas. Bring the student you're partnering with. They can join us for drinks before the meal."

"No." I shake my head instinctively. "I mean." Fuck. Tyron is going to be there. Five members of each Brixham U team will be in attendance. Tyron is one of the Bears' five. "He's on the basketball team, so I assume he'll be training." Dad's going to jump all over my ignorance, but I don't want more focus on Tyron than necessary.

In my mind's eyes, I can see Dad narrowing his gaze at my response. "Nonsense. Since several of the team will be attending the gala dinner, as is their coach, there won't be a practice. Did he play last season in the championship team?"

I wince, realizing I should have lied about Tyron.

Since the research project is a figment of my imagination, it shouldn't have been difficult to say I was spending time with someone else.

This is the thing with my father. It's a battle not to cower and revert to the yes-man he thinks I am. But sometimes, like now, I react and bumble. Panic. Sure, I'm playing the yes-man game until I graduate, but my excuses for staying away from visits home and my controlled reactions have generally improved over the last year. Admittedly, even before that… when I met my grandpa.

"Yes," I admit, not knowing how to backtrack without digging the hole any deeper or making this conversation a big deal.

He hums, a sound that makes the hairs on my arms stand on end. "Which player has the intelligence to be working with you?"

Nausea whips around in my gut. My father's such a prick.

On the edge of nausea, irritation bubbles at just how condescending he is. Tyron is incredible. Yes, he's a genius, but he's so much more than his IQ. He's kind and fun and a bit of a loveable dork. He's also fierce and protective and hilariously grumpy and defensive to the outside world.

And here I am, running out on him, ignoring his

calls, when he's done nothing to make me think he'll reject me.

Anger pulses to the surface, trailing a red-hot blaze across my skin.

I'm angry with myself. But most of all, I'm fucking livid with my dad that he's helped shape me into a man who's been too afraid to trust, speak up, and believe in genuinely good people.

"Tyron Channing." The urge to say more and list Tyron's amazing attributes sits on my tongue. I swallow the words back, not wanting to give my father anything.

"The power forward. Interesting. I've seen the attendance list, and his name is on it."

I'm not even surprised Dad knows who Tyron is or that he's seen who's attending. He's told me often enough he's invested a lot of time and money in me and my education. Brixham U's championship team will be something he can brag about.

"Six thirty sharp, Logan. Wear a suit, and be sure to leave any rainbow paraphernalia locked away in the closet where it belongs."

The line cuts off. A whoosh of air escapes me, and I suck in the fresh air, hating how much my hands shake. I stare at my cell that's trembling in my hand. Six missed call notifications.

Shit.

I need to give Tyron a heads-up and let him know about the mess I've created.

CHAPTER 11

TYRON

I can't get to Logan's place fast enough.

As soon as he raced out of our place, worry pushed against my chest. His behavior all night's been odd.

In his text I finally received not long ago, he mentioned his dad coming into town tomorrow for the annual dinner, which is a surprise.

Last year, Devlin Bryce, who offers a sizable donation to the school, didn't attend. I know because I was there. When Coach told me I had to go to the gala meal this year, I did a little research into Devlin's donation history, wondering if he would be coming this year. Not that I told Logan.

Devlin became a donor at Brixham the day after Logan was accepted into his program. Based on what

I know, Logan didn't choose the school because of its ranking but rather its distance from his hometown. I expect his grandpa being based in Georgia was a big pull too.

I have no doubt that annoyed his father, who attended Dartmouth.

Historically, donations are a big business. As in fifty-million-dollars-a-year business.

Of course, there are many whose reasons are far from nefarious—the gratitude donors, those rooted in positive values and principles. But for the likes of Mr. Bryce, I have little doubt his donations—under the bank he's vice chairman of—are more about controlling his son and wielding power, should he ever need it.

Now that I know he's coming, I'm extra curious to meet him and figure out what kind of man he is.

Maybe Logan's jittery nerves are him simply knowing his dad's going to be in the same time zone as him. Hopefully, as soon as he answers the door, I can find out.

After I know he's okay.

The paleness of his skin earlier isn't a complexion I like on him.

I shoot off a message to Kieran as I turn onto Logan's street after picking up his concerned text about Logan.

As if I wouldn't. Concern is dominant rather than being pissed off that he ran.

I wish I could roll my eyes and tell him he's wrong, but we all know I'd be full of shit.

If I have answers, have all the information, then I can help. Sure, my need to solve and fix isn't always the best solution for others, but it's who I am. I've learned in some relationships to step back, with my sister, for example, but Logan… I shake my head and tuck away my phone without responding to Kieran.

My relationship with Logan is more than him turning me on or getting my dick hard. Spending time with him rivals the time I spend with my friends, and it absolutely is a contender with the fun and contentment I get from playing basketball.

That means he's important.

A firm knock on his door follows, and I wait impatiently for him to answer. While I'm relieved he reached out to me and asked if I could visit, I'll be much happier when we've talked out his obvious upset.

"You came." There's a flush of surprise in his cheeks.

"You asked me to, so of course."

Logan nods. "I know"—he draws me inside—"I just… I don't know."

He goes to close the door, but before he can, I snag him around the waist, chasing his mouth and heat. That he falls into the kiss and sighs against me eases some of the strain in my shoulders.

Breaking the kiss, I pull my head back just a few inches. "If you need me and I can get to you, I absolutely will."

Logan searches my gaze, his own softening at whatever he sees there. "Thank you." He steps back and clutches my hand. With our palms joined, he squeezes. "Do you want a drink?"

"No thanks. I'm here to talk and make sure you're okay."

A soft smile curls his lips.

I follow him to his room, not willing to let go of his hand. Not that he tries to release me. Once we're in the privacy of his bedroom and his door's locked, I sit on his bed. I leave plenty of space for him to join me, though my lap's always free.

Something tells me now isn't the time for that, though.

Patiently I wait him out as he hesitates about where to sit, ending up on his office chair. At least he wheels it my way rather than there being more feet than I like between us.

"So, there are things I should tell you about my family, my dad especially."

I totally called it, which I won't share since I don't want to sound like a dick. "Okay."

"I've already explained how we're not close and how they're not exactly thrilled about my sexuality."

The creak of my jaw echoes in my head. I hate that his parents are assholes.

"But that's all kind of secondary to what's going on."

My brows dip.

"So you know my dad's now attending."

"Did you know before I saw you earlier, or did this just happen?"

"Just before I texted you, asking to see you."

I nod. "Nothing like last minute."

A humorless laugh escapes Logan. "I expect he decided a few weeks ago but just told me about it now to throw me off my game."

"Why would he feel the need to do that?"

The pulse in his neck throbs so hard it catches my attention. "I was told to go home for Christmas, but I refused."

"You don't usually go home for the holidays?"

He shakes his head. "Never. This past summer was the last time I ever planned to go home."

With this new information, I sit up more rigidly. Fresh concern rakes over me.

"Will you explain why that is?"

Logan's nod is slow as emotion flickers across his features. "Dad has expectations. A condition of me attending school so far away, and not one he wanted me to attend, is that when I leave, I'll join the team at one of his friends' corporations, stay for at least five years, before taking on a more senior role at the corporate bank he works at."

"But you're joining FinCEN, right?"

"Yes." A thread of steel punches out that one word, and understanding takes shape in my mind.

"Your parents don't know." It's not a question, but he answers anyway.

"No, they don't. They won't know until it's already happened and I've completed my degree."

"They've threatened not to pay your school tuition."

"One of the conditions." The resigned sigh hits

me in the solar plexus. I'm not a fan of his upset, but the steel in his "yes" earlier still rings in my mind.

"Okay, so tomorrow and the holidays?"

"They're linked." His mouth twists, his embarrassment obvious, but he doesn't look away. "I told my parents I couldn't come home because I was tasked with a bonus research project, and you're my partner."

I nod, rolling with it. "Okay. That makes sense that you came up with a story." While I can't relate to his distress or the need to lie to his parents, I understand why he feels he needs to.

"You're not pissed?"

"That you pulled me into your deception?" When he nods, I reach out and drag him, chair and all, closer to the bed. "While I'm not an advocate for lying, and I'm not keen for people to bring me into whatever lies are being told, for you and for this, I don't mind."

His shoulders practically melting, Logan looks lighter and less stressed. When he responds with "Thank you," taking me at my word rather than double-checking my sincerity, I tug him again. This time he stands and clambers onto my lap, a position I'm ridiculously fond of.

"And tomorrow?"

Logan winces. "Dad knows you're going to be there tomorrow and expects you to join us at six thirty for a drink."

I raise my brow. "He's assuming I don't already have plans?"

"I'm sorry. He's a prick. I didn't commit you to join us for drinks. I wouldn't do that to you, but he knows you're there, and I have no doubt he'll grill you about the research project."

"So, he's checking you really do have a genuine reason for not going home for Christmas."

Logan nods. "Yeah. He's pretty pissed off. I've spoken a handful of words with him, but that much is obvious. The friend of his I was meant to meet with is apparently the perfect mentor for my first few years. No way do I want to meet him and dig myself in any deeper."

I nod, getting my head around everything he's shared with me. I have so many questions about his dad and who this future employer is, but there's something more important I need to know for tomorrow.

"Does your dad know we're dating?"

"No."

Even though I'm not surprised, bitterness slices at my chest. "So, you're just doing drinks, or are you now attending?"

"I'm his plus one."

I nod as Logan studies my face, happy at least I get to spend more time with him, even if it's at an event I'd rather not attend. Especially now.

"I don't plan to hide who you are to me."

I freeze, the thump of my pulse racing to my ears.

Logan surprises me by capturing my chin and angling my face. My breath catches at the contact. It's a move I've pulled on him more than once, and I like it a hell of a lot that there's a fierceness in his gaze that matches the possessive touch.

"That we're dating isn't something I'm willing to conceal, especially not from my dad, and that's not about pissing him off or getting a dig in, despite how much he wishes I'd lock myself in the closet."

His dad's annoying me more and more. And while I won't be a prick to him tomorrow and call him out for being a sorry excuse of a father, and a worthless human being, one thing you all know about me is my inability to roll over.

I certainly don't intimidate easily.

"And if you introduce me as your boyfriend?"

The hesitation and knowing each of Logan's secrets no longer seem significant. Not when he's so fucking resilient and working on paving his own way, despite his shithead parents. Sure, he's privileged, as am I, but he's not entitled. He's also desperate to break free from the restraints, and I expect emotional abuse he's been dealing with since he was fourteen and came out.

Red hits Logan's cheeks, and his eyes practically light up at my words. A good sign. But he's mute, staring at me.

"I'm asking you to be my boyfriend. I think we've got this dating gig locked down," I tease, despite the edge of seriousness in my words. "I like you a lot, Logan."

"I like you too." The words caress my skin.

I smile at his confession. "So, what do you say? Interested in being my boyfriend?" Would I ask if I thought there's a chance he'd say no? I'd like to think not, but it doesn't stop the fast fizz of anticipation pushing against my rib cage.

Here, in the stark lighting of his messy bedroom, I swear I'm at his mercy.

I want him to say yes so fucking badly, I can barely think straight.

"I'd like that a lot."

My breath whooshes out of me. The sound lifts with an unsteady chuckle. "Yeah?" I shouldn't be questioning him or giving him a chance to take it back, but I want to keep him. Make Logan mine.

We're good together, and from the wide grin and

the way he scoots forward so his groin rubs mine, I expect he thinks so too.

"I definitely want to be your boyfriend." A sweet kiss follows, lighter than I anticipated. Every kiss with Logan is phenomenal, though.

There's a gentle glide of his tongue to mine as our mouths move, still slow and tender. He cups my cheek, his fingers dancing over my skin, but all too soon, he's pulling back.

"I hate to say this, but you have gym time in the morning."

I grunt and chase his mouth for another kiss instead. He allows just one swift brush of our lips before he angles away with a soft chuckle.

"Do you have to be so sensible?"

Our gazes meet, and he quirks a brow. "Should I be concerned that you're not being?"

I roll my eyes even as I clamp down on his waist, so we rub together. When his lids flutter closed, I grin.

"Nuh-uh."

Apparently not.

"Really? Why?" I shift my hand, placing it over his groin, squeezing the hard outline of his cock. "We should always make sure we find time to be satisfied."

"Epididymal hypertension, or blue balls, isn't actually dangerous."

Fuck. Me. Dead.

Moving so fast he doesn't have the chance to protest, I hold tight, spin, and have Logan beneath me. He's laughing by the time he wraps his legs around my thighs.

"Keep talking dirty facts to me."

"A single sperm contains 37.5 MB of DNA information."

I drop my head with a groan, burying my face against his neck. He smells so good and sexy. Add in the facts, and I'm going to struggle to move off him.

The asshole's still chuckling, even as he angles his head, giving me better access to his neck. Obliging, I drop kisses there.

"Eating pineapple doesn't make your cum taste better."

A wide grin has me pulling back and looking down at Logan. Shadows from my larger body spill across his face, but they don't hide the amusement or the tender expression he's sending my way.

He's gorgeous. Sure, I think his body is hot, complete with its paleness and softer skin, and his face is perfection. This, what's going on between us, is so much more than a fling. While my asking him out proves that, I want long-term and serious with this guy.

Logan yawns, and I recall what time I arrived.

"I could spend the night." It's late, and Logan's not wrong about my early start. "We can cuddle and go to sleep. No funny business." I quickly add, "As long as I can be the big spoon and my hand on your junk all night is okay."

His lips quirk. "And that's not funny business?"

"It doesn't have to be." I smile back. "I like your dick a lot. Holding on will help me sleep well. Maybe even give me sweet dreams."

He studies me a beat. When he licks his bottom lip, I know he's going to say yes.

"Don't wake me up in the morning when you leave at the ass crack of dawn."

"Not even to kiss you goodbye?"

"Well, maybe a small kiss."

"On your dick?"

Logan snorts and taps my ass to get me to move. "Maybe." He shifts before I can drag him back to me. I groan and reach out for him. "Nuh-uh. It's late. Tomorrow is going to be a shitshow with Dad"—I sober a little at that—"and I need my wits about me." Once he's on his feet, he faces me, his gaze intense. "It'll be better with you there, so thank you."

I don't point out I'm going anyway. He knows

that. I understand what he's saying, so instead, I nod. "How about we meet for lunch and talk about this awesome research project that's taking up so much of our time?"

A sweet smile is sent my way. "That sounds great. Now, I'm going to shower." I make to stand. "Alone," he says quickly, darting to the door and unlocking it.

"Fine," I grumble, tugging out my cell to set my alarm a little earlier and sending a group message to my housemates.

> Me: Staying over at my boyfriend's. I need to talk tomorrow with those of you going to the gala. Got some shit to arrange.

> Kieran: Sure. Don't be late in the morning.

> Leon: Boyfriend! Totally called it. CU 2mo.

> Sammy: The hell!!! You're all going down like flies. Fuck. But yeah. I'm not going 2mo but tell me something interesting enough and I might crash. :P

> Bentley: Tell me what you need, and I'll make it happen.

Happy my friends will support me, no matter what I ask of them, I tug my clothes off, reluctantly keeping my boxers on, and get under Logan's covers.

I hope he realizes I was dead serious about cradling his junk. It's an image I can't get out of my head, and palming his jewels seems like a spectacular way to fall asleep.

SNUGGLING WITH LOGAN WAS EPIC—ONCE I WORKED out the best way to sleep without getting a dead arm or an elbow in my face. While he's not quite as fidgety as my aunt Alice's cat, who twitches like she's smacking at glasses of water to knock as many of them off the table, he could give the orange tabby a run for her money.

But still, I managed to sleep eventually, palm cupping him, which went a long way to stop the imaginary glass-swiping. Sure, there was twitching elsewhere, but he slept soundly once I had a handful.

Since I left him sleep-rumpled, I sweat until I could no longer grip the dumbbells, caught up with the guys, who ribbed me mercilessly about having a boyfriend, and I told them a little about Logan's dad.

While I didn't set out to overshare and betray Logan's confidence, I spilled enough to let them know Devlin Bryce is a homophobic asshole who, unfortunately, donated a lot of money to Brixham. The bonus is, with this being Logan's final year, I can't imagine that level of donation continuing.

Why's this a bonus?

Well, I figure the school won't be too disgruntled if I piss Devlin off.

"Looking good, Ty." Leon stands in my open doorway, eyeing my painted fingernails. I hold them out, admiring Lexi's handiwork. My sister and a couple of her friends came through for me, my teammates, and the football, soccer, and lacrosse team members turning up tonight.

The rainbow colors, complete with the final three nails blue, pink, and white, actually look kind of cool, but there's no chance I could see myself wearing color again, unless it's for a good cause.

I chipped at least two nails by the time my sister had finished with Kieran's, so she had to reapply. Whoever finds the time to look after themselves with color and cosmetics has my absolute respect. It takes a shitload of dedication.

"Thanks." I narrow my gaze on his nails, wondering why they look sparklier than mine. "Why are yours different?" I frown, envious of how the light catches them.

He waves his fingers and grins. "This glittery stuff. Cool, huh. Dean put it on for me."

I gasp. "Why the hell didn't he give me any? This stinks of betrayal."

With a snort, Leon rolls his eyes and leaves the room, saying, "Take it up with him if you're feeling brave enough."

When he puts it like that, maybe not.

Dean, Kieran's boyfriend, may only come up to my chest, but what he lacks in height, he makes up for in personality. And sass. A whole lot of it.

"You've got two minutes before we're heading out," Leon hollers as he goes downstairs.

Taking one last look in my floor-length mirror, I reposition my rainbow pin on my lapel and button up my suit jacket, grinning at the waistcoat I'm hiding away.

They're all little things, but they make our position and support clear. While the need to spell that out for Logan's dad is at the center of my rallying my sporting family, it's something I'm ashamed to say we haven't done enough of.

I plan to rectify that.

I'll definitely talk to Coach about doing something with the team. Ideally not just for the opening game but for the whole season. Even better if we could make it permanent.

Doing a final check of everything, I pat my wallet in my pocket and snag my phone.

This feels a little like preparing for war. Sure, that's majorly overkill, but I'm definitely expecting to have to handle Mr. Bryce. Not physically, obviously. The feeling remains, though. I can't imagine the man will be pleasant. That's me totally being polite, when the truth is I'm envisioning him being a giant fuckhead.

Thankfully, I can control my expressions and my tone. Believe it or not—contrary to any slips you may have witnessed—I can also be super subtle when the situation calls for it.

How freakin' awesome would it be, though, if I could time travel and get my FBI training squared away and seriously put Devlin through his paces? Depending on how tonight goes and how he treats his son, maybe I'll be sure to remind myself when I'm in the agency.

I find my friends in the hallway, all waiting for me, apparently. They're all dressed in their formal post-game suits.

Grinning when I see their polish, I shoot off a text to Logan, letting him know we're about to leave. He doesn't know anything about the LGBTQIA+ apparel. I can't wait to see his reaction.

It doesn't take long for us to get to the school's events center. The large room is decked out with huge round tables, and the walls are draped in swaths of school colors. But first, it's drinks in the foyer, complete with canapés and a mass of suited middle-aged and older men and dressed-up women.

While I couldn't meet Logan beforehand, courtesy of having to see Coach first, I take a surreptitious glance but don't spot him or his dad. Not daring to annoy Coach, I make my way over with the other guys.

Coach doesn't even raise a brow when he notices our pins. There's a small eye twitch when he takes in our nail polish, though. "Best behavior," he grumbles. "No antics, curb your cussing, and remember you're representing not only the school but me and your team."

"Yes, Coach," we chorus.

"No ditching the meal. I expect to see every face until desserts are finished."

We all nod. There's not a chance of us going against the man. He runs drills hard and is all too cozy with the timer and adding on those minutes when we're asshats.

Before he dismisses us, his attention falls on me. "This your doing?"

While I'm not the captain, it's no surprise he calls me out. I'm known for getting shit done.

"Sure is." I offer a shit-eating smile. Aiming for wide-eyed innocence is pointless. His narrowed gaze means he's not buying it. "I've got a bunch of ideas for our games."

"I just bet you do. Talk it through with Assistant Coach Krestle. As long as there's no makeup, jewelry, or the like, I don't see a problem. But he has to give the okay."

"Thanks, Coach." I nod respectfully, grateful he's had Kieran's back since day one especially, and mine since I told him about who I'm dating. Maybe it helps that he's a proud dad of a gay son. Either way, there's a whole lot of attention on our team—with our win and the flurry of rainbow announcements—and he's taking it all in stride with a healthy dose of "don't mess with my team" attitude.

Yeah, we're all lucky as hell.

Dismissing the team, he calls my name. "PDA at a minimum, you hear me, Channing?"

There's little point in pleading ignorant. He'll be fully aware of the attendees tonight.

"To clarify, minimum means no tongues but—"

"Channing." He looks to the ceiling.

I chuckle. "I got it, Coach. I won't embarrass you."

"Uh-huh. Just keep your head in the game, okay?"

"Sure thing, Coach." I offer a nod before heading away, thinking about his words. They're similar to

Pops's at the start of the semester. The difference being their goals for me aren't the same.

The literal game is important. I have no intention of ever letting my team down. But my long game doesn't include basketball. That means I have to always think bigger and beyond the season.

Now, there's the inclusion of a third. Logan. I like to think he's part of my endgame too.

A person who can not only put up with my awesome peculiarities and intensity but embrace them is someone I want to keep.

I like my chances.

With renewed purpose, I seek out Logan, making sure to stop and shake a few hands along the way. I finally spot him next to his father. The photographs on his company site are accurate. There's a carefully placed, barely there smile, which absolutely doesn't reach his eyes. It's the sharpness in his gaze that already rubs me the wrong way. Though, to be fair, my impression of him has already been formed. It would take a miracle for me to be swayed.

Shifting my focus to Logan, I embrace the thrum of awareness and the fizz of delight at seeing him. What I don't like is the strain around his mouth.

A few feet away, his eyes widen when he spots me. There's no hiding the purpose and intent in every step I make. In the few seconds I have, I read him as best as I can, looking for any sign that he doesn't want me to greet him as though he's mine.

A slight shifting of his mouth, a curl of his lips, is all it takes.

He's happy I'm here.

"Hey," I greet as I hold his hand, squeeze, and press my mouth to his. It barely lasts a heartbeat and is G-rated, though it does its job of letting anyone who cares know that we're together.

Funnily, Logan is the person who matters the most. The need to let him know I'm here for him—regardless of my basketball player duties—is my priority.

"You okay?" I hold his gaze, wanting the truth in his eyes, knowing his words might not match.

"I am, yeah." That his words aren't strained is a testament to his control. The lines between his brows smooth out a fraction.

I nod, squeeze his warm palm again, and turn my attention to the looming presence of the man at our side.

The polite smile of his hasn't wavered. Impressive. If there was a way to capture bitterness in someone's gaze, though, it would be his.

"Mr. Bryce." I hold out my right hand, having deliberately held tightly to Logan's with my left, so there's no need to let go. "I've heard a lot about you." Yeah, there's not a "good to meet you" here.

"Tyron Channing." He grips my hand and shakes. I'm disappointed there's no squeeze or toxic masculine bullshit of trying for dominance. "It seems my son's been keeping secrets from me." He releases my hand, his gaze landing on my nails, and side-eyes Logan.

"No secrets" is Logan's only response, his attention on me. A small smile hovers over his mouth. "Nice polish."

I grin. "Lexi's done a great job."

"Impressive." He eyes my rainbow pin, his gaze softening. "It looks good on you."

"You're a positive influence on me." I wink before I drop my smile and turn my steely gaze on his dad. "You must be proud of Logan's work with the LGBTQIA+ group. I know how valuable he is."

"Quite." Mr. Bryce nods, that tight tilt of his lips still present. "He's always had a way with numbers. It's wonderful he's using that talent for such a good cause while he has the extra time at college. I know it's a social club, but the group supports two deserving local charities."

The tightening of Logan's grip draws my attention to him. He's slack-jawed and staring at his father like he's an alien being. "You know about the charity work we do?"

"Of course I do. The youth center and the outreach program. I've ensured our company has matched your club's donations every year."

"You have? I didn't know." Logan shakes his head, and I have to admit, this isn't a conversation I expected to overhear.

When Mr. Bryce attempts a careless shrug, I grasp the thread dangling before me, begging me to understand what he's not saying. There's no chance Logan's dad does anything carelessly. Hell, even a shrug doesn't marry with what I know about him.

"Sometimes it's not necessary to make bold, loud announcements about philanthropy."

Are you buying this shit? Yeah, I'm not sure I am either.

"That's certainly honorable," I say, watching him carefully. "Showing your support for your son this way is admirable too."

"It's important to recognize where my son invests his energy and try to connect with him when the opportunity arises." He turns his focus to Logan. "Such charities begin to rely on donations. I believe the youth group has even set up a new program recently. Without the commitment of donations, that would never be possible. It's so important they continue, especially when they're doing such good."

The fucker.

From the way Logan's palm flexes and his muscles jerk, there's no way he missed the threat of his father's words.

"I understand why you're too busy to visit for Christmas now, with all of the extra... studying you're doing," Mr. Bryce continues, gaze still on his son. "It's not a concern at all, as long as you know how vital it is you stay the course, and you don't neglet your commitments."

He turns to me, and it takes every ounce of control I have not to tell him exactly what I think about him. Not wanting to give him the opportunity to continue to control the dialogue, I say, "I'm interested in discovering more about the Harrington Group." The twitch is the only tell that I've caught him off guard.

I hold back my smirk, loving how my few hours of focused research on the internet last night can unravel a wealth of factual information, in addition to hearsay.

"Next term I have a paper to write on fraud, and I think I'll focus on charitable fraud. It would be great to have some insight into someone who has connections with the group."

Pink touches the tips of Mr. Bryce's ears. "I don't have connections with that group."

I can feel Logan's gaze on me, but I refuse to break eye contact with his dad. "But weren't Creshman BCL a main donator to their charitable work?" It goes without saying they were. Sure, they were cleared of any involvement, but Simpleton and Gravings, the directors of the firm, were charged with conspiracy to commit wire and mail fraud and subscribing to false tax returns. The two directors were also at more than a handful of events and parties with Mr. Bryce, with photographs of smiles and handshakes.

If I were closer, I'm sure the sound of his grinding teeth would reach me. The clench of his jaw is evident, though.

"It goes without saying the whole situation was terrible, and the involved parties were identified and brought to justice. It's not a subject suitable for polite conversation. Nor is it something I'll be discussing."

I quirk my brow, ensuring there's no tone change in my words. "Embarrassing, I expect. Understandable." I nod. "I imagine that makes any charitable contributions you make susceptible to more scrutiny and that you ensure there's never the potential for anything, let's just say… untoward or to cause any bad press or scandal." I angle to look at Logan. His cheeks are flushed and his eyes bright. "Your dad's a smart man, Logan. I can see why you aligned with those two charitable groups. No chance of fraud. Certainly no chance of projects being dropped due to donors pulling… not when your father's involved."

The swell of voices draws my attention to more students entering the room. I grin, spotting Denny, the football captain. The rainbow nails contrast with his dark skin so perfectly, they may as well have a spotlight shining on them.

"If you'll excuse us, Mr. Bryce, I promised to introduce Denny Kilroy to my boyfriend. I'm sure there are many other generous individuals who you'd love to catch up with." Dipping my head to make it clear I'm going to be leaving with his son, I fix my gaze on Mr. Bryce for a steady beat before pulling Logan away.

"What the hell just happened?" Logan's words are a rushed, breathless whisper.

"No way was I letting your dad threaten to hold funding for charities over your head."

"You read that threat too?"

A humorless snort escapes me. "He was as subtle as a rhino in a china shop."

"Not sure that's how that simile goes, but yeah… he's an asshole."

I pause a few feet away from Denny and turn to

face Logan. "I think it's safe to say he expects you to renege on your agreement to follow in his footsteps."

A deep furrow appears between his eyebrows, and his lips tighten into a thin line. "At least it shouldn't come as too much of a surprise, then. Maybe he's already drawn up a new will to disinherit me."

Glancing around, I'm aware this isn't a conversation for now. No one appears to be within hearing distance, especially as we're talking quietly. With my gaze back on his, I ask, "Will that matter if he has?"

"No." He shakes his head, and I believe him.

"But it makes you upset." There's no question, just a statement that hurts my gut.

"Yeah, I suppose. It would be great if I had these amazing parents who supported me. I suppose I should be grateful they didn't cut me off when I told them I'm gay."

This is too much, too personal, and clearly too raw for Logan. Locating the closest exit, I tug him that way and don't stop until we're alone. When we are, I enclose him in a hug, wrapping him in my arms and squeezing.

He sighs against me, locking his arms around my back. It's the first time we've hugged like this— taking comfort this way—and I can't help but wonder when the last time for him was.

I hold tighter, not loosening my hold when I whisper, "You shouldn't need to be grateful that your parents haven't cut you off for being true to yourself. I wish you felt their love every day, because you're unapologetically you. Because you're kind and amazing. You're compassionate and intelligent."

Somehow, Logan draws me even closer, burying his face against my neck.

"Parents shouldn't need to threaten or force or change you. Not for them to love or support you. You're incredible."

A shuddery breath brushes against my skin, leaving goose bumps behind.

"You're going to be okay, whatever happens."

"Thank you." Logan angles away and brushes his lips against my jaw. When his gaze catches mine, his struggle simmers at the surface. "Not sure I can handle you being any more amazing. You're going to make it impossible to keep up with this perfect-boyfriend gig you have going on."

"Let's not worry about perfect. Let's just be defiantly us."

I barely finish speaking before his mouth crashes to mine, kissing me with such intensity, my brain turns to mush, and I can't quite remember why it's not a great idea to find a closet somewhere so I can finally fuck him.

"For the love of God. Channing."

Coach's voice is as good as a bucket of ice-cold water. Breathless, I jerk away. Logan's still in my arms, but there's a little space between us. He goes to move, but I hold on tight, looking away from Coach, who's rubbing the bridge of his nose, to Logan. Wide-eyed, I raise my brows in silent warning.

He seems to understand my need to not use him as a shield. There's no concealing my rock-hard dick, not in these pants.

"Sorry, Coach. Just working a couple of things through. I'll be there in a minute." At Logan's mouth twitch, I amend, "Make that two."

"Two minutes, Channing."

And then he leaves, and Logan's laughing loudly, back in my arms and hugging me again. "We best get ourselves under control and head back inside. Didn't you say something about when your coach is annoyed, he kicks your ass at practice?"

"That's an understatement." I force myself away, giving us space, and look down at my crotch. "Maybe I need to think about the laps he's going to make us do so my dick behaves."

"Will that work?" Amusement colors his words.

"Maybe if I think about the stench of the guys and the locker room afterward, then yeah." I scrunch my nose in concentration and don't have to recall too deeply just how awful the smell gets.

"Do you need me to let you have some space so you can go do your thing with the guests?"

My gaze snaps to his. "No space necessary. I'm sure you can do ample schmoozing, and it'll keep you away from your dad."

"I wonder if I can get the seating plan changed. Shift the name tags or whatever."

My grin is instant. "Seriously, Logan, it's like you don't know me at all. Let me show you how the master works and gets shit done."

It does the trick. He laughs, the sound light and free. There's a brightness in his eyes that wasn't there a moment before.

"A master, huh?"

"Fact."

"Not sure that's how facts work," he teases.

"Facts, smacts!"

He snorts. "Isn't it meant to be schmacts?"

"Hush your traitorous mouth. The master's speaking, remember?" I wrap my arm around his back, my palm landing on his waist. "Come on, baby." I catch the way his brows shoot high at the endearment. The way his mouth curls upward is an added bonus and makes me want to use the term all the damn time. "Let me strip out of this jacket, and you can watch the magic happen."

He's snickering at my side, rolling his eyes too, but his flushed cheeks and happiness that's all but radiating off him are worth all the silliness, my teasing, and the fucking amazing rainbow waistcoat I'm just about to reveal.

CHAPTER 12
LOGAN

"Smart isn't the word I'd choose." Glaring at the offending shoes that clearly hate me, I take stock of what hurts.

I saved my face, so that's something.

My fishnets are toast, and from the look of horror on Dolly's face, my outfit didn't survive the tear I heard when I plummeted.

Attempting to move my ankle is a fool's move. Pain blooms, and saliva floods my mouth.

Hurling now is not an option. Nor is an injury of any kind.

Everything I've worked so hard for can't disappear with a stupid slip, a wobble, and a twist.

"Fuck." Giving up on dealing with any of this, I ease myself back on the floor, hiding my face with my forearm. Deep breaths, nice and easy. That's all I need to focus on. Then I'll restock.

"Hey now, girl. None of that. Your mascara will trash that pretty face of yours. No hot basketball player's going to want to feed you cock if you look like a smoosh-faced skunk."

I snort out a laugh.

"There we go. Much better. Now, while you brace and I put some ice on this ankle of yours, tell Aunt Dolly a fun story about your sassy grandpa."

Grateful for the distraction as I hear someone pass Dolly what I assume is an ice pack, I consider which of the many stories to share with her. There are many. The two years I spent getting to know my grandpa, he didn't waste a second. Regaling me with stories of his misspent youth or the fun he had while performing was a weekly event.

Not that he shied away from some of the stories with a much harsher reality of being a gay man who started doing drag in the seventies.

"One time his dick tuck came unstuck in the middle of a Cher performance." Cold hits my foot, but it's the pressure of the heavy pack that has me wincing. I shudder out a breath, feeling just a little pathetic at how much a twisted ankle has knocked me about. I refuse to believe it can be anything more serious than that. "You know the infamous black outfit that left nothing to the imagination, it was so high cut?"

"Oh, honey, I do. I wish I had the ass to carry that outfit off." Dolly chuckles. "My chunky deliciousness just won't be contained by something so skimpy. Did your grandpa play a game of peek-a-boo with his one-eyed snake?"

Uncovering my face, I angle up to look at Dolly, snickering at her description. "Sounds like you know the game well," I tease.

"That I do, honey. Just ask Jakey."

That has me bracing myself on my hands to stare at her. "What? Seriously? The bouncer?"

"Oh, how that man likes to bounce." She waves a hand in front of her face and puffs out her cheeks. "Anyone who can throw me around, then let me take him on a wild ride, now that, girl, is a man you want to play the game with. Often."

"Jesus." I clear my throat, bombarded with visuals I'm not sure I want. "So, how's my ankle looking?"

Dolly shifts the pack and tentatively touches my foot and examines it. "I'm confident it's not broken, but you may want to consider an X-ray."

"Not unless I really have to." I can imagine the questions that will arise from my dad when he receives the details from my insurance. He's been unnervingly quiet since he visited a few days ago, but I don't want to give him a reason to make contact.

"In that case, let's get it strapped and keep it iced. I'll go and grab the first aid kit."

"Thanks." I watch Dolly go, grateful she's not only amazing but that she's a paramedic. Her day-job skills have come in mighty handy over the four months of training I've had. I'm getting a bit of a reputation for damaging myself.

It doesn't take long for Dolly to get me fixed up and for us to get dressed into our street clothes. We're edging closer to our performance night, which means the pressure's on, and we're practicing in almost full costume.

The group are incredible humans as well as performers. They're also passionate and are rocking their drag queen training. Not only that, but they've also welcomed me with open arms, despite knowing this is neither a hobby nor a passion for me. But the stories about my grandpa opened up their hearts and had them tucking away their manicured claws to help me to fulfill my promise.

"Let me drop you home."

Since I'm limping badly and my ankle's throbbing, I happily accept. "You're a star. Thanks, Donnie."

"Have you got crutches you can borrow from anyone?" he asks as we make our way slowly to his car.

"Maybe. I'll try and sort something when I get home."

"If you struggle, let me know, and I'll drop some around."

Donnie really is the best. He's also super easy on the eyes, his oversized chunky ass included. Even with all that, there's never been any zing of attraction between us. And now, with nothing but a hot basketball player at the center of my world, I can't imagine anyone else ever catching my attention.

I smile to myself, more than happy with that.

"Did you hear there's just four tickets left to our show?" Donnie grins as he buckles up and waits for me to do the same before he starts the engine.

It takes a moment for me to compute, my thoughts traveling to Tyron and his friends. They wanted tickets. My grin stretches wild. With just four tickets left, it means they won't be going, right? Tyron tends to be the organized one out of the guys, and he hasn't mentioned anything to me. No way they'd leave anyone out and not attend as a group.

"That's great," I say, still smirking, a relief I haven't felt in a while coursing through me.

The drama of my dad coming to town completely

overshadowed my telling Tyron, as well as pushing down my panic about him and his friends attending our graduation performance. Now it doesn't look like I have to worry. Not that I don't plan to share with him what I'm doing, but right now, I can't deal with anything else.

What I do have to consider is what to tell him about my ankle.

Lying is not an option. I'm fully aware I'm keeping my drag queen training from him, but I haven't outright lied. Not even that day before school officially started did I lie. Not that I wouldn't have. I'm not that much of a saint. But I still get the most delicious goose bumps and warm tingling in my stomach when I think about how he not only helped me up but cupped my face and asked me who hurt me.

Holy shit. I'm still surprised I didn't melt into a puddle of goo.

What's funny is Tyron talks about the ridiculous alpha vibe, and we banter and joke about it, but fuck me dead. That night he nailed it.

Hell, if I'd been in my right mind and not so sore, I'd have asked him to nail me too.

"You know, you're grinning more and more each time I see you."

I side-eye Donnie, struggling to hide my smile. "That right?"

"You've come a long way from the young, slightly dorky, and painfully shy guy who rocked up for the late-spring school."

"I was so not dorky."

Donnie snorts. "Whatever you need to tell yourself, handsome, but you were. You could barely look any of us in the eye. Now look at you."

Heat touches my cheeks as Donnie continues. It should come as no surprise that I'm a stranger to praise, so when I do receive it, I feel awkward as hell. Not that I'm not grateful.

"You can hold your own, even against Dixie. That takes tits of steel. You even have a bona fide basketball-star boyfriend."

I shrug, my face still flaming hot.

"I'm proud of you, Logan. I know you'll be hanging up your breasts after the performance, but I hope you remember to hang on to the inner diva Dewanna brought out in you. Keep mirroring that inner goddess and that backbone."

I clear my throat and cast Donnie a look, humbled. "Thank you," I settle on. "I don't think I could have got through any of the classes without you."

As he pulls up outside my place, he squeezes my

arm. "No problem. I just want you to promise not to be a stranger when you're a high flying whatever it is you want to do in the government."

I chuckle, more than okay with making that promise. "No chance of us losing contact."

Throwing me a wink, he pushes open his door, and I do the same. I haul myself out, grunting in pain when I put my weight on my bandaged ankle. I'm shoeless, and my toes are cold.

"Let me help you inside."

Scooping his arm around me, Donnie holds me steady, letting me get my balance before we edge away from his car. Thankfully, there was a parking spot right outside the house, so I don't have to hobble too far.

As I shove my hand in my pocket to get my keys, I startle at the door opening. Surprise ripples through me. Tyron's in the doorway, his face so void of emotion that one thing is clear. He's wondering what the fuck is going on.

When he scans Donnie, his hold on me, there's not even a twitch.

Since I still haven't considered what I'm telling him, I stare, my brain farting and aware the jig is up, and it's time I come clean. I'm so intent on Tyron, I misstep, stumble, and hiss in pain.

I don't even have enough time to open my eyes

before an arm, combined with a scent I know so well, is wrapped around my waist, and Tyron's warmth is pressed against me.

"You're hurt." The concern in his voice has me opening my eyes and taking a calming breath.

If he's concerned, it means he's not pissed off, right?

"I'm okay. Just a sprain."

"Maybe," Donnie unhelpfully adds. "Ice, painkillers, then see how you're faring tomorrow."

We still haven't started moving, and I don't think we're going to yet. Tyron is laser-focused on Donnie.

"Who are you?"

"Donnie. A friend of—"

"My boyfriend's?"

Is it wrong to swoon and find that bite to his words hot as hell?

"The one and only." I don't need to look at Donnie to know he's grinning. Tyron is a big guy, in every conceivable way. Donnie not only has ten years on us, but from some of the stories he's shared about work, he's not easily intimidated. "And you, handsome, must be Tyron. You're every inch as lickable as Logan's described you to be."

I jerk my head in Donnie's direction. Mortified. "I didn't describe him as lickable."

"You don't think I'm lickable?"

Like a swinging door, I whip my gaze back to Tyron. The asshole has his sexy brow quirked, and those annoyingly gorgeous eyes have the perfect amount of intensity to get me hot under the collar.

"I didn't say that you weren't, nor would I tell anyone if you were."

"So I am lickable." A total statement. "On a scale of one to ten, with ten being irresistible and as addictive as those cherry drops you love, what number would you land on?"

"Ooh… what would number one be?" Donnie chirps. "Outdated licorice-flavored condoms, with dulce de leche lube rubbed in?" I turn to him as he shudders. "That would be a total one for me."

I can't not respond. "I don't want to know more, as that sounds worryingly specific."

"Screw that. They make dulce de leche lube?"

I yank my gaze back to Tyron and recognize that look in his eyes. Curiosity. It means he's going to research the hell out of it. Something I adore about him, but I know full well he doesn't have time for.

I need to get this conversation moving.

I also need to get off my foot. It's throbbing something fierce.

"I could really do with some ice."

Those words do the trick. Tyron pretends not to

be, but he's one hell of a caretaker. "Shit, let's get you inside."

"Thanks." I lean into him, grateful for his strong hold.

"If you've got him, I'm going to head out. I have an early shift tomorrow." Donnie backs away, and I roll my eyes at his appreciative last once-over of Tyron. "Let me know if you need the crutches, and I'll see you next week."

"Thanks." I nod, grateful he doesn't elaborate. "Get home safe."

"Will do. Good to meet you, Tyron." He waves and makes his way to his car.

I focus back on the path before me and getting inside.

"You need me to carry you?"

I smile softly at the offer. "I should be okay. It's only a few more steps. Thanks."

Slowly, we head inside, where Tyron gets me set up on the couch and disappears into the kitchen. While he's gone, my housemate enters the room.

"Shit. You've damaged yourself again?" Bradley stares at my ankle. "Is this going to affect… you know?"

"I should be okay. Just a sprain. As long as I look after it over the next couple of days, I should be good."

Bradley winces in sympathy when I grimace, moving my foot so it's more comfortable.

"How'd you get home?"

"His friend Donnie, who I'm eager to hear more about," Tyron says as he returns, a bag of frozen—I lean forward to get a better look—hash browns in his hand. "It's all I could find that's not in a box." He shrugs as he settles the bag on my foot.

"And on that note, I'm heading back to my room." Bradley offers a kind smile before abandoning me.

"Do you know Donnie from your secret project?"

I bob my head and take the glass of water he passes me. "Thanks, and yes."

He stands and tugs out a packet of tablets from his pocket. "Take two of these."

"Thanks." I pop two in my mouth, hoping the painkillers touch the edge of my pain quickly.

After swallowing my water, it's no use. I have to focus on Tyron. He's waiting me out, his gaze harder than I'm used to seeing these days—well, directed at me. Honestly, I want to share this with him and get it off my chest. Sure, it's my choice, but he's my boyfriend. I'd like to think he won't hightail it out of here.

"I've told you a fair bit about my grandpa. Our family's estrangement. My dad disowning him."

"Because he was gay."

"That's part of it."

"Yet your dad's not done the same to you." He tilts his head and studies me. "He's an asshole, and I know he's not exactly supportive, but I'm curious why he rejected his father but not his son."

A bitter laugh escapes me. At the sound, Tyron settles on the floor beside the couch and holds my hand. Jesus, he's so damn good and kind.

"My grandpa was a performer. A drag queen." When he offers no tell, no sign of surprise or shock, I pause, my brain ticking at his lack of reaction. "Did you already know?" There's no bite to my tone, but there's an undercurrent of accusation that I'm sure my boyfriend doesn't deserve.

"No, I didn't."

Tyron has never given me a reason to doubt his honesty. Closing my eyes, I nod. "Sorry, I know that… know you wouldn't look into things behind my back." When his thumb brushes my cheek, I open my eyes. It takes a moment to focus since he's closer than I realized.

"I may have considered looking into what you've been up to for a beat, which, full disclosure, I did a search on your dad, read news reports, investigations, and such, but everything was public record, and that was so I knew what I was walking into when it came to meeting him."

"I kind of figured." That whole discussion at the gala had thrown me off, until Tyron dominating the conversation and putting my dad under pressure reminded me of the type of man my boyfriend is. And his career goals. "Why didn't you find out about me? What I've been up to?"

Tyron runs his thumb over my bottom lip, but his penetrating stare is locked on mine. "I wouldn't betray you like that, dive into your privacy without your permission. Clearly whatever you've been doing matters to you… is personal. Me going on a mission would make me an asshole. If I wanted to know badly enough, I'd come right out and ask. I believed you when you said you'd tell me when you're ready."

Each word presses against my skin, hitting its mark and finding residence behind my rib cage. It's difficult to speak without emotion. Difficult not to blurt out how close I am to falling for him.

Completely.

Irrevocably.

I could. Maybe I should.

But Tyron isn't trying to distract me with how big his heart is, and after those words that weave between us, I don't want to hold back anymore.

"To say I was stifled by my upbringing shouldn't be a surprise." His hand is back holding mine, and he squeezes in encouragement. "When I met Grandpa, he made it his mission, even through his cancer treatments, to help me become the man he knew I could be."

"He did an amazing job. I wish I'd got the chance to meet him."

Tears blur my vision. "Ty, shit, stop being so damn perfect." I snort out a watery laugh. The fucker disarms me with his picture-perfect smile, lifts my hand, and presses a sweet kiss there. "But I wish you had too. He was amazing. So fun and wise. He showed me more love in those couple of years than I'd felt in a lifetime."

A whoosh of air punches out of me when Tyron drags me into his arms, his chest smothering me in a giant, tight hug. After my surprise, I sigh into the touch.

"Anyone tell you, you give the best hugs?"

He somehow holds me closer and seems to breathe me in. "I'm so pleased you found your grandad and had the chance to feel that. You deserve to feel love every single day."

Holy shit. I struggle to inhale. Struggle to get my thoughts together.

"Please come home with me at Thanksgiving."

He pulls away, waiting for my answer as I clutch on to the subject change and my whirlwind of emotions.

"Okay." Any reservations I've been having disappear. I want this with him. Want to get to know his family. Want to see where he grew up. "I'd love to."

"Yeah?" When I nod, he stops me with a brush of his mouth against mine. "Thank you." He clears his throat before settling back on the floor and readjusting the frozen bag on my foot.

"Grandpa challenged me," I continue, knowing Tyron wants to hear the rest, "encouraged me to push my boundaries and discover new things, as well as tease out the more confident, braver version of myself." I chuckle, thinking about how I somehow managed to promise to try drag once he'd passed. "He was a savvy man. Basically, I agreed to give drag a go… in honor of him."

I get a reaction. Finally. Tyron's brows shoot so high, I'm not sure if I should be concerned they're going to pop off or something.

"But me being me, and I suppose not wanting to disrespect the hard work I know it takes to be a queen, I enrolled in drag school."

Five long seconds pass before Tyron's brows finally lower, his gaze struggling to land on any fixed position on my face. "Drag school. Holy shit." Two silent beats follow. "The showcase in a couple of weeks… that's for the graduating drag queen class. You're there, performing."

I nod, my alarm wrestling with my relief that rather than being confused or horrified, he seems excited.

"I want to know everything." Bright-eyed, his eagerness trickles over me, making my lips twitch as relief finally wins the battle. "Can we head upstairs, though? My ass is going numb."

"Sure."

With a smile, Tyron helps me into my room, and we settle on my bed. Close together, he strokes my arm, tiny gooseflesh springing up. I explain about the flyer in the diner and how the school started just after Easter. How my summer break put me a little behind the rest of the class. I tell him about the characters, some of their entertaining bitchiness, and the full-on support of my classmates.

"When I found you at the side of the house at the party, that was the result of you falling on your ass in one of your classes?"

"Well, face, technically." My cheeks heat at the memory.

"Why were you at the side of the house to begin with?"

"I really was waiting for Michelle. I told her I'd go to the party after practice, but that was before I hurt myself. She wasn't answering her phone, so I turned up anyway but didn't want to go inside."

"And you fell why?"

I roll my eyes at myself. "I didn't see the second trash can. Rookie move when attempting to be stealthy. I should have just used the light on my cell."

"You'd been drinking."

"Donnie gave me a couple of shots before I left. Pain management. I wasn't actually drunk."

Tyron studies me, his fingers still roaming. They feel comforting. "What type of drag queen are you?"

"As in, what do I look like?"

"Yeah."

I shouldn't be embarrassed but describing Dewanna to my boyfriend isn't a conversation I ever expected to have. "You know Violet Chachki?"

"From season seven." Tyron's eyes widen before his lids lower to half-mast. His tongue darts out as he swipes at his lower lip. Still on his side, his fingers pause before starting back up again. This time moving to my chest. "You do burlesque?"

My shrug is so minuscule most might miss it, but not Tyron. "I try to." I swallow hard at the intensity blazing in his gaze. "I spent the first month working on styles and acts, trying to figure out who my queen persona was, and well, Dewanna likes Dita Von Teese's style."

"And moves?"

I'm not even surprised Tyron knows who Dita is. This is a man who embraces research and enjoys traipsing along whatever random path that steers him.

"You like the thought of that?"

"I like the thought of you being Dewanna. Getting hard for you is what gets me going. You being happy and confident, hopefully having fun, fuck yes, it's hot."

That shouldn't sound so sweet, right? That he gets hard for me? But fuck if my dick doesn't jump in delight. I'm totally fishing when I say, "Yeah?"

From his arched brow, he knows it too. "Oh yeah." His features contort, turning serious. "You know me and the guys have tickets for the show, right?"

My pulse stutters before turning frantic. "But they've only got a few tickets left." As soon as I speak, I realize how silly that sounds. There are only four tickets left because the team has snagged a fair few.

"I now understand why you said you were busy that weekend. Are you going to be okay with us being there?" Genuine concern radiates from him. If I told him no, I'm convinced he'd stop the guys from attending.

"Are you okay with them being there, knowing I'm going to be performing?" This is me being brave, trying not to worry that people I know will see me as Dewanna.

He seems taken aback. Confusion flashes in his gaze before understanding dawns, and he narrows his gaze. "Just how hot do you look? Am I going to have to threaten the shit out of the guys? Not sure if I like the idea of you being spank-bank material, but as long as you'll be coming home with me, then I can handle it. For you."

Surprise has my lips parting. I slam them closed and shake my head, willing my brain to compute.

"You're worried I'm going to be too sexy, but you're not worried about your friends knowing what I've been doing or that I'm going to be Dewanna on stage?"

"I'm not embarrassed by you. I could never be." He peers into my soul. "Are you?"

Shame is an ugly emotion, but I accept the truth of everything I've felt over the past few months, admitting, "There was a time I was. It's not like this is a calling or anything for me, but since knowing the girls, it was easy to respect them, their passion, their art."

They're an incredible group and work their asses

off. It only took a couple of classes for that reality to hit home. Tyron listens intently.

"I think with that came a new appreciation, but I'm not a performer. It started off with me doing this just for my grandpa, but it's become more. I want to do this for me. I suppose to prove I can."

"Is that why you haven't told anyone?"

"Michelle and Bradley know, but yeah. I don't need cheerleaders or, hell, praise and recognition. That's not what any of this is about."

"Were you really going to tell me after? I mean, if I hadn't been here and seen you injured, was this something you would have kept to yourself?"

"No," I say quickly. "I would have told you. I said I would. I suppose there was a part of me that was anxious about how you'd handle it. It could have influenced me to wait till afterward." I don't feel great about sharing this with him, but Tyron is all about honesty and cutting through the bullshit.

Not only have I witnessed it for myself, but he's made his position clear on telling the truth.

"What exactly were you anxious about?" Thankfully, he doesn't appear upset or frustrated.

"Background checks are pretty thorough when you join the FBI, right?" There's a note of teasing in my voice, attempting to keep this light, but with the tension in my shoulders, I expect he sees right through me.

"They are, and I don't think that you doing one drag queen performance, or even twenty, is something to worry about. I'm certainly not ashamed or would hide this part of your life away." Warm fingers track down to my waist and squeeze. "I think what you're doing is admirable. From what you've told me, I think it's probably good for you, too, especially if it's helped shape this version of you."

My breath catches when he positions himself between my knees, hovering over me.

"Just to be clear, I like this version of you a whole lot."

"I'm a fan of you too." A smile lifts my lips when he grins down at me.

"And if you honestly don't mind, I can't wait to see you perform." Angling down so his stomach brushes mine, he continues, "And you performing burlesque, having a sexy-as-fuck drag queen persona…" His gaze searches mine before dipping to my mouth. "I can hardly wait."

Punctuating his words with his mouth on mine, Tyron kisses me.

CHAPTER 13
TYRON

There's a loud crack as my jaw practically unhinges. I shake off my yawn, rub my eyes, and stare at the screen. The blurring words tell me it's time to stop, but a glance at the time tells me I need to put in more. I have at least four hours before it's my cut-off to get some sleep.

That may sound ludicrous—giving myself a bedtime—but the minimum amount of sleep needed to live is four hours. For the past couple of months, I've been giving myself at least five when I have an early training session and at least six when I don't.

It means I have more than needed for simple survival. I can totally function on that. I have no other choice. And ignoring the jaw-cracking yawn and my sore eyes, I'm nailing multitasking.

Between classes, studying, practice, spending

time with my friends, and as many hours as possible with Logan, each minute I have is precious. But I've got this.

"Are you going to answer that?"

I jolt at Logan's voice, having spaced out. As I turn to look at him, my ears tune in to the ringing of my phone.

"Fuck." Grabbing it from my bedside table, I ignore Logan's dipped brows and his concerned gaze and see Pops's name. "Hey, Pops." Another yawn lurches out of me.

"Are you not getting enough sleep?"

I sigh and flop onto my back. "I'm fine. Practice was brutal today, is all." We all tease Dad, saying he's the worrier of the family, but Pops can give him a run for his money. He's usually a little more subtle about it. "I'll have a quick break," I say, not pointing out that my break will hopefully include my mouth on Logan, "finish off this last bit of studying, then head to bed."

"In like four hours," Logan mumbles beside me, and I shoot him a wide-eyed look.

"Is that Logan?" Pops asks. "Did he say you're not heading to bed till midnight?"

"Nope. He didn't say those words at all."

"Tyron." Exasperation colors his words.

"Pops…" I drag out. "I'm fine. How'd Brody get on?"

"Brilliantly," he says, but I'm sure he's not going to let his concern go. "It was a decent warm-up game. I'll leave him to tell you all about it. Blocked a few shots, was fast on his feet."

"Yeah?" I grin and peer over at Logan, who's chewing the end of his pen. I'm tempted to tell him about the number of germs but think better of it when he narrows his gaze at me. He does roll his eyes and drops the pen. "It's a shame I can't pick up a game."

"I know. Your brother understands. He's holding on for you making at least one game next year, though."

I exhale, relaxing on my mattress and into the conversation. "I'll make at least one game. I promise." Next year during basketball season, I'll have graduated. While I have no real idea where I'll be located, finally watching my brother play is something I'm willing to commit to.

"Did you get Logan's plane ticket organized?"

"I sure did." At the mention of our upcoming trip home, my stomach fizzes in excitement. Logan gets to meet my family, and I can't wait. Just the thought has me reaching for him and tugging him toward me.

He lands half sprawled on me with a grunt and a chuckle.

"I didn't see a notification from the credit card company."

"That's because he insisted on paying for his own ticket." Angling to reach Logan, I drop a kiss on his head, enjoying how he snuggles into me.

"No problem. If something comes up, though, the card's there."

"Thanks, Pops," I say softly. It's not like we're wading in money. My parents work their asses off. Pops has the reality of a cop's wage. While my dad earns a little more, now the gym is established, it's a business with no guarantees. There were a few years growing up there when cash was pretty tight. Knowing this and that they're offering to pay for Logan so they get the chance to meet him, is not something I take lightly.

"Have you spoken to your sister recently?"

When he asks such a question, he never needs to clarify. "She did mine and the guys' nails a couple of weeks ago."

"She did what now?"

I snort. "Don't worry about it. Just something for the gala and wanting to make a statement."

"Of course it was." Pops doesn't conceal his amusement.

"Other than that, we've texted a few times."

While we attend the same school, it's not like we live in each other's pockets. Plus, since the beginning of the year when she said she was going to buckle down, it's been easier to let go a little and loosen those reins that I pretend I never held.

"Why?"

"Just curious if you know anything about this new guy she's seeing?"

I freeze, not liking the unfamiliar sensation of not knowing what Pops is talking about. Especially when it's about Lexi. "What guy?"

Logan shifts in my arms and leans up to meet my gaze. I shake my head at him, needing to focus on this conversation.

"She's apparently been seeing him for about a month." My brow furrows as Pops continues, "She mentioned that she wouldn't be coming home for Thanksgiving, intending on going to his parents' place. You don't know anything about this?"

With my muscles tense, I can no longer lie down comfortably. I sit up, and Logan shoots me a concerned glance. "Nothing, no." The words taste bitter, and unease stirs in my gut. If she's been seeing a guy for a month, it's not like she hasn't had ample time to tell me about him. For me to meet him.

Pops's silence speaks volumes. He's wondering

why the fuck I have no idea who Lexi's dating. My promise to him—that I'll look out for her—sizzles and flares, threatening to turn to acid and simmer in my throat.

I don't do not knowing well.

Fuck.

"I'll handle it." The words are quiet, but I know Pops hears the promise.

"I'll leave it with you." His voice is calmer, losing some of its steel. "Obviously, I'm not about to force her to come home." The "if he's a decent guy" remains unspoken.

"I hear you, Pops."

"Thanks, Ty. Make sure you're getting enough rest."

"Yeah, sure. Love you, Pops."

He says goodbye while I'm wondering why Lexi kept a secret from me and trying to figure out when I'm meant to get enough rest with all the shit that needs to get done.

Admittedly, last night I spent two hours researching some tech Kieran wants to get Dean for Christmas. Not that he asked me to, but I did nonetheless.

I throw my cell on the bed and clasp my head in my hands.

Seven months. That's all I have to get through. The juggling can then stop.

"Hey." The tentative voice matches the soft touch. It's uncertain. Worried. "I heard a little of what was said. What do you need?"

Peering at him through open fingers, I take Logan in.

This man right here is sweetness and warmth. He's everything that I didn't know I wanted or needed. When I'm tired, I still find the energy to be with him, basking in his company. When my brain is buzzing, a simple word, look, or gentle caress calms me in a way I've never experienced before.

Holy shit. Is this what love is? What it feels like?

Happiness clutches at my chest and sinks deep when he reaches out and takes my hand. A timid smile, which despite its size is full of affection, crosses his mouth, and my heart thuds beneath my ribs. The sound fills my ears. I welcome it, knowing it beats extra hard for him.

"Have you ever been in love?" The question's out there, even though I'm sure it shouldn't be. But whenever have I followed the rules? Okay, so all the damn time, but more like society's rules and relationship expectations? Those I like to bend as often as I can successfully get away with.

There's a widening of his eyes, and his palm jerks in my hand. A slight dip of his tongue across his bottom lip follows, and I happily trail its journey. For a fraction of a heartbeat, I don't think he's going to answer. The flush of his cheeks clues me in, though, so I wait him out.

"Maybe."

"Being in love is a feeling, a sensation. A secondary emotion. Never a fact." I can barely hear my words over my racing pulse. "But the way it's described, the millions of words and actions dedicated to it over the centuries, makes it feel like it should be able to be substantiated by having the status of a fact."

"Emotions can produce measurable signals, though, right?"

My breath catches as his words hit their mark. Elation, legit, motherfucking elation, pulses through me with such force, an abrupt laugh spills from me. That I look slightly unhinged is the last thing I'm worried about. How can I be worried about such nonsense when those five words tell me all I need to know.

Logan knows me.

I trust him.

I want him to be the center of everything.

"Emotions can produce memorable signals," I

repeat. "Fuck." I shake my head, more than aware Logan's radiating concern. "I love you."

Worry phases to shock in the blink of an eye. And I hold my breath that it's hope I see peering back at me.

One, two, three seconds, but I'll wait as long as it ta—

"I love you."

Joy spirals, an all-consuming force as I tackle Logan to the mattress with a grunt. Beneath me, he's warm, with the perfect combination of soft flesh and hard muscles. I don't give him a chance to say anything else. For now, I need to kiss him. Savor him. Capture this moment, these emotions.

The concern for my sister and all the shit I need to do prods at me, but it can all wait.

Nothing's as urgent as my need for Logan.

Eagerness has us tearing at each other's clothes. Our kiss is messy, but our laughter as we snag on our clothes and bump noses is worth it.

"I want you inside me," I say as I kiss his neck.

We've talked about fucking, and Logan's told me he's vers. I think I'm into that too, but just the thought of Logan dicking me is enough to have me leaking on his thigh.

Gone is my exhaustion from earlier. My eyes are no

longer tired or sore. And here, in my organized room that's filled with Logan's disarray, I want to finally seal the deal. "I want you to fuck me. Just so we're clear."

"Oh, I didn't misunderstand that." His chuckle is breathless, and he's never looked hotter. "I haven't come prepared." A sweet, embarrassed wince follows.

"It's a good job I am."

I launch off my bed, almost tripping on the discarded clothes. Snagging the condoms and lube from my wardrobe, I hold them high and bounce my brows.

"Aren't you just a regular Boy Scout."

"Yep, for all of three weeks." I check the door's locked before stopping in front of the mattress. Pink-cheeked, wild-eyed, and naked, Logan is incredible. My cock jerks in appreciation, and I'm struck with not knowing what the fuck I'm doing.

"Hey, why don't you pass me those and come and lie here next to me."

I huff out a laugh and shake my head. "You can read me that well, huh?"

"Sometimes." Clasping my hand, Logan settles me next to him, fingers skirting across my chest. "You're not the easiest person to read, but I like to think I'm getting better."

"You definitely are." A rumble follows my words

as he nibbles at my nipple and ghosts his touch over my hip. "I like that you can."

"You do?" he asks, not pausing from tracing patterns on my hip. Every time I think he's finally going to touch my cock, he changes direction. I fucking love it.

"Yeah, and if you can't, then you should ask me." The feel of his smile against my chest has me closing my eyes. "I'll remind you of that when you're being wily."

I chuckle. "Probably a good thing I never said I'd always tell you. But what I won't do is lie to you."

When Logan pauses, I snap my eyelids open, settling on his penetrating gaze.

"You okay?"

A slight nod is his answer before he silently reaches for the lube and squirts a generous amount in his palm. At the sound, my stomach tightens, asshole tensing.

Leaning up, his lips skim mine as he says, "I'll take care of you."

Any words attempting to form sizzle away at the firm touch on my dick. The slick is wet and warm and feels so incredible. And then he's moving, gaze on me for a second longer as he makes his journey south. Then I lose it.

And fuck, I'm okay with that.

His mouth's on me. An errant thought of flavored lube enters my mind, but between his tight sucks and his roaming fingers, I'm lost. Taut yet boneless. Hyped up but so relaxed.

I relinquish to him, sigh into his touches, his suction, his caress. Gasp when he penetrates me—a tip, a knuckle, a whole finger, then more.

I'm barely holding on. Close to whiting out, my head filling with white noise, I can't keep still, riding his fingers like they're the only thing keeping me here. Alive. Grounded.

"Shhh…."

The comfort has the opposite effect since I lose his fingers.

"Need you." I rock my hips, empty and chasing Logan.

"You're so fucking beautiful like this." Tenderness lights his words and cuts through my writhing. Thank fuck I hear a foil packet. It's enough to have me opening my eyes and staring at him.

"You ready?"

Captured in his unwavering gaze, I nod. "Yeah. So ready."

His sweet smile is at odds with his blown pupils and shaking limbs. Somehow, he's keeping control. I have just enough wits about me to consider I should be embarrassed about being so needy. But screw that.

Trust. It's all I need to remind myself that Logan really has got me. He'll take care of me.

And quite possibly, for the first time ever, I let him take it all. The control. My ability to think.

I just want to feel.

A shuddery sigh breaks free from deep in my chest when he positions himself at my entrance.

"If it's too much, tell me to stop, and I'll—"

The shake of my head stops him.

"No," I say quickly, looping my limbs around him. "I want this, you so fucking badly. Just do what you know will feel good and right."

Logan's breath is uneven as it washes over me, and when he nods and says, "I hear you. I'll make sure you're okay and it's good for you. I'll never hurt you," I sink deeper into the mattress in relief.

He knows me. Understands even what I'm struggling to ask for.

That alone is enough to wonder if forever will be long enough.

CHAPTER 14
LOGAN

THE SENSATION OF ENTERING TYRON, BEING SHEATHED so fully I feel almost a part of him, is all-encompassing. But I have to focus on him.

At the center of the pleasure surrounding my dick is the need to care for him, make this moment so good that he'll want this with me, always.

I want to wreck him. Unravel him. Give him the peace from his thoughts he so desperately craves.

That he wants this, me... more than that, that he loves me feels like a dream.

My breath catches in my throat, and I still at the tight heat and the gasp that escapes Tyron. His eyes are closed, so trusting that I'll make this good for him.

Using every ounce of restraint, I carefully sink an inch further and grip his cock. Tyron shudders at the contact. It's what I was after. I smile, praising him, "You're so hot, tight… fucking amazing." I move my hand over him as I speak, keeping up the momentum until he thickens in my hand.

His groan and shift of his hips tell me he's ready for more.

I push in further, focusing on his cock while watching his expression. "I'm almost…." A deep moan punctuates my sentence. My groin brushes against his perfect ass. "Holy fucking…" I want to ask him if he's okay, if he wants me to move, but I don't. Won't.

He wants me to control this. Is as desperate for me to sweep him away as I am to plow into him and make this so incredible for the both of us.

There's a subtle shift of his muscles, a loosening. I reward him with a kiss, distracting him as I ease out before slowly pushing back in.

I capture his gasp, reveling in the sound and the slick heat of entering him before pulling away. And then he's gripping me, clinging on, big hands clamping on my ass, and if I had it in me to laugh at him topping me from the bottom, I'd do so.

But I can't. Incoherent babble mixed with sweet praise spills past my lips instead. "So good." I press my mouth to him again, barely controlling the kiss.

My hips take over, driving into him, reacting to every delicious curse and plea for more.

"Fuck… that… do that."

I grunt out a laugh, and he opens his eyes. The grays have turned storm-like in their intensity. They're wild, just like his spirit that he allows me to see. The smile forming is fast, at odds with the force of his gaze.

When I cant my hips in the same motion that earned me this smile, his mouth slackens. I nail him again, and Tyron throws his head back, burying deeper into his pillow.

Needing him to fly, to finally soar, I keep going, working my grip on his dick while pegging his prostate over and over again. I can barely hold on. My orgasm is within reach, so close that my spine tingles and my toes are close to curling.

But not this time. Not now.

Tightening my hold on his shaft, I move faster. On every third sweep down, I reach out my fingers, touching his balls before returning my attention to his cock.

He grunts. Sighs. Fucking writhes so much that I've got no choice but to send him over. If I don't, I'm likely to be bucked off.

Breathless and strained, I manage, "I need you to come, Ty. So fucking much. I need you to blow so fucking badly that I can catch your cum in my mouth." I double down, thrusting my hips, focusing on the sting of sweat in my eyes, hoping it'll keep my orgasm at bay.

"Fuck—ing—come." Each syllable is broken by a fast punch of my hips, until a soundless shout has his lips parting. Tyron becomes taut beneath me, his limbs shaky, and soft groans finally break through.

One drive of my hips is all it takes for me to spill, filling the condom. I tremble as I keep myself upright. My hand jerks around his cock as I shudder with the last pulse of cum leaving me.

"Fuck. I'm sensitive."

Not able to manage more than a snort, I press my head against his throat and smile. Inhaling the scent of Tyron and sex, I don't want to pull away, but this delicious mess isn't going to clean itself.

I angle up and hold on to the condom as I ease out, watching Tyron's expression carefully. Other than a whole-body shudder, he seems content. Spaced out. Perfect.

I drop a kiss on his puffy lips and get rid of the condom, grabbing the wet wipes Tyron keeps in his drawer. "These are going to be cold," I warn, "but better a clean cock than a crusty one."

His laughter is abruptly cut off when I wipe him clean.

"Motherfucker."

I snort and roll my eyes before gasping when I clean myself up. "Jesus, that's cold."

"No shit," Tyron says as he tugs me next to him. "We need to snuggle."

No complaints from me. Snuggling with Tyron is always incredible. I can only imagine how much I'm going to like after-sex cuddles. I tug the duvet on top of us and plaster myself to his side.

With his large arm wrapped around me, it makes sense just to rest my eyes for a minute.

"Fuck. Shit."

The hammering at the door accompanies Tyron's cussing.

"Huh, what's wrong?" Sleep refuses to release its grip, my words barely coherent.

"Ty, the fuck! Two minutes, else you're going to be late." Sammy punctuates his sentence with one final bang to the door.

I hear the words, but it's not until Tyron curses and jumps out of bed, almost taking me with him, that I pry my eyes open fully.

My grunt isn't pretty, nor is my breath, but my

complaint dies on my tongue when my gaze lands on Tyron.

He's frantic. Disheveled. It's actually kind of hot, but there's no chance I'll tell him. Not when he looks like he's ready to commit murder.

"I didn't turn on my alarm." Each word is venom, intended to hit its mark.

Startled, I sit up, wide-eyed and not sure how to respond without his head exploding. "It'll be fine."

With the way his gaze snaps to me, it's the wrong thing to say. Last night already seems like a million lightyears ago, and with his legs now covered in sweatpants and his head disappearing in his training top, any sweet vision of waking Tyron up with a bj turns to dust.

Sighing, I pull myself out of bed.

It's shit that he's running late, but with the speed he's changing, he'll make it to training in time.

"What are you doing?"

I jolt to a stop, naked in my search for my boxers. Flicking my attention to Tyron, I say, "Getting dressed and going home."

His gray gaze rakes over me as he grabs his cell and steps into my space. "I'm sorry. I'm never late. You don't have to go."

Unfreezing at his apology, I smile. "It's fine. I'm up now. You need to leave."

Tyron searches my face before dropping a kiss on my waiting mouth. When he pulls away, I totally don't stumble, my lips seeking more. His chuckle is worth it.

"I'll text as soon as I'm finished." The last word trails after him, his ass already out the door.

With my hands on my hips, I look around at his bed and the rumpled sheets. Happiness settles in my gut. Last night was incredible. While I don't have a heap of experience, I know when my world has been officially rocked.

And damn if Tyron hasn't tilted mine on its axis.

Feeling lighter and pushing aside the abrupt wake-up call, I get dressed. It makes sense to head home and shower. It's Friday, so there are just two more rehearsals before the showcase, but a lot of studying needs to be done.

Plus tonight, there's an LGBTQIA+ social with the club members.

We've grown exponentially since I joined. Nothing to do with me, though. As the treasurer, I have little to do with the fun part of the club. If you ask Bradley, he'll tell you that my being in charge of the purse strings is a fun killer.

If he does, go and tell him to screw himself.

I just know what money's available and refuse to let anyone get carried away.

I make sure the front door is locked after I pull it closed, then head in the direction of home. It's still dark. It's also unseasonably cold.

Tugging one of Tyron's hoodies on before I left was a smart move. My jacket barely fits over it, but worrying about what I look like is the last thing on my mind. No, beyond the autopilot moves of walking, my thoughts are on Tyron.

They usually are.

Rather than luxuriating in the memory of last night, how tight he was, how he told me he loves me, my thoughts snag on his expression this morning.

We must have fallen asleep by nine last night, after incredible sex and cleaning up. While we clearly needed the extra hours, Tyron especially, based on his honestly disturbingly packed schedule, we lost out on three hours of study.

If it was anyone else, I wouldn't be worried.

Tyron running late and being behind—even though technically I know he's way ahead—has me gnawing my lip in worry. While I've never seen him like this morning before, it doesn't bode well as to how he's going to react.

Not outwardly or aggressive or anything like that. More about his berating himself.

You know as well as I do how focused he is. Me coming along has shifted his plans, which isn't meant to sound conceited, but finding time to spend with me has impacted his schedule. I just hope he's able to rationalize his timing blip, and maybe I'll need to make sure we don't fall unconscious after an orgasm.

I can totally do that.

Keep Tyron awake after bone-melting sex. Check.

I wait at the crossing for the lights to change, thankful I can bounce on my feet with no pain from my ankle. With my hands tucked in my pockets, my gaze snags on a guy holding a takeout coffee. That's exactly what I need. If I grab caffeinated goodness, it means I can probably get a couple of focused hours of studying before classes.

And if I focus on the subject I have with Tyron, I can hopefully take some of the pressure off him.

When the lights change, I cross the street and head toward my favorite diner. It's a little out of the way, but the coffee is worth it.

Warm, coffee-scented goodness greets me when I step inside. The tinkling bell announces my arrival. Unsurprisingly, it's quiet.

Taking a seat at the counter, I smile at the server, a little disappointed that my favorite waitress isn't here.

"What can I get you, darlin'?"

"Coffee with cream to go, please."

There aren't any fancy coffee machines at this

place, and while I like a good cappuccino, this coffee is a serious rival.

"Sure thing. Anything to eat?"

I eye the pastries, thinking about my bank account. The tickets to Tyron's went on my credit card, which my dad pays for. Since he's never mentioned what I put on there, as I try to be sensible, I'm confident the payment will fly under the radar. "A bagel will be great, please."

"Bacon and cream cheese?"

"You know it." I smile as she writes down my order, then accept the coffee with thanks when she brings it over. I love that everyone knows my favorite breakfast food here. Bacon isn't the normal combo for bagels and cream cheese. I freaking love it.

"The bagel will be out soon," the server says before she steps away, coffee pot in hand.

As I sip my coffee, I tug out my phone and open my email.

I sort through the newsletters that I never open but refuse to unsubscribe from "just in case," read through next week's agenda for our social club's meeting, and pause on an email that has me stilling.

It's from my mom. Legit, she's sent me one email, ever, and that was about an RSVP to a Thanksgiving meal in my first year away. Yeah, she RSVP'd her son. Needless to say, I rejected the invitation.

"Here you go, honey." My food's set down in front of me.

"Thanks," I say as I pay. Distracted, I pocket my phone, grab my order, and head home. The unanswered email from my mom weighs on me.

Sure, it could be another invitation, but since I've not received another over the last couple of years, I don't expect it to be. As much as I'd like to ignore it, I won't.

It doesn't take long to reach my place. My hands are cold, and the sun's still not risen, but I begrudgingly think it's kind of pleasant being up when most of the world is sleeping.

Except for poor Tyron and his teammates. I shake my head as I unlock the door. Their dedication is impressive. I can understand why Kieran, who plans to go pro, is so devoted. The rest of the guys, not so much. That commitment to a sport is alien to me.

I roll my eyes at myself as I step inside, close the door, and tug off my jacket. Come a week's time, my own commitment as a spectator will no doubt rival that of hard-core fans.

With my coffee and bagel in hand, I go straight to my room, kick off my shoes, and settle on my bed. Phone. I need to check that email.

It takes but a moment to open it. The contents make my heart stutter.

Logan.

Your father doesn't know about this.

That she's opened a letter addressed to me pisses me off, but for the first time ever, I'm grateful she did, especially concealing it from Dad. It's possibly the single kindest thing she's ever done for me.

Something I'll overthink another time.

I open the attachment, scanned in by my mom.

Dear Mr. Logan Bryce,

Please find attached the court's estate settlement notification and assisting paperwork.

We can confirm that the will and settlement of Mr. Terence Bryce is complete.

As the beneficiary, the sum of $75,500 will be deposited in your chosen account within one working week.

As per the decedent's wishes, please also find enclosed a personal letter—instructed for delivery at the time of settlement.

Kind regards,

Reggie Cullen

Tears blur my vision as I read through the letter a second time, not yet ready to look at the words gifted to me by my grandpa. Seventy-five thousand. I blink, trying to clear my vision.

I wasn't expecting anything. Hell, as far as I was aware, Grandpa had nothing monetary to give, and as far as I'm concerned, the unconditional love he offered is more than I dared dream.

But seventy-five thousand.

This can change everything.

Visions of what this final year of school could look like play on fast-forward. No commitment to a job organized by my dad. No pressure to fight off his demands and requests.

No threat of not paying my final semester's fee.

I inhale deeply, releasing a shuddery breath a moment later.

Dad not having a hold on me will likely mean him cutting me off completely. The financial implication of that isn't what I'm focusing on—not with Grandpa's generosity.

Despite all the shit, the underhanded sneers, he's my dad. While there's little I like about the man, I love him. Maybe it would be easier if I didn't.

And what about Mom? That she intercepted the letter has to mean something, right? That she has a heart. That she can actually think for herself outside the role of socialite she works so hard at.

Jesus. I pick up my coffee, wishing it had a shot of something harder in it. That it's not even six doesn't matter. How can it be when my world is imploding… melding into something I can hardly believe.

Financial freedom.

My silent phone calls to me, but I think better of it, opening my laptop instead.

Grandpa, for all his progression and forward-thinking, wasn't a fan of technology. Fondness swells in my chest as I navigate through my home page. I expect he handwrote me a letter. I hope Mom kept it.

Once my inbox is open, I click on another attachment. This one's something from the estate. I close it and open another, my breath snagging in my throat.

Grandpa's scratchy handwriting fills the screen.

Logan.

Here's hoping you don't have to wait too long to receive this letter, but no doubt the Powers That Be have been in no rush to get everything settled. Think about that when you commit to that career you have planned, my boy.

I chuckle, finding it easy to hear Grandpa's voice and his wonder and horror that I want to work for the government.

Who knows how much will be stolen with taxes, but whatever's left, I lovingly gift to you. You never quite broke free from those heavy clouds constantly pushing down at you. Repressing as shit, those things. And yes, I'm totally talking about my son.

It's not much, I expect, but maybe enough for you to dance on those damn clouds rather than suffocating under them.

You are light and good and kind, and I have loved

every moment of getting to know you. The day you knocked on my door rivals the night when Cher herself attended the club I performed at.

My tears are back, spilling over with my laughter. God, I miss him.

I love you, Logan. You're enough. I'm proud to call you my grandson, and I hope you've found it in yourself to be brave and complete the task I set you.

Pushing yourself is never easy, but greatness can't be gifted. It has to be earned.

Keep being the man who holds his head high, knowing he did everything he could to live his best life. And remember, Logan, you're tough and belong under no man—with the only exception that he's good enough to make you happy and deserves your smiles.

Love always.

Grandpa Terry

Crying is never pretty. Well, not on me. But I embrace every single tear, dedicating each one to my grandpa.

CHAPTER 15

TYRON

BLAME SITS ON MY SHOULDERS.

Practice was a clusterfuck of epic proportions. Everyone knows it, but since no one's actually making eye contact with me, they're keeping quiet about just how off my game I am.

I leave the locker room without engaging in any conversation. If I do, I'll end up losing my cool and go into a tirade about how I screwed my team over. Since I don't want to do that, it's best I find my sister before my class starts.

That's something else under my skin. Lexi with a new guy I know nothing about. While I hope I'm overreacting and have nothing to worry about, that she didn't tell me about him has alarm bells ringing so loudly, I'm eager to do some damage.

Since I don't have time for a martial arts session

where I can do that safely, it looks like I'm going to have to keep myself in check. I flex my fingers as I head toward the design studios where she's set up pretty much full-time. I crack my neck, relaxing into the pop.

What I need to do is get control of my frustration. It's more difficult than you'd think, especially when I'm the reason for my fucked-up emotions. As I get closer, I force the memory of last night to the surface.

Something good, pure in the dirtiest of ways… it's what I need to cling to. Maybe it will help me accept why the craptastic practice was worth it. Not that I want a repeat of this morning again, but last night… hell yes.

All through practice, muscles I'm not used to being sore twinged, and my asshole… fuck if it didn't burn. Who knew that could be a good thing?

I want to do it again. For Logan to take me. Maybe I could ride him. Logan fucking me from behind is definitely on my must-do list. And all of that, I'm eager to do to him.

My muscles relax, despite desire swirling through me.

All of this, my plans and fantasies, are totally doable. As long as I don't fall asleep in a blissed-out haze, run late, and mess up. In the future, it makes sense for us to wait until just before I fall asleep to fuck, preventing any chance of it happening again.

I feel better already, figuring it's the most logical option.

The studio is bustling with students. It's a large building, split into six areas. There's a graphic design studio to my right that I pass. My focus, though, is on the double doors that separate the architecture studio.

It's a relaxed space, I expect for the creative outlet. It also means they have an open-door policy, with students free to come and go between 8:00 a.m. and 8:00 p.m. Since Lexi doesn't have any formal lectures today, she should be in the computer lab at the back of the room or at her large workspace used for practical assignments.

I spot her at the 3D printer. She's focused on her iPad, flicking her finger across the screen.

"What are you working on?"

Startled, her head jerks up, a smile quickly overriding her surprise. "Hey, you. What brings you here? More nail art?"

I snort. "Not at the moment, but you could have told me how hard that stuff is to get off. Nearly tore my nails off."

"Never heard of nail polish remover, asshole?"

"Obviously, but that would have meant a trip to

the store. Who has time for that shit?" I change the subject. "You have time to grab coffee?"

"Not really. Tomorrow works."

My eye twitches, something she spots based on her narrowing gaze.

"You've spoken to Dad." It's not a question.

"No."

With a roll of her eyes, Lexi sighs. "Pops then."

"You want to have this conversation here?"

"I told you I'm busy. It'll have to wait until tomorrow."

I pull out the big guns and offer her legit puppy-dog eyes.

"Fine. You have ten minutes while the printer's finishing off."

Quirking my brow, I indicate for her to lead the way. She shakes her head and tuts. First, she heads to her workspace, where she places her iPad in her drawer and picks up her cell. I follow her outside to the small courtyard.

Once she sits on the wall, away from a small group of students, she stares at me in expectation. The thing about my sister is she can give my stubborn ass a run for its money. I also believe her when she said she only has ten minutes.

I figure it's best to go with honesty rather than playing any subtle games. "What's going on? Who's this guy you're seeing, and why don't I know anything about him?"

"We agreed I was fine and you'd back off."

"That's not what we discussed at all. You said you were going to stop partying as hard and focus on your final year."

"And I'm doing both of those."

"Yet you're dating."

"And you have a boyfriend. So what? Why's it different for you?"

I set my jaw, trying hard not to grind my molars. "Because I'm organized, and I know what I can handle and what's important."

"Wow. Fuck you, Ty." Her brows shoot high before they lower as she narrows her eyes. There's a stubborn set to her jaw. I've pissed her off, and I get it. What I said was shitty, but seriously, you don't know her like I do. The scrapes she's got herself in... I shake my head, knowing it's a miracle I haven't been locked up. There've been too many guys I was close to beating the shit out of.

"Fuck you, Ty. I'm nailing my projects. My advisor's really happy, and I haven't been partying at all. All of which is none of your business. I know you like to think you're the boss of me, but you're not."

"That's not what I'm trying to be." Frustration blooms in my gut. "Pops asked me to look out for you, and even if he hadn't, you're my sister, so of course I want to make sure you're okay."

"And I am." She huffs out a breath and stands. "What about this situation even suggests that I'm not okay or I'm not focused?" she challenges.

"Because you have a boyfriend who you've been with for a month, and this is the first I'm fucking hearing about it." While I'm not raising my voice, there's an edge sharp enough to cut diamond.

"Everything okay out here?"

I whip my gaze at a guy who's maybe thirty. From his smart, designer jeans and his button-up shirt, I deduce he's not a student. His gaze is also fixed on me, assessing, clearly weighing me up.

I shift and stand in front of my sister. "Yeah. Private conversation." I stare him down, telling him silently to fuck off. Am I being an asshole and unreasonable? Maybe an overbearing dick?

Shit. I totally am.

I relax my shoulders and step to the side so I'm not completely blocking my sister. Balancing being protective without being overbearing is a struggle.

Concern etches his features, and while he's not walking away, the lines of tension tell me he's wary.

"Lexi, are you okay?"

I want to answer for her, not liking this douche or

his interference, but I keep my mouth shut. He seems a little young to be a lecturer. Well, at least compared to most of the other teachers on campus. It forces me to keep my manners in check. Plus, it's likely my sister will nut punch me if I carry on being an asshole.

"Yeah, I'm okay," Lexi says, edging to my right.

The douche hesitates, and just when I think he's going to finally go, he surprises me and takes a step forward. "Are you a student here? I haven't seen you in any of the classes."

"Yes." It's all I offer.

"What is it you study?" When his gaze narrows and rakes over me, I'm mildly impressed by his balls, not that he'll have them attached for long if he does that again.

"I've got a boyfriend," I deadpan, and he jerks his attention back to my face, lips parting in surprise and quite possibly embarrassment from the flush of his cheeks.

"I'm not— That's not what—"

"You're such an asshole, Ty." Lexi smacks me on my arm as she shoves me to the side, but it's when she mentions my name that the douche reacts. This guy's heard of me. Good. Hopefully it means he'll fuck right off.

"Ty," he says, stepping forward, reaching out his

palm for me to grasp. "It's good to finally meet you. I've heard a—"

"No." It's all it takes for me to figure out what the hell is going on. "Fuck no. You are not dating my little sister."

"By three minutes, dickhead." Lexi steps fully away from me and takes the douche's outstretched hand. "This is Christian."

It's a struggle to look away from their joined hands, but I do, only to focus on the guy's face and throw him a death stare.

"Are you one of her teachers?" My tone is ice.

"No," he's quick to say while Lexi punches out, "Jesus, Ty. No."

"So, who are you and *how* old are you?" That I'm being rude is the last thing I'm worried about. This whole exchange has thrown me for a loop and put me completely on the back foot. I don't like it at all.

"Ty," Lexi starts, but I shake my head.

Christian clears his throat and stands a little straighter, catching my attention. "Our relationship isn't a secret. Your sister's in control of who she wishes to tell and when." He pauses and looks at Lexi. "I'm sorry. I'm speaking for you. Do you want to handle this?"

Her smile is sweet as she shakes her head. "I'm good. Ty's letting his toxic masculinity show."

That pulls me up short. "That's not what—"

"That's exactly what this is." Her stare tells me to do better.

Fuck. This is worse than being an overbearing asshole. "Shit, I'm sorry. You're right. I'm a dick."

"A prize dick." Lexi arches her brow.

"So, uhm… how did you guys meet?" I'm not backing down completely.

"Christian's an architect. He works for Pratchett and Limpton in Atlanta. He's working with the college for the semester, offering real-world support and guidance. Something of an outreach program."

"The firm I work for has been working with Brixham for fifteen years," Christian adds.

"So not a teacher, then."

"Definitely not a teacher." Christian peers down at Lexi. It's a look I recognize as I stare at Logan the same way.

"Okay. Fair enough." A glance at Lexi and her pointed stare tells me I need to fix this. I reach to shake his hand. "Good to meet you, Christian. I'm the slightly protective brother you may have heard of."

With a chuckle, he has the grace to shake my hand. Letting go, I focus on Lexi and silently ask her for a hug. After a second, she relents and steps into my arms. "Sorry." She bobs her head. Speaking quietly so only she can hear, I say, "I just don't understand why you didn't tell me. We don't keep secrets."

With a softening gaze, Lexi squeezes my arm as she steps back. "I know we don't, and I hate that I felt like I had to." She heaves in a breath and blinks a few times, shoving away her emotion. "This reaction right here is textbook Tyron. I didn't want to deal, especially when things are so new. I am sorry I didn't tell you."

Considering how I reacted, I can see things from her point of view.

"He's so much olde—"

"Six years." She rolls her eyes. "There's seven between Dad and Pops."

"And what about you bailing for Thanksgiving?"

"That'll be my fault." Christian interrupts, and Lexi releases my arm. "I asked Lexi to stay and join me and my family." When he hesitates, I wait him out. "My mom's undergoing chemo for breast cancer. She still has seven weeks left of treatment, so I'm not willing to not be with her, and I selfishly asked Lexi to stay."

And don't I feel like a prize fucking asshole. "Shit." I wince. "I'm sorry to hear about your mom. I hope the treatment's going well." I focus on Lexi. "I understand why you're going to miss Thanksgiving."

"I'm going to miss you too." A small smile appears on her lips.

I narrow my gaze at her, and tug her into another hug. I'm full of the feels today.

She squeezes me tightly, her words muffled when she asks, "Hey, is everything okay?"

Instead of answering, I hold her tighter, ignoring everything else around us.

The thing is, I'm not convinced I am okay. Even admitting that to myself has my chest constricting in concern, because I have to be okay. There's too much for me to do and keep on top of for me not to be fucking awesome.

Last night, after Logan's revelation, which I've still not fully processed, and our spectacular sex, and telling him how I feel, I should be feeling the best I ever have. And I do. But shit. I fell asleep. Hours of work I didn't get done. Plus, running late this morning completely put me off my game and earned three extra minutes of laps.

That may sound like nothing, but three minutes may as well be thirty. It's a killer, and the worst thing is, the whole team suffered because I couldn't get my shit together.

"I'm serious, Ty." Still holding on, Lexi eases away to peer up. The worry staring back at me sits heavily on my chest. "Is something wrong?"

I huff out a laugh. "Never." When she doesn't let me go, I roll my eyes, saying, "Practice wasn't the best, is all."

For a beat, she studies me before she lets go. "Perhaps we can find time for you to meet Christian properly?"

Knowing she really likes this guy, I manage a smile. "Sure."

"Find out when Logan's free, and we'll go out one night or grab coffee or something. Whatever works for you."

I like that she's included Logan. It immediately loosens the thread of discomfort weaving itself around me. "Yeah, okay." I peer over at Christian and give him an up-nod.

After a quick goodbye, I retreat, proud of myself for not giving Christian not-so-subtle warnings or threats about how to treat my sister. Fuck toxic masculinity. Dad would kick my ass if he witnessed how I behaved. She seems to genuinely like the guy, and that he's clearly not a stoner and has a steady job is a leg up from some of the previous guys she's been interested in.

A quick check of the time lets me know I can spend half an hour in the library before my next class. Heading that way, I shoot off a text to Logan, smiling as I type, arranging to meet for lunch. It'll be a quick one, sure, but any time I get to spend with him is worth the effort.

Logan surprises me in the library a few minutes later with a kiss on the top of my head.

A grin replaces my frown of concentration as I turn, hook an arm around him, and drag him close. I press my forehead against his stomach. Inhaling his fresh shower gel and body spray, I relax into his hold. It does the trick of soothing me.

"Did you get to practice on time?" he whispers, his fingers raking through my hair. When I nod against him, he digs his fingers against my scalp and massages. "That's a relief."

I finally glance up at him, capturing his gaze. Pretty hazel eyes peer back at me, and I smile, happy to see him. "You came early."

He nods and swipes a finger across my cheek-bone. PDA with Logan feels natural. Any chance I have to touch him and be near him, I'll take. The last thing I'm worried about is the few stares that I know are aimed at us.

"Something's happened."

My body locks up, and I ease back, studying him more intently. I zero in on his eyes, noting the slight puffiness and tinges of pink surrounding them. He's been upset, but from the brightness in them now, whatever upset him seems to have passed. "You want to find a quiet place?"

"Yeah." An emphatic nod follows as he steps out of my hold and waits for me to stand and gather my things.

Making fast work of packing away, I keep a watchful eye on Logan, curiosity making it difficult to concentrate on anything else. It's been a shit of a morning, and while seeing Logan already helps make that better, "something's happened" tends not to be the greatest phrase ever.

Hand in hand, we leave the library and head toward an empty bench. It's not exactly warm out, but the sun is shining and there's little wind. Our asses shouldn't get too numb.

As soon as we sit, we angle toward each other. There's been a shift in his eyes. Something close to an excited sparkle fills his gaze and peers back at me. The sight warms my stomach, loosening another thread of worry.

"What's going on?"

"Mom sent me an email today"—since he's not frowning when he speaks, I don't let concern brew at the mention of his mom—"with letters sent home about my grandpa's estate settlement."

"Wow, okay. Were you expecting that?"

Logan shrugs. "I knew it was in the system and

that I'm the sole beneficiary, but honestly, it was forever ago the process started, so I sort of forgot about it, you know?"

I nod in understanding.

"Grandpa didn't own any property or anything of significance, so I suppose I wasn't expecting much, and honestly, you know he already gifted me with more than I could hope for."

A spike of anger flares in my chest that he grew up feeling little to no love. I really do wish I'd had the chance to meet his grandpa, the one person who he felt he could be himself around and from whom he received unconditional love.

Instead of sharing any of that, I squeeze his hand. "I know, baby. So, what did the letters say? Were they from the lawyers or government?"

"A collection of papers that the lawyers finalized. After the estate settled, there's some cash left." Fresh emotion floods his features. "Grandpa left me $75,000."

"Holy shit."

"I know." A chuckle that's light and full of disbelief escapes him.

"That's incredible." My brain's already working, considering what this means for Logan. "Is your dad pissed?"

"As far as I'm aware, he doesn't know." When my

brows dip in confusion, he clarifies, "Mom scanned in the letters and sent them to me. Told me Dad hasn't seen them."

"No shit?" There's actually very little I know about Logan's mom. Before marrying, she worked for her father's printing company and then became a stay-at-home mom. Which sounds super normal.

There were no nannies or anything from what Logan told me, and that Logan is such an incredible person means that he had to have received some kind of nurturing, right?

"The last time Mom went to bat for me was when I was eleven and didn't want to play baseball anymore."

"You played baseball?" Imagining him all cute and decked out in his gear has me smiling.

"I'd use the term 'play' very loosely. I have zero athletic ability."

Logan's smirk is impossible to ignore. I capture it in a kiss, enjoying the softness of his lips and the way he sighs against me. "It's okay," I say, pulling away, "you have so many other incredible abilities."

A quirked brow and a loud snort fire out of him. "Is that right?"

My dick twinges, as does my tender asshole. I shift a little uncomfortably. "It sure is. My asshole can attest to that."

Heat flares in his eyes, and Logan swallows hard. Seeming to remember where we are and the craziness of this morning, he asks quietly, "Are you okay? I didn't get the chance to check this morning."

"Yeah, tender, but it's totally worth it."

A smile immediately wipes away his concern. "Last night was incredible."

"It was." It's so easy to get distracted and drawn into Logan, thinking of all the ways I want to blow his mind and make him come. I ease back, putting a little distance between us. His smirk tells me he understands what I'm doing, and like the good guy he is, he sits back a little. "So, your inheritance; what are you going to do?"

When his expression loses all playfulness, I wish I hadn't said anything, but this is important to Logan.

"I'm not sure."

"So you're not just going to tell your dad to go fuck himself?"

A tight smile forms. "If I have to, but I...." He teeters off, and his struggle is evident in his taut shoulders and the way he worries his bottom lip.

"But you what?" I prompt, adding, "You know, whatever you decide, I've got your back, right?" Damn straight. I'd go into battle for Logan.

"I know. I think I'm just going to sit on this for a

while. If he keeps putting pressure on me about work, then I'll tell him the truth."

We both know it will be "when" rather than "if." We also know next semester's invoices will be sent out by the end of the month. "Are you worried about him cutting you off, not wanting to see you again?"

"He cut Grandpa out of his life."

"You have no plans to go back home, though, right?"

Logan's sigh is heavy. "I know, but it's knowing I can if I want to. Knowing I still have parents who maybe sort of care about me and will… I don't know, be there if I really need them. This money changes everything. And it's so amazing and incredible and gives me a freedom I never dreamed of, but it could be the reason I lose my parents for real."

"But you following your dreams could do that too, right? Which is your plan?"

"Urgh." Logan narrows his gaze at me. "You talking sense right now isn't helping." There's no bite to his words.

"I know, sorry," I offer, giving him a sympathetic smile. "I suppose this money means you no longer have to pretend, which makes everything real."

An emphatic nod is his answer as he stares a little miserably at me.

"But your mom, how she's handling this, that's a

good sign, right?" I want to rub away his distress, so I'm happy to latch on to any hope I can find.

"I suppose. Maybe. I suppose only time will tell."

Hating to interrupt, but knowing our time is limited, I check my phone.

"Class?"

"Just about," I answer. "How about simply taking each day as it comes, and any fallout, I'll be there?"

Standing together, I hold his hand, enjoying the sweet smile directed at me.

"That sounds great, thank you. I'll see you in an hour for lunch." A kiss follows before he steps away.

"See you soon," I call, watching him leave.

CHAPTER 16
LOGAN

THE SOUND OF TYPING FILTERS THROUGH MY consciousness. I sniff and turn over, trying to ignore it, but the tapping isn't stopping. Reluctantly, I force my eyes open, the small light from the desk slamming into me.

Jesus, how can one tiny lightbulb destroy my retinas so effectively?

Prepared for it, I try again, knowing it's not going to be a perfect pitch-black greeting me. The light's a little easier to digest. It spills out in the corner of my room, landing on Tyron at my desk. His fingers are flying across the keys, his gaze glued to the stark glare of the screen.

"What time is it?" I croak, my voice scratchy with sleep.

My question captures Tyron's attention. While his

face is partially cast in shadow, his expression is clear to read. A wince precedes "Two thirty."

I sit up, the sheets pooling at my waist. The cool air pebbles my skin, and I shiver. "Couldn't you sleep?" I passed out before midnight, about an hour or so after getting home from hanging out with the social club. Tyron had already been in my room, studying and waiting for me. And when I went to bed, he told me he planned to finish up some revision for an upcoming exam, and he'd be right with me.

I take in the strain in his eyes, the tired creases surrounding them. "Haven't you been asleep?"

When he shakes his head, I get out of bed, grateful for the spongy carpet under my feet. By the time I reach him, he's turned fully on my swivel chair, legs wide, and gaze on me before he yawns loudly, his eyes squinting shut.

"You're exhausted." Standing between his spread thighs, I touch his cheek. "You need to come to bed."

Seeing the hesitation peering back at me, I angle a glance over his shoulder, trying to see what he's working on. I frown at what I see. "Is that for next semester's course?"

"Yeah." Even tiredness wraps around that one word. "Just trying to get ahead before the season kicks off."

"You're already way ahead. I think what's best right now is for you to sleep."

"But I have a day off tomorrow."

More than aware he has a super rare day off, something I'm ridiculously excited about as I get to spend the whole day with him, I nod. "Exactly. It means we can get a lie in. I can wake up with you wrapped around me and no alarm to interrupt us."

"Even more reason that I can get in extra study tonight."

I frown. "I think you're missing the point here. You're exhausted, Tyron."

"I've got this."

Pursing my lips is never a good look, but I can't help it. Not when he's being stubborn and blind. He's got this whole head-in-the-sand thing going on. It threw me at the beginning, when I first witnessed it. I suppose I ignorantly just thought he's smart—genius IQ—so of course he can manage everything and not take on too much.

Oh, how wrong I was.

He's juggling so much. But what's worse is he takes on responsibility for shit he doesn't need to. It's like a compulsion or something, which I don't quite understand.

"Perhaps you'll have everything *better* if you get at least eight hours sleep."

Studying me, he's tempted to argue. There's a slight tightening in his left eye that tells me as much. I can't budge on this, though. That he's going to get ill by taking on too much and not getting enough rest has me fretting.

"Bed. Now." My voice is firm and does the trick. His large hands clamp down on my hips and squeeze. Even though I'm seriously tired, too, I wouldn't mind if my boxers magically disappeared. But that would not get Tyron asleep any quicker.

"Okay." When he stands, I back away barely an inch, so he's all up in my space. Hard planes and warm skin press against me. While it'll delay him getting into bed, I can't resist wrapping my arms around him.

Touch-deprived, I get my hugs in as often as humanly possible. Plus, by the way Tyron leans into me, burying his face against my neck and breathing me in, I figure he needs this too.

"I'm worried you're doing too much," I admit, and not for the first time.

I'm surprised when he doesn't tense in my arms —his usual go-to reaction. That or he brushes me off completely.

"Perhaps we need to look at your planner together." It's a risk saying this, as Tyron is seriously attached to his schedule, but something's got to give.

I also think I need to teach him the value of the word "no" and that it's okay to use it with friends and loved ones.

But one step at a time.

Tyron's "Maybe" startles the hell out of me.

Relieved he hasn't shut me down, I dot a kiss to his cheek and lead him to bed. Once he's under the covers, I grab my phone for a light, then switch off my desk lamp before snuggling in beside him.

Another loud jaw-cracking yawn tears from him.

"Jesus. That sounded painful," I whisper.

He grunts beside me and pulls me tighter to his body. "Love you."

Those words are becoming my favorite. "Love you." I sigh against him, content he's finally settling, and in 3.2 seconds, I kid you not, Tyron's breathing changes.

He's fast asleep. Thank God.

Today's been a bit of a shitshow for him, and he's struggling to forgive himself for falling asleep early last night, which made him late today—or I suppose yesterday, since it's technically now Saturday morning.

The plan when we wake up later, at a more reasonable hour, is to do as little as possible. We'll undoubtedly get some studying in. That goes without saying. The good thing is there are no parties, no events or fundraisers going on, which means I can keep Tyron all to myself and maybe talk him into looking at his planner together.

It's the only thing I can think of doing to make sure he keeps himself in check.

Worry churns my gut, thinking about what's coming up. I'm not even referring to my solo and group performance at the drag club next Friday. Tyron's helped to ease away the remaining fears I have about that, and hell if I don't love him the more for settling my nerves.

That he doesn't care about his teammates seeing me, either, has helped put my own fears in perspective.

No, what's playing on my mind is Tyron's upcoming game schedule. We've talked about it. Even Dean's warned me how crazy it is to have a boyfriend on the team. The difference is, Dean gets to go wherever the team plays. I'm kind of envious.

I try to relax and cut off my thoughts. The room is perfectly dark, the house silent except for the occasional rustle of my curtains from the breeze coming through the open window. It's peaceful, and I'm tired, but my thoughts refuse to quit.

I'm tempted to scroll through my phone, perhaps find my headphones and watch some TikTok videos. No chance I'm shifting and disturbing Tyron, though.

I've never known anyone to fall asleep so quickly. Not that I have any real experience to compare it to, beyond school camps and sharing dorms.

Maybe when basketball season starts, I'll figure out I worried over nothing. As long as we make video calls and see each other a couple of times a week, we'll be fine. Plus, we do have a class together. Next semester, we actually have two, so it'll be even better.

Happier with that thought, I expel a long breath, counting down from ten and relaxing my shoulders. Believing we'll get it sorted is essential. I don't want to consider the alternative.

It feels like I've barely closed my eyes before Tyron kissing my neck wakes me. With the light spilling through the room, piercing my closed eyelids, it's clearly morning.

"You taste especially delicious when you're not properly awake." The words are whispered between kisses along my neck.

Smiling, I sigh into his touch. "Best keep going then before I open my eyes."

A light chuckle flutters over me as he traces his tongue over every available inch of skin he can reach. Traveling lower, he nips along the way, and still, I keep my eyes closed. A playful Tyron is one of my favorite versions of him, but since I love every single part of him, even the grumpy form, it's not much of a contest.

His lips do the asking when he reaches the waist of my boxers. Immediately I lift, not holding back my grin when he tugs them off me. Before my ass settles back on the mattress, the wet heat on my dick has me gasping for breath.

My eyes spring open. Glancing down, I part my lips at the satisfaction on Tyron's face. Hollowed cheeks, a slight widening of his eyes, and he wraps one hand around my cock, right near the root, and sucks, coming away with a pop.

His grin is one hell of a thing.

"Morning, baby."

"Morning," I rasp, which quickly turns into a groan when he laps at the end. I have no doubt there's already a bucketload of precum there, ready for him to drink down. "Fuck, that's hot." It's impossible to tear my gaze away, especially when he makes eye contact and envelops me once again.

Sensation floods through me, quick and so hot. I need to hang on so I don't fall off the precipice too soon, but oh, how I could.

"You're so good at this," I pant. In response, he pushes further, and I swear my dick's wedged in his throat. "Holy fuck... nngh," I garble. All I see is white as I spurt directly into his throat. He pulls away quickly, coughing a little, but there's nothing I can do. He's milking me, tearing every drop of cum out of me as, watery-eyed, he returns to sucking my dick.

I pant, writhe, and am not quite sure how to get my words to work. Still latched on to me, Tyron doesn't stop, doesn't give up until my brain's short-circuited and he's licked all traces of my release away.

Goo. I swear that's what I am. Here, in my bed, my limbs are noodles, and I can barely lift my hand to encourage Tyron over to me.

"Rendered you speechless, huh?" His voice is scratchy and sexy as sin.

I flick my gaze at him and let it drop until it lands on his hand, which is stroking his cock. "Come in my mouth." Cheering silently at my ability to create words, I grunt when he shifts, knocking my sensitive cock.

"Fuck yeah." He scoots forward, kneeling over my chest, dick so close I wish I had the energy to lift and suck him down. "Nuh-uh… no sucking."

My brows pitch low, but pouting isn't possible, not when my mouth's open and my tongue's out, ready to taste him.

"You want to taste me that bad?" Tyron's eyes are wild, full of heat and fire, as his hand moves faster.

"All the time," I say quickly before reopening for him. I savor his groan, wanting him so badly that my cock's already hardening. Finding some energy, I hold on to his ass, loving that this position means he's spread open. I dip my fingers between his cheeks, my focus on his expression.

The shudder rippling through him is immediate, and my dick swells. A groan escapes from me, remembering how he felt on my dick.

"You hard again?"

I nod.

"Fuck. I wanna ride you so bad, but I want you to drink me down."

"We can do both." Full and hard, my dick's absolutely on board with this.

When his eyes glaze over and his rhythm falters, I think I have him. Lips parting briefly, he then licks his bottom lip. "I haven't," he starts, a fresh flush crawling up his cheeks. His hand slows too.

"What?" I ask gently, squeezing and rubbing his ass.

"I just woke up. I haven't cleaned up."

Understanding dawns, and I smile softly at the pink-cheeked man above me. "How about you come in my mouth, then we take a shower together?" I quirk my brow. "There are some things we just have to accept are going to happen. And washing away any evidence of that isn't a big deal."

Once again, his pace quickens, and he nods.

"Now, come in my mouth so I can fuck you in the shower."

Another shudder racks through his body. A breathy groan breaks free when the first shot of cum lands on my chin. The second hits my tongue.

It's the only incentive I need. I tilt my head, lifting it off my pillow, capturing his cock, not willing to miss anymore.

Tyron gasps and groans, his hips jerking during the last of his release. By the time he's finished, his limbs shake like jelly. I encourage him down to me. He comes willingly, mouth meeting mine, tasting himself while I savor the joining of our two releases.

Breathless, he pulls away. Peering down at me, he gives me a dopey, blissed-out smile. "Two minutes and shower."

Since my cock is crying out for attention, I nod eagerly. "Yes. Rest, then, your ass is mine."

He smirks as he buries his face against my neck. It's something he does a lot, and I'm more than okay with that.

THIS PAST WEEK HAS BEEN CHAOTIC.

I've had two extra rehearsals, which means I see Tyron less. Plus, with his first game next week, there's more hours watching game footage or something that the team has to do.

The good thing is I've turned in two assignments already. The others aren't due until next month, but I do have a couple of exams before Thanksgiving.

What's not been so great, on top of the above busyness, is Tyron's not let me discuss his planner. Also, last night I heard him agree to help Sammy with an assignment. Not only that, he decided to problem-solve some sort of issue with the mascot's rehearsal schedule or costume or something. Honestly, I was too frustrated to really listen. All I know is Tyron didn't need to get involved, and the couple of hours it took him to sort it out are ones he'll inevitably end up stressing about losing.

I have to admit, I'm curious about meeting his parents. Maybe getting to know them and seeing the family together—minus Lexi, which is a whole other drama, apparently—will help me understand Tyron even more.

From what he's shared, his family is stable, his parents in love, and he's experienced nothing but support and affection from them. They sound incredible, and I'm envious and so happy his childhood was so different from my own.

But none of that explains this pressure he puts himself under.

"I'm so excited, I think I'm going to pee."

Dolly tugs me abruptly from my thoughts of Tyron. Something I've willingly grasped on to because I need the distraction. It was either worry about Tyron or fret that tonight is going to be dreadful and something I'll end up regretting for the rest of my life.

But peeing. That's what Dolly's talking about.

"Aren't you already strapped down?"

Dolly's deep, masculine snort is not at all in line with the leopard-skin, super-sexy costume she's wearing. "Girl, you think I'd be able to get my fruit and veg in this getup if they weren't?"

Fruit and veg? I roll my eyes, not looking for a further description that I'll never be able to erase. The show officially starts in fifteen minutes. I'm close to vomiting. Seriously, I feel it sitting high up in my stomach. Every time I think I'm going to make a fool of myself or fall or, hell, reveal my junk, it scoots a little closer.

The reflection staring back at me in the mirror shows none of that, though. There's no sign of the ashen or perhaps green-tinged skin you'd expect.

Instead, my features are contoured to perfection. This time last year, "contour" and "makeup" were barely in my vocabulary. They're words I was aware of, since I don't live under a rock and TikTok's algorithms go funky sometimes. Me perfecting both in my four months of schooling is one thing I'm surprisingly proud of myself for.

I look fucking hot.

Between my long lashes, red over-drawn lips, which I finally mastered to look sultry rather than clown-like, and my carefully styled wig, I'm confident no one I know will recognize me.

I could pass by my parents with ease for sure. I'm half convinced I could fool Tyron too. Since he has an idea of my style and who I mirrored myself on, though, he'll recognize me straightaway.

The thought starts a fizz of excitement bubbling in my gut. Damn straight I'm going to embrace the feeling. It's much better than fear.

I recall Tyron's glazed-over expression when I told him how I styled myself. That he legit was turned on helps to calm my nerves, my pulse spiking for a whole other reason.

The ping of my phone makes me jump.

"Humping monkeys, don't jump like that. One false move and your titties are going to fly free." Dolly fans herself and eyes my cleavage.

I stare down at my fake chest, not at all a fan of breasts. They help me embrace this character that I'm playing, but after my two performances, never again. As in ever.

The same goes for makeup and these pain-in-the-ass stockings.

The only items I'm begrudgingly partial to are the lace and satin panties, which I reluctantly bought after all my classmates gasped in horror when I wore my regular old boxers in drag.

Damn them all for being right.

The panties make me feel sexy. They also help me get into character.

Maybe I'll even get the nerve one day to wear a pair in my everyday life… and for Tyron.

"Five minutes and places!" is hollered from somewhere.

"Shit." I fumble with my powder, wanting one more touch-up, as I'm shit scared and sweating. Finishing off, I scoop up my phone, checking the message that's come through.

Tyron: We're here. I haven't told the guys and I won't. Break a leg, and I can't wait to see your performances. I'll be cheering the loudest, but not too loud so I out you. 😉

Smiling is so easy with Tyron. He makes my heart melt and brings such fun into my world. And that he feels the need to reassure me that he won't out me as being one of the queens on stage is all levels of endearing. Unnecessary, as he already promised once, but I appreciate it all the same.

"Dewanna, are you ready?" Dolly scoots beside me, face next to mine, as she looks at me through the mirror. She looks freakin' amazing.

"Let's do this," I say with as much confidence as I can muster. Standing, I take one last look at my reflection and spare a thought for my grandpa.

This one's for you, MaryLou.

CHAPTER 17
TYRON

"Dude, what's wrong with you?" The expression on Sammy's face matches the disbelief in his voice.

Shit. What happened to me keeping my cool and my shit together? How the hell am I going to make it in the FBI if I can't even act casual? Sure, my boyfriend is going to appear on the stage any second now, and I can't tell anyone, but I should at least be able to control my bouncing leg and concentrate on whatever it is Sammy's trying to talk to me about.

"Just tired. Looking forward to relaxing." Neither is a lie, so I don't mind using them as excuses for my behavior.

"In that case, do you want me to talk the bartender into making you something special?"

"No," Bentley says immediately, clamping his

hand on Sammy's wrist and stopping him from bolting to the bar.

"Fine," Sammy mumbles. "But I swear when I have a club of my own someday, whenever you assholes visit, you'll all be my guinea pigs, and I'll charge you double."

"As long as Key's buying the rounds, that's fine by me."

Kieran flips me off. "No chance will I be drinking any of Sammy's dodgy brews. Not sure how I've survived the past few years intact."

"Whatever, assholes." Sammy flicks a beer coaster in Kieran's direction. "We all know you're going to be begging to be on the VIP list."

"You said our names were automatically and always on there," Leon says, staring Sammy down.

"You actually have it in writing."

I chuckle at Bentley stepping in and getting one over on Sammy. He's usually the one saving his ass.

"The fuck, Bent. There's a code, man. Jesus, just stab me in the back." Sammy shakes his head, looking honestly horrified at Bentley's interference.

We all laugh as Leon holds out his hand for a fist bump with Bentley, which apparently pisses Sammy off even more.

"You're all assholes. I'm getting another drink before the show starts. Anyone else?" Sammy glances around the couple of tables our large group has managed to grab. There are nine of us in total. Our whole house, plus Dean, Tiller, and a couple of the guys on our team. When we all say no, Sammy leaves, grumbling about us not having any vision or some shit.

The important thing is that Sammy got distracted by bullshit, so no one's attention is on me. I refuse to mess this up for Logan. I'm proud as hell of him. Even if he sucks and his performance is lousy, I'm still proud of him for pushing his boundaries and doing this in honor of his grandad.

The place is packed tonight. Sold out. The line at the bar is three deep, and every chair is taken. It's hot as heck, too, with all these bodies crammed in, but it makes for one hell of an atmosphere.

The place is buzzing. There looks to be a bunch of regulars and several groups of women, one a bachelorette party, obvious by the sashes and plastic tiaras. There's a real mix of people, but undoubtedly, we caused many heads to turn when we entered.

Even now, we're getting more than a couple of looks.

Sure, we've been here before, but it's been a while, and there weren't so many of us. It's understandable that a few of the looks are a little wary.

When a large group of jocks walks into a drag

club, it's going to cause a stir. And no, we're not wearing our sports jackets, either, but it's pretty obvious from our builds—with the exception of Dean, who I could pop in my pocket.

I told him that once, but his death stare had me backing off.

"You know, on *Drag Race,* the finale's recorded three times, with each contestant being the winner," I say, my gaze on my phone, waiting to see if Logan has time to text me back.

"I read that somewhere," Dean says. "Something about who the actual winner is not getting leaked before it airs."

Pulling my gaze away from my cell, I smile at Dean, liking that he appreciates such tidbits. "The winner finds out at the same time as the audience."

"That sounds messed up." Leon shakes his head.

I shrug. "I suppose it sucks for the losers, but I get why it's done." Buzzing in my hand has me almost jumping. Jesus. I need to cool my shit. I clear my throat and glance around, hoping no one noticed that I half jumped out of my chair. Thankfully, no one's paying me any attention, since Sammy's already returned with his beer and is saying something about being chatted up.

I leave them to it and open my messages.

Logan: 🩶

It's not poetry, but a love heart's enough for me. Feeling happier now Logan knows I'm thinking about him, I smile and pick up my Coke. No way am I drinking tonight. I don't want to miss a single thing.

The lights flash off and on a couple of times before they start to dim.

This is it. Fuck, I'm excited and terrified for Logan. He tried to play it down earlier, but there was no hiding his fear.

With my gaze rooted to the stage, I grip my glass and wait, not quite sure what to expect or how this is going to go down. Not that it matters. I'm here for every moment.

The emcee is hilarious and introduced themself as Dixie. They're fun and feisty, if not a bit fierce. They also easily rival my height and size, and their dark skin practically glows under the stage lighting.

They explain about the drag queen school and its graduating students. Fun things about their stage lives are shared. Absolutely nothing personal.

The first three acts are entertaining. And so different in looks, style, and performance. The guys are having a blast, clapping along, cheering and supporting like the rest of the crowd. Of course I'm doing the same, but half of my attention remains on knowing Logan could be next.

When Dixie takes the stage again, they're wearing a feather boa, and there are giant nipple tassels over their costume. Shimmying and moving in a way to get the tassels spinning, Dixie eats up the attention before finally saying, "A hint of what's to come from our next incredible diva."

My heart leaps in my throat.

"Please welcome, Dewanna Boner."

Cheers break out in the room, and while I join in, my vision narrows to the side of the stage, where a spotlight appears.

Holy shit. This is it.

Bitter:Sweet's "Dirty Laundry" sounds over the system, a song I only discovered last week courtesy of Logan.

A long leg appears right before Logan—fuck, *Dewanna* saunters onto the stage. Each step fits the tempo, and I zero in on every detail I can commit to memory.

From Dewanna's red glittery stilettos to the corset, long gloves, and floor-length skirt, which splits all the way up, she looks fucking amazing. And I'm sticking with this pronoun after being asked to by Logan.

The dance is sultry. The smirk and the way she

eats up the audience with the occasional wink, and she's not only sexy as fuck, but looks to be having fun. Something the crowd reacts to.

The cheers virtually blow the damn roof off as she starts to strip in time with the beat. The long skirt goes, the corset too, revealing delectable flesh with just the right amount of softness that I love tasting.

And fuck me dead. Fishnet stockings wrap around Dewanna's skin, showing each curve and arch of her calf.

The guys around me are whistling and cheering. Me? I touch my mouth to make sure I'm not drooling or gaping. Thankfully I'm not. But I am wearing the biggest smile ever. It rivals the one I sported when we won the championship last season.

"Fuck, she's hot," Kristof says off to my right.

I snap my gaze to the freshman, wondering why the fuck he was invited. Narrowing my eyes, I glare at him.

"Ouch. The fuck?" I shoot Kieran a pissed-off look, rubbing at my side where he jabbed me with his elbow.

"Stop trying to set Kristof on fire with your death stare." Amusement fills his words, but I hear the confusion too.

"No idea what you're talking about." Best if I return my attention to the stage. I can play ignorant. I also don't want to engage in conversation and miss a second more.

I pointedly ignore Kieran's snort, but I can't resist giving him the middle finger, positioned perfectly next to my face so he can see.

Logan is rocking Dewanna's persona. My smile's back until my face turns slack. A lack of oxygen has me spluttering when the bra is whipped off, revealing two tassels concealing nipples I love to nibble.

There's nothing I can do about my hardening cock. The confidence in the gaze of the person I adore is staggering. Like this, she's mesmerizing, and it's impossible to look away.

Pride swells in my chest, wrapping around the love I have for Logan.

Long legs eat up the stage as the music hits some sort of crescendo. Not a lyric is missed as Dewanna keeps up pretty spectacularly. Front and center and working hips that look almost shapely with the style of what remains of the costume, Dewanna's hand shoots up in the air, and with the final key, that hazel-eyed gaze I know so well snaps to mine.

I'm lost in beautiful eyes and am smiling so damn big my cheeks hurt.

Dewanna bows, and I'm already standing and clapping. I'm not the only one. The guys join in, and I want nothing more than to hunt Logan down and kiss the shit out of him.

Obviously, I can't. There's still a couple more performances, including the group act. It's the only thing forcing me to sit my ass down.

"Ty, man. You'd be in so much shit if Logan saw how you were eye-fucking Dewanna." Sammy, the asshole, sounds super amused with himself.

"Fuck off." My death stare is back.

"Whatever, man. I wonder if they do photographs after, you know, with the audience," he goes on, speaking to our tables at large.

Dean answers, "Maybe. Since it's the school's showcase, it's probably great publicity."

Does Logan know that? Expect that? My gut tightens, wondering if it's compulsory and, if so, will he be okay.

There's no way any of my friends will recognize him, even up close. They haven't so far, and with the way all their attention was fixed on the performance, there's not even an inkling.

I force myself to relax and excuse myself to go and get another Coke just as Dixie reappears. There's no line, since most people are focused on the stage.

"Hey, handsome, what can I get you?"

"Coke, please."

The server's gaze roams my face, and the asshole

I am offers nothing but raised brows. Yeah, love may have made me giddy for Logan, but my guard's still firmly erected and will remain that way.

Hell, I said "please." I'm not a complete douche.

The Coke is set before me, and I nod my thanks, paying and leaving a tip.

"Dark, broody, and a sexy jock who tips. Maybe you need to place that hot ass of yours on one of these stools and get to know me better." I have to give it to the guy; he's got impressive confidence, especially as he apparently knows who I am.

"I don't expect Tyron's boyfriend will be too excited about his relocation, but I'm more than happy to keep the barstool warm." Bradley's at my side, wearing a smirk and giving me an up-nod. The bartender smirks and wanders away. "Enjoy the performance?"

"The best of the night," I answer, holding back the loved-up smile that's threatening to escape.

"No surprises there. Are you hanging back after the show?"

"No. Made a promise to head home straight after."

Bradley nods in understanding. Logan told me that as soon as the show was over, he wanted to change into his street clothes and meet me at his place. After some persuasion, he agreed to meet me outside so we could share a ride together. The guys plan to stay out tonight and have a few more drinks, so I won't have a problem slipping out early.

"Thanks for next week's tickets."

"No problem. Pleased that you can make it with Logan." The crowd's cheering has my attention shifting. The next performer is on the stage. "I best get going. I'll see you in the morning, maybe."

I say goodbye and leave Bradley to flirt with the server. While I haven't exactly loosened up around Logan's housemate, apparently I smiled at him last week. Bradley made a big announcement about it while Logan was dishing up the Thai takeaway we'd ordered.

The next two performances are enjoyable. The last makes me laugh, especially when the queen leaves the stage and rubs up against Bentley, whose face goes bright red. It's Sammy's reaction that I get the most fun out of. I'm nothing if not a sadistic fucker at times.

Sammy's unimpressed. He goes his own shade of red and even folds his arms, his pissed-off stare rivaling my own.

And finally, the last performance of the night starts. The queens dance their way onto the stage in step with the music, all with a costume change. And they lip-synch and do a choreographed piece with only a couple of fun missteps that the queens big up and make their own. At least, I assume they weren't choreographed.

For the most part, my attention is solely on Dewanna. During this performance, there's a clear goal of having fun. Damn my heart, and the way his second wink makes it flip over. I'm so gone for this man and can't wait to get him home.

Confidence looks so sexy on him.

The music cuts out, and we're all standing and hollering. The queens are hugging, and Dixie is closing the show.

"Our amazing queens are going to freshen up and be right back out for photo opportunities. Be sure to tag @divaqueenschooled, one word, in all your social media. And if any of you are feeling inspired, registration for the start of April's school is open. I'll meet you all at the bar, and if you're buying, I like cum shots to celebrate."

All the guys are chuckling and chatting. Tiller and Leon head to the bar to get drinks while I wonder what Logan's going to do. I fire off a quick text.

Me: Are you doing photos?

We already decided Logan would text me when

he was ready, so I could retreat and make a run for it. Photos, though, change things.

I'm proud as punch of Logan, but I'm not sure how he feels about photos of Dewanna everywhere. However, I need to give him some credit, as he surely will have expected it. But him being in touching distance while guys get close to take photos... I scowl, not liking the idea. There's plenty of good-looking men around, and while they don't know what Logan looks like, I've no doubt plenty will think Dewanna is sexy.

Yes, I know I need to get over myself, especially as I've appeared in so many photos with Bears fans, but still, I'm protective.

"What are you smirking at? It's freaking me out," Sammy asks.

I roll my eyes, yet it's totally directed at myself, knowing Logan will laugh his ass off if I call myself an alpha again. "Just thinking about Logan," I answer honestly.

"Why couldn't he come tonight, again?"

This one I rehearsed. "Prior commitment." Admittedly it was an easy one to practice, but again, I don't want to lie, per se. Being flexible with the truth, however, I have no issues with.

"Sucks, man."

The commotion to the right pulls our attention away. It's the queens.

Game face activated. Hopefully.

I swallow hard, watch, and wait. The group stands near the stage so people can take photos with the backdrop. Sammy's moving immediately, grinning wildly and seeming completely into this.

"You not going with him?"

Bentley shakes his head but doesn't stop staring after Sammy. "Nah. You know photos aren't my thing."

I nod, knowing that. Bentley actively avoids photographs at games. The only exception is when it's a team photo. We all know he has a complex about his busted nose. It never quite fixed right two years back, and he refused to get it straightened up.

Total respect to the guy. I wouldn't choose elective surgery just to look a certain way either. The slight misalignment of his nose suits him.

Hearing Sammy's loud laughter, I seek him out. He's right next to my boyfriend, his arm wrapped around Dewanna. I bite back a smile at the look flashed my way. Terror and amusement seem to battle for dominance on Dewanna's face.

As soon as the line goes down, the queens spill into the room, talking to each other and the audience.

I don't lose sight of Dewanna as she's dragged along toward us. A wide-eyed expression is on her face as she mouths something to Dolly. It didn't take me long to figure out Dolly is Donnie when she hit the stage.

"Oh my, we have basketball royalty in our midst." Dolly fans her face, grinning at our tables, skimming over me without a double take. "Cute asses up, gentlemen. We need a photograph with all your gorgeous muscles."

Sammy, who's already standing, claps his hands. "You've got it." He then wrangles us into action, and obediently we follow. From the second glances, it seems like the whole team's expecting me to tell them to fuck off. So when I stand without a word, keeping half an eye on my boyfriend, Sammy makes a big deal of shoving me next to Dewanna.

Apparently, he's not letting go of the apparent eye-fucking.

Body tense, I woodenly stand next to Dewanna. When there's a brush of fingers at the center of my back, I settle, side-eyeing her. Bright eyes peer back at me, and the twitch of painted lips has me smirking.

"You were amazing," I say quietly. The rest of the group is noisy as hell and still getting themselves into position. A photographer has also appeared. "You okay with these photographs?"

"Dewanna can handle it" is Dewanna's breathy

response. If I hadn't committed Logan's voice to memory and captured every tone, there's not a chance I'd recognize his voice.

At ease with Dewanna's response, I wrap my arm around her, palm meeting skin. The other arm I wrap around Kieran.

"Okay, looking this way and smiling," the photographer orders. A couple of flashes follow. "Can we have a couple of kisses on the cheek?"

My teammates chuckle and are all for it. Me? I have no issues as long as Dewanna's lips are mine.

Lips press against my cheek, and I flex my fingers a little against Dewanna's skin. It's a struggle to ignore my quickening pulse. I wish I could turn my head and capture the familiar lips. Lipstick or not, I can't wait for a taste.

"Perfect. Thanks, guys. We'll have these up on the website." The photographer steps away, and our group parts.

I turn to Dewanna, whose attention is already on me. "Thanks. I hope you're able to relax soon," I offer, more than aware Kieran's at my side.

Dewanna nods, gaze flicking to Kieran and smiling. "About to finish now." With that, she finger waves and steps away.

There's more than a few smiles and requests for photographs on Dewanna's journey to the door. I look on, checking no one oversteps. Finally, Dewanna's out of sight.

Relaxing immediately is a peculiar sensation, but that's exactly what I experience when I know Logan's okay. That he fulfilled his promise.

With tonight being all ours, I plan to show him just how brilliantly he did.

CHAPTER 18
LOGAN

Knowing just enough about basketball makes enjoying the game easy. What sucks is when an asshole from the opposing team fouls. It's pretty shitty being so invested when I see players who I'm beginning to consider as friends get the wind taken out of their sails.

What's worse is the clear focus on Kieran.

This is his first official game since coming out. Sure, it's Tyron's, too, but I have no idea if Tyron has used magic or something, but our relationship so far has stayed out of any press or gossip columns.

Not that we're keeping our relationship a secret.

The team are wearing rainbow bands on their arms and matching shoelaces. Proud was barely the cusp of my emotions when the Bears first entered the court and I spotted their nod to the LGBTQIA+

community, all showing their absolute support to their two out players.

There's no surprise that Tyron made it happen, because of course he did.

Selfishly, I let this one slide, considering the affiliation, but these past few days, the man hasn't stopped. Last night was the first night we've slept apart in at least three weeks too. Something I insisted on, which Tyron complained super vocally about.

There's no chance I'm going to get in the way of him having a good night's sleep. This first game is important.

"Ouch." I wince, unable to look away as Carolina fouls Kieran again.

"Bastards," Bradley grunts at my side before booing loudly. "It looks like Tyron is preparing to tear limbs from bodies."

Bradley's right. Tyron is pissed. If this were a comic, there'd absolutely be steam coming out of his ears. Plus, those little zigzag movement lines showing his temper is close to boiling.

Kieran's up before I can respond, shaking himself off and saying something to Tyron.

I know it's not going to happen, but I will Tyron to look my way. I want to reassure him somehow. Send him some sort of plea not to lose his shit.

Tyron may have a rep for being the epitome of

cool and distant, unaffected even, but nothing about his expression gels with that image. He looks murderous.

While my mind control doesn't work, he does nod at whatever Kieran is saying. After they carry on with the play, there's no more time to worry. Fast legs, lightning-speed passes, and points happen so quickly, I feel dizzy from watching.

The team is rallying, taking no shit from Carolina. The home crowd feels it, the buzz like electricity as we cheer and chant. The Bears push hard, racking up points while defending their net like it's the holy grail in need of protection.

"I'm out of breath just watching these guys. They're on fire," Bradley says just after another point is scored.

I agree. Not that I'll admit seeing Tyron so focused and passionate is a turn-on. The last thing Bradley needs is more fuel. The moment he saw me wearing a fan jersey sporting Tyron's name and number, he ribbed me mercilessly.

If he only knew that yesterday afternoon, Tyron fucked me while I wore it. My asshole twinges at the memory and the slight burn I still feel.

"Yes, go, Channing!" It was only weird the first time I called him by his last name. Now, with the number of times he gives me a reason to celebrate and support him, I have no hesitation cheering so loud that my voice is going to be screwed by tonight.

With two minutes left on the clock, I don't bother sitting down. Since the whole arena is standing, there's no worry about me blocking anyone's view.

Unless Carolina has some sort of magic wand under their sleeve, there's not a chance they're going to win. Let alone even the score.

The ten-second countdown begins, and I bounce on my feet, already cheering. When the buzzer sounds, the Bears fans go crazy. A few rainbow flags appear, and happiness swells in my chest. Tyron's fueled all this love by organizing the team's official social media pages to encourage love and support and embracing diversity.

"This is incredible," Bradley gushes from my side. His phone's out, and he's snapping photos. No doubt they'll be featured on our social club's pages too.

"Right." I grin while searching the team. It takes a few seconds to finally spot Tyron. "Fuck." He's practically nose-to-nose to number seventeen, one of the assholes who fouled Kieran at least three times.

"Oh shit."

Reacting immediately, I push my way through the line, apologizing along the way. Tyron doesn't do shit like this—get up in people's faces. Even if people deserve it, almost every word or action Tyron makes is thought through. He might say random shit sometimes with people he has a connection with, but never this.

Background checks are a very real thing for his career. Hell, both of our careers, but his is absolutely crazy rigorous. Tyron in a public argument or worse, getting into a fight, is beyond bad.

Not only that, he could be banned from future games. That's a thing, right?

"Sorry," I say as I push past a couple of women, but at least I've reached the steps. I'm only three up from the front, so I make quick work of getting down.

I spot Dean first. Though officially, I shouldn't know that it's him. "Uhm… Bryson," I call out, remembering myself at the last second. While I just want to race onto the court, there's security around. Being tackled isn't on my to-do list.

Thank fuck, Dean spots me immediately and encourages me over, shutting down one of the security personnel.

"Thanks. I need to get to Tyron."

His big bear head nods, and I rush past him, doing a quick walk so as not to draw attention.

At the moment, there aren't cameras flashing, and I don't think either of the coaches have noticed. But it's been less than a minute since I spotted them, and all it takes is another for this to blow up.

I don't even care that I'm possibly being dramatic or stepping over some invisible line.

This is Tyron. That he's behaving out of character worries the shit out of me.

"The fuck did you say?"

Two steps away, I hear Tyron's growled question. Bentley's at his side, I think trying to get him to step away. But whatever number seventeen is saying doesn't seem to be helping.

"Tyron." I don't want to shout, but I need him to hear me. Bentley shoots his gaze at me, and I see him visibly relax. "Tyron," I repeat, reaching his side and placing my hand on the arch of his back. Damp material connects with my fingers.

At the contact, Tyron straightens. While his jaw locks, he angles his head to look at me.

"You ready?"

For two long seconds, he stares at me before he nods. The movement pulls a smile from me, one that's all for him and filled with relief.

"Let's get going."

Surprise jolts me when he takes my hand. Not that he hasn't before. Heck, we're practically always touching. But we're at the edge of the court. Eyes and cameras are everywhere.

If this is what he wants, he can have it. Gladly.

I squeeze his hand and tug him away.

"Fucking f—oomph."

I turn in time to witness number seventeen's *oomph*, surprised and relieved as hell it's one of his teammates in his face, and from the looks of it, he got a smack to his stomach with a basketball too.

Tyron witnesses the moment too. His grip is tight in my hand, but he allows me to tug him away, Bentley at our heels.

"That was Lucas Marshall shutting him the fuck up," Tyron states with no inflection.

"Kenny is a loud-mouthed homophobic shit."

My brows shoot high at the anger in Bentley's tone. Understandable, for sure, but I've never heard Bentley cuss anyone out before. He's absolutely the quietest member in Tyron's shared house, possibly the team.

"He is that." Tyron glances at me. "Did you think I was going to lay him out?"

"Weren't you?"

He shrugs. "Thought about it."

"It looked like you more than thought about it," I say quietly, aware we're getting closer to his coach and the rest of his team.

"He pissed me off."

"I see that."

"He would have deserved it."

I agree totally, but Tyron can't be the one to do that. "I'll wait for you outside," I say as soon as we're close to the main action. I stop and make to pull away, but Tyron's hold stops me. "What?"

"Can I kiss you?"

Nerves punch at the wall of my chest, right along with a fluttering of butterflies. "You want to here? Now?"

"Only if you're okay with it."

There's no saying no to that, right? How can I when he looks so kissable and stares at me like I could so easily be the center of his world?

Taking action, I step into his space and brush my lips against his. It's totally G-rated, considering our surroundings, but it's enough to have Tyron sighing and his shoulders loosening even more.

"I'll be as quick as possible." He finally releases my hand. "You still good to go to the party?"

"Yeah, of course." That he's exhausted is clear, but it's tradition apparently—a party after their first game of the season. No chance I'm messing with that. "We'll stay as long as you want." I don't hide the undercurrent of my words. Sure, I want to get my mouth on his as soon as possible, but I've taken it upon myself to cluck around him.

That means I want him to catch up with sleep.

Finals are coming up, and while he's trying to hide it, the signs of stress are becoming more and more obvious to me.

"Maybe we should just miss it?" His lids lower to half-mast, and I'm tempted to agree, but Sammy appears at Tyron's side, wrapping an arm around him.

"Come on, Casanova. Don't keep Coach waiting. Keep it in your pants for a while longer."

I snort and back away quickly, chuckling when Tyron shrugs him off. "He's right. And you all need to celebrate. You won and were brilliant."

His smile is so big that I swear my knees go weak. "I think it was with the help of your lucky charm."

My brows crinkle. "What lucky charm?" I hope he's not talking about the bj I gave him earlier; not in front of everyone anyway.

From his smirk, I figure he knows where my thoughts have traveled. "Your origami bear."

Heat hits my cheeks. It's something I made him earlier and hid in his training bag.

"I love it, thank you."

I don't have time to respond as Sammy's dragging him away, and I'm sure if I don't get off the court, I'm going to get in trouble. With my heart full of Tyron's sweetness, I practically float back to a grinning Bradley.

I don't even mind so much that there are extra lingering stares. Tyron is worth the attention, and an origami before every game if it makes him so happy.

"CAN'T YOU SLEEP?"

I've lost count of how many nights I've woken up with Tyron not sleeping next to me. Each time my concern becomes more tangible.

With basketball season well and truly started, his time is stretched so thin, our sleeping together seems to be the only closeness we get. But he's awake half the time, studying rather than snuggling.

"I managed a couple of hours, woke, and couldn't get back to sleep. Sorry if I woke you."

He's at my desk, his laptop open. A familiar position.

"You worried about something?" Even though I'm bleary-eyed, I see the strain on his features.

"No." He shakes his head, a yawn ripping out of him, long and loud.

It goes without saying I'm not convinced. "You've got another game tomorrow."

"I'm aware."

"Which means you need energy and sleep."

Standing, he sighs. "I know." He drops down on the bed next to me.

"Maybe you need to lay off the coffee."

Needless to say, that earns me an eye roll.

"I'm serious. Something's going on for you to be struggling to sleep. Insomnia is no joke."

"I don't have insomnia."

"Uh-huh." Total bullshit.

"I don't."

"You don't think waking at all hours of the night, struggling to get back to sleep, and surviving on five or six hours a night isn't insomnia?"

"Five or six hours is fine. Studies—"

"Broken hours, Ty." I cut him off. This isn't the time for him to spout facts that he chooses to cling to for his own benefit while pointedly ignoring other facts. Usually the ones that call bullshit. "You know, for a smart guy, you make me question what's going on in that brain of yours a lot."

He shoves off the bed so abruptly it takes me a moment to catch up.

"What are you doing?" I clamber out of bed, wide-eyed, as he grabs his clothes and starts dressing.

"You're a *smart* guy. I'm sure you can figure it out."

Fuck. What the hell is happening here? "Whoa." I

lift up my hands, more awake than I want to be at this time in the morning. My brain's still foggy, though, and I have no idea why he's pissed. "Are you leaving?"

"Looks that way."

"Hey." I reach his side as he grabs hold of his laptop. "Please don't go. I know you're tired, and whatever I said, I'm sorry, but... just come back to bed and sleep."

There's a tic in his jaw I'm not used to seeing when he's with me.

"Please." I'm confused as hell. His reaction's come completely out of left field. It's so abrupt, I don't even know what to say. He has stopped packing his laptop, though. That's something.

I reach out and wrap my arms around him. Tense muscles give way and relax when finally, thank fuck, he drops his bag and hugs me back.

"You want to talk about it?"

The sound of him swallowing is loud against my ear. "I'm just tired."

"What did I say that pissed you off?" It would be easier not to ask, but Tyron is one of the most self-aware people I know. Even when he's exhausted. And I absolutely don't want to piss him off without meaning to again. I'm not a saint, and there are times he deserves a razzing.

He leans away, his gaze so tired and sad that my heart aches.

"Let's get back in bed. Then you can get it off your chest, yeah?"

Bobbing his head, he strips off his shorts. When he's just in his boxers, I tug him back to bed and cuddle him.

"What's going on?"

"There's this expectation that I have all the answers about everything, just because my brain works the way it does." The dejected tone claws at me and has me hugging him even closer. "I'm twenty-two. I'm only a couple of years out of puberty, for fuck's sake. For the first time in over three years, I've discovered the hottest sex, and love, and that I'm attracted to you, a man. And my dick's hard all the time, and I think this is what normal sixteen-year-old boys deal with all the time, yet I'm not fucking normal, am I? It's like I'm going through some sort of sexual puberty or awakening now. Six years late. So I'm dealing with all this shit with my body and my dick, and my heart, yet I'm still meant to keep up, but do more than that... do better. And I can't fuck up, as in ever, because my brain should know better, but I'm twenty-two, and I—"

He cuts off so abruptly that it takes me a couple of

seconds to realize he's breathing heavily and rubbing against his heart. Fuck, he's in pain.

"What's wrong?"

He shakes his head, though there's no hiding his wince. "I'm fine."

"Tyron." I punch out the word. This isn't the time for him to be a martyr.

"My heart's just beating fast."

Fear clogs in my throat as I press my hand against his chest and two fingers against the pulse in his neck. It's racing.

"Shh…," I say, somewhat pathetically, while I try to swallow how fucking scared I am. "Just take a deep breath for me. *Ty*." The word's sharp, but it needs to be, as he's not paying attention. His gaze snaps to mine. I have to keep it. "Breathe with me, okay? You're fine. You're with me, and you had a lot to get off your chest. That's all this is."

Jesus, I'm talking out of my ass while hoping I'm right.

He nods, and I exaggerate my breaths, encouraging him to follow. When he does, I nod in encouragement.

"You're doing great, but let's keep going, okay?"

He follows my lead, and we keep breathing. We keep eye contact, and I urge his pulse to slow, sending all the positive thoughts I can muster out into the ether.

When he finally settles, his eyes droop. He can barely stay awake.

"Is your chest hurting?" I whisper.

"No, it's okay."

"Do we need to—"

"No. You're right. It was my version of imploding."

I nod, not sure what else to do beyond be here and discuss this with him tomorrow. He has an away game, though, so will be leaving school at ten.

Hell, Tyron got it right about only being twenty-two. We're college kids. And I feel that often… being a kid, despite how much I might pretend otherwise or sometimes have to deal with shit some real fucking adults don't have to deal with.

"You just sleep. I've got you." I press my lips against his brow and rearrange us so his head's against my chest and I have him wrapped in my arms.

There's no chance I'll be sleeping tonight. But at least I'm beginning to understand even better the pressure that Tyron's under.

CHAPTER 19

TYRON

Bleary-eyed, I managed to get through team breakfast, something of a tradition before jumping on the bus to take us to tonight's game. Clearly I was giving impressive "fuck off" vibes, too, since nobody sat next to me on the four-hour journey. It meant I kept my promise to Logan and rested.

Three hours of sleep, and by the time we arrived at our accommodation, I felt more refreshed and a damn sight more embarrassed about my early-hours outburst with Logan.

It's been years since that happened, and I've been doing a lousy job of heeding the warnings.

The atmosphere buzzes in the locker room. Last season we had a close game against the Tigers, so we expect it to be a tough game. We're up for the challenge, though.

I stretch out, eyeing the guys around me. I catch Kieran's eye and he smiles, giving me an up-nod. With the extra sleep on the bus, it's easier to return his smile. I'm confident we'll keep doing our thing and score as many points as needed to create a happy distance between the win and loss.

"Everyone got their bands?" I glance around the room, receiving nods and a few waves of the rainbow bands. When my gaze lands on Monroe, I pause, taking in his shifty look. "You got a problem there, Monroe?"

A deep flush colors his cheeks, and he rubs a hand over his shaved head.

"Five bucks, he forgot it," Sammy hollers.

Leon snorts. "I don't think anyone's taking that bet."

Rather than getting into it or cussing Monroe out, I grab a spare from my bag and throw it over to him. "Don't lose it," I say pointedly.

"I won't."

From the snorts around the room, it's clear I'm not the only one who doesn't believe him. Monroe's a good kid. This is his second year with the Bears. Last year he warmed the bench a fair bit, but Coach seems to be giving him a go at it this season. Maybe. Since we're only on our fourth game, who knows what will happen.

"What time's your flight tomorrow?" Kieran asks. We still have ten minutes before we have to be on the court, so shooting the shit is normal for us.

"Two in the afternoon. My feet are barely going to touch asphalt before Logan and I have to leave for the airport." Up and out by 6:00 a.m. isn't too unusual. At least it means we'll be back by ten, so plenty of time to grab my bag and head to catch our flight.

"How's Logan feeling about meeting your dads?"

"Good, I think."

"You think?"

I shrug. "I asked and he said yes to visiting. We haven't talked much about it." From the look he's giving me, he thinks that's odd, but it's not, right? I've already told him a heap about my parents and my siblings. There are not going to be any surprises. There's nothing I need to warn him about.

Though I did tell Dad my expectation is for us to share a room. That's the only possible weird parent blip that I could foresee, so I made sure to get ahead and deal with it last week rather than embarrass Logan when we're standing on the porch.

"Fair enough. You're not nervous?"

I snort. "No. What about?"

"It's a big deal, meeting the parents."

Not sure I agree with that. Since I've already met

Logan's dad and my only concern was being there for my boyfriend, Logan meeting my dads seems like a breeze. My folks have their quirks for sure and can be personalities, but they love me. "Maybe. You know my dads are cool. Thankfully I don't embarrass easily," I say with a chuckle.

Kieran grins. "True for both."

"Okay, gentlemen," Coach says as he enters the locker room. "Time to get your asses into gear and show the Tigers exactly why we're the champions."

After our usual warm-up routine, I eyeball the opposition, using the moment to get my head firmly in the game. The embarrassing stuff from this morning has to go.

I shove it firmly in a box in my brain, compartmentalizing the crap out of it.

Instead, I focus on Barry, the asshole last year who made our win so close. He's not paying attention to me, which gives me time to see who he's focusing on and consider what his possible plays are.

When on the court, it's easy to ignore everything happening off the court. The cameras and film crews, the spectators, none of them matter during the play.

The only opening I allow is Coach's voice. My senses are tuned in to listen out for him.

Kieran's in position. Already the intensity in his eyes is there. His focus is a thing of beauty. He's a legit powerhouse and well on the way to going pro next year. Supporting him like this, helping him on the way, is a mission I cling to.

I'll work my ass off to make that happen and do what needs to be done to support him.

I may not be the captain, but I'm the eyes and ears of our team.

The start of play has me racing, thinking, moving. Springing into action to get the basketball in my hands, to our guys, and racking up as many points as possible.

The leather connects with my palms, settling just right before I shift and pass to Leon. Kieran frees himself, taking control and all but gliding down the court. Barry's close to intercepting his layup.

Not on my watch.

I'm there, blocking, shifting, there for the pass before I'm able to return it to my captain. The basketball flies through the air, slipping through the net, and the first three points are ours.

We don't break our stride as we keep moving, stealing when we can.

There's barely time for breaths, let alone a word.

We communicate by a look, a positioning of a foot, a spring forward, and the shift of a hand.

Like a well-oiled machine, we keep moving

forward. No stumbles, few blocks, and none of the bullshit from that first game of the opening season.

While this game isn't my life or my dream, I love it.

THE TRIP BACK TO CAMPUS FELT LIGHTER. WITH THE WIN under our belt, we all had something to celebrate. I still slept for shit last night, though.

I'm also struggling to tuck away everything I said to Logan.

Having to leave yesterday for the game gave me a reprieve. Playing last night gave me room to focus on getting the points and being in position.

Even on the drive to the airport, I get a slight break. Not from overthinking but from talking things out with Logan. Sammy's driving us, Bentley in the passenger seat. They're dropping us off before heading to Sammy's parents' house for Thanksgiving.

Sammy's been filling up the conversation in the car, so it's been easy to settle back, my hand in Logan's, and simply enjoy touching him.

That doesn't stop me from saying, "You know, nearly one in five Gen Zedders identify as not straight."

Sure, that statistic could be smashed to smithereens considering the number of people interviewed, but let's keep that quiet for now. It defeats my purpose.

"Is that figure from that global survey a few years back?"

I nod at Logan. "Yeah. So statistically speaking, our team is right on average."

I've got a point, honest. And it's to do with the two boneheads in front. I suspect Sammy is the bigger bonehead of the two, though. And I know I said I'd leave it be, but it's reached the danger zone.

"I like to think we're better than an average team, though," I continue, drawing a snort from Logan. Unsurprisingly, Sammy and Bentley remain quiet.

You know I can push and pick—a bit like someone does an itchy scab. Gross, sure, but so damn satisfying. It's all with the aim of being helpful and, in this instance, cutting through the brewing problem I'm 99.9 percent sure is going to implode by the new year.

Since I had my own implosion in the early hours yesterday, you can trust me on this.

Logan snickers next to me. Do I feel slightly guilty that he has no idea of my mission here? A little, sure, but some thoughts, goals, and suspicions are important to keep to myself.

Ask Leon if you don't believe how annoyingly

helpful and perceptive I can be. If I asked for a review rating, five stars all the way.

But back to Sammy and Bentley.

"Not to say bromance isn't a thing."

Logan has the good grace not to scrunch his brow at my shift in direction or call me out that clearly no one mentioned bromance to begin with. How awesome is it that he's accepted this is who I am! I totally scored in the boyfriend lottery.

Damn straight I'll be telling him later, probably when I'm licking his dick and he's trying not to be loud. I feel a new plan forming.

But bromance…

"Because it is, but let's look at Gale Sutton and Jayden Moore. Ultimate bromance goals right there."

Moore and Sutton play for the Eagles in the League. They've been a power duo for the past few years. Have had the whole BFF thing going. This past summer, right after the first pro player came out—their teammate Ryan Broadwater—they did this whole FU kiss to the media.

It was epic.

Not long after that, news about them being engaged broke. Neither has actually been reported as officially coming out or even labeling their sexuality that I know of. Since I read a heap of articles, I don't think I would have missed it.

But still. They're an engaged couple in the League. Hell, they're even playing for the same team.

So back to my point.

"They were friends, inseparable, and I assume at some point secretly crushing on each other. Had a whole relationship on the down-low too. A hell of a thing to keep that a secret from the media so long, since they're in the spotlight."

I have a point. Seriously I do. And while Logan's curious about me making it from the way he's searching my profile, Sammy's rigid and staring straight ahead.

My next words take a moment to form when I focus on Bentley.

Shit. His stare is hard, but not on me. The way he's staring at the side of Sammy's face is… I want to say fierce, maybe even challenging.

It also feels intensely personal. I glance away, smiling at Logan. Have I pushed too far?

"Were you going somewhere with your bromance and statistics speech?" As Logan asks, his brows tug down a little.

I relax my features, trying to conceal my stumble of conscience. "Don't I always have a point?" I jest.

"No," Sammy scoffs.

I meet his gaze in the rearview mirror. He's staring daggers at me, so I grin, lifting my eyebrows in surprised innocence. Screw it. "Well, in this instance," I continue, "all I'm saying is my own sexuality came as a surprise, and the whole team has been fucking awesome."

"Well, of course we have." Sammy's gaze is back on the road.

"And there's been no 'why didn't you tell me before' bullshit. Just complete acceptance."

Shifting in his seat, Bentley angles a little so I can see more of his face. "Did you surprise yourself as well?"

There's a total fist-pump moment happening inside me. "I figured out I saw sex and attraction differently when I was about fifteen," I start, happy to share this with him and Sammy. They're details of my journey I've only shared with my dads and Logan before. "I put it down to the way my brain worked and didn't think any more about it, honestly."

"Seriously?" Sammy looks at me in the mirror again. "You didn't go into research mode?"

"I didn't feel the need to. That I wasn't interested in anyone, I accepted as being my normal. Told Dad that I didn't want to date anyone, and he was ridiculously happy that I was focusing on studying rather than risking getting a girl knocked up." I snort, thinking about Dad's excitement and acceptance.

"And you've hooked up before with a girl, right?" Bentley asks, color flushing his cheeks.

"I had a female best friend, which developed into more when I was seventeen. First boner for another human being."

Capturing my attention by squeezing my leg, Logan offers me a soft, sweet smile.

"That relationship didn't last, though."

"Then Logan came along, and you were like, what, *swing*?" That it's Bentley asking this question and not Sammy takes me a moment to catch up. It also has me busting a gut.

"Not quite that fast. But I'd noticed him over the years. Paid attention."

"I'm a catch," Logan says, bouncing his brows at me.

"Then that first night back, the first party of the year, we… connected. Had a proper conversation."

Snorting beside me, Logan shakes his head. I grin, recalling his injuries and my instant need to protect and care for him.

"Then the stalking began."

"Hey, now. Stalking can get you arrested. Let's not throw words like that around."

My boyfriend rolls his eyes. "Insistent in his pursuit to get to know me better."

"Yes, that."

"So you didn't know you were interested in men before Logan?" Mission accomplished, right?! You must be thinking it, too, what with all the questions Bentley—yep, the strong and practically silent Bentley—is firing off.

"Remember, attraction works a little differently for me. I can appreciate a face and a body, regardless of gender. They can be interesting or Hollywood beautiful. But that chemistry, that forming a connection, that *friendship*, it meant I was open. I like jacking off to a guy on OnlyFans."

"You… what… you do?" Sammy splutters.

"Hell yes. I'll send you the link."

"That's not what I—"

"That was one of my research projects going way off track. I was looking up security and international relations, and boom, four hours later, I'd watched this guy's whole one-man-and-his-hand backlist, read his blog posts, which I think is a nice touch, and his interactions with his fans. Yeah, I was one of his top fans there for a while."

The airport is up ahead, so it's time to wrap this up.

"Friends that fuck is a thing, and I'm sure it can be fun." Three wide-eyed stares are instantly directed my way. The blinker echoes in the car, and Sammy pulls over. "But it's inevitable that one person is going to get hurt, and likely the friendship's going to be ruined. A bit of self-reflection and honesty could change all that." I open the car door, leaving the quiet of the car. "Pop the trunk."

I hear the soft snick, and a second later, Logan exits the car. I grab our duffel bags and go to the passenger window.

The window lowers. "Thanks for the lift. See you in three days." I grin, examining their expressions.

I just hope to hell they get things sorted out.

As they pull away, Logan's at my side. "What was that all about?" Before I can respond, he says, "Holy shit, you think something's going on with the two of them?"

Shrugging, I turn to him. "I wouldn't like to presume anything."

Disbelief floods his features and has him shaking his head. "I sure as hell hope you know what you're doing. Meddling doesn't always work out great."

I take hold of his hand as we head inside. Let's hope I didn't screw up.

CHAPTER 20
LOGAN

"I don't understand." I hate that my fingers shake. Pointing again and waving my open booking in front of the check-in person, I say, "It's right here."

"I'm sorry, sir. It says here your booking was canceled nine days ago."

"But it can't have been since I didn't cancel it. I haven't received an email either."

This has been the longest five minutes of my life. It's also a conversation that's going nowhere. Hot-cheeked and becoming increasingly pissed off, I'm close to losing my shit.

The worse thing is, I know it's not this woman's fault. That doesn't get me an explanation or on the plane, though.

"Have you checked your credit card statement? Your spam folder?"

The wind is knocked out of me when I absorb her words. I never check my credit card statement, since I don't pay the bill.

"Just give us a few minutes." Tyron leads me away from the counter and the numerous eyes already focused on us. Once we're a distance from the line, Tyron plucks my phone from my hand. I let him do so willingly, my brain already traveling to what I know gut-deep has happened.

"It's my dad. The fucker's canceled it."

I don't even need to find evidence to be sure. Tickets don't just spontaneously cancel.

"Three hundred and twenty-nine spam emails. Seriously, Logan."

Not needing any sort of lecture about how to handle my email, I shoot him a stink eye. "Saying that is helpful, how exactly?"

Luckily for him, he has the good sense to wince. "Sorry, you're right." He holds out my phone. "The ticket was canceled, like she said."

"The fuck did it go to my spam folder for? I received the original confirmation in my inbox."

"Because you have a shit email provider." At my glare, he adds, "Which isn't your fault and totally nonessential information."

I take my phone off Tyron and consider calling

my dad. The urge to have him answer just so I can tell him to fuck off builds. It's a growing need.

Since receiving my inheritance, which is now safe in my bank account, nothing's changed other than a loosening of pressure in my chest. There's been no increased calls home and no shift in my relationship with Mom, despite her doing a decent thing for me. There also hasn't been a conversation yet where I tell my dad about my career plans.

I've not been quite ready to possibly sever our relationship forever.

Now's a whole different story.

"Maybe don't."

"What?"

"I know you want to call your dad, but perhaps wait till you're not as angry."

His words add kindling to my growing frustration. "Why the fuck would I do that?"

"Because I don't want you saying anything you may regret."

Gasoline is thrown into the mix. "Fuck off, Ty. I'm allowed to be livid about this. That asshole deserves hearing what a— *Oomph.*"

Strong arms hold me so tight, the air is squished out of me. "Hey." Warm breath brushes across my cheek. "I'm on your side here. Always."

"Fuck." I sag into his arms, hugging him back. "I know. I'm sorry I told you to fuck off."

A flutter of a laugh dances over my skin. "Sometimes I need you to tell me that, so it's okay." Pulling away, Tyron doesn't release me fully, his hand shifting to hold mine. "How about we just get you a ticket, get our asses on the plane, and we'll focus on having some time with my family?"

How is it that such sweet words can make me so unbelievably happy while sadness rolls through me?

"My dads can't wait to meet you."

Swallowing down my emotions, I nod. "Okay. Sounds good."

The intensity and depth of his concern remain as he searches my face. "I love you."

"Love you." The man sure does know how to make my heart overflow.

"Come on." He leads me straight to the front of the line, ignoring the few complaints as he sidles back to the woman we were just dealing with. "We'd like to book another ticket, please. Same flights."

The check-in operator smiles. "Let me see what we have available." She clicks around, furrows her brow a couple of times, and the longer she takes, the more my gut sinks.

"Is there a problem?" That Tyron asks doesn't bode well.

"Unfortunately, there are no seats available on this flight."

"Are you sure?"

"Positive. It's sold out." She clicks around. "There's availability on the twenty-fourth."

"That's Thanksgiving," I say. My gut's officially falling and scrunched up into a tangle of defeat. All of this because my dad's a fucking narcissist.

"And the only date we currently have available."

Since we're heading back the day after, it's pointless to book. Plus, the whole point is to spend Thanksgiving with his family.

"Thanks for checking." Crushed, I tug Tyron's stiff form away from the desk. We're just holding up the line, stopping everyone else from getting on with their holiday plans. "It's fine," I say, turning toward him. "I'll see you on Friday. It's no big deal."

We both know I'm full of shit. My heart hurts, and disappointment isn't a strong enough word.

"Just go and see your family."

"Fuck that."

"No." The word is loud and so strong, I take us both by surprise. "No," I repeat, lowering my voice. "You promised them, and this is the only chance you'll get to see them. You're going."

When he releases my hand and folds his arms, I prepare for battle, standing my ground.

"This is nonnegotiable, Tyron."

"I'm not going. Not without you."

"Urgh. I'm serious. I'm not going to be the reason you don't see your family." His dads hating me before they even meet me… no thanks. "Two months ago, I wasn't even going."

"Two months ago, I wasn't in love with you."

Damn Tyron's ability to melt my heart.

"Please, Tyron. I need you to go." Emotion clogs my voice. Between my excitement, my worry for Tyron that's still not settled, and my anger at my dad, this is all too much. "*You* need to go. You've been looking forward to seeing your family. I get you the rest of the time. We can have three nights apart without this being a big deal."

Some of his muscles lose tension. He's wavering.

"Please just go. You need a break, and I promise you I'll be fine. If I make a call now, I can catch Sammy before he gets too far. You know how his family invites everyone."

"But I wanted you to meet my family." He drops his arms, and I step into him, wrapping my arms around his back.

"And I can't wait to. It'll happen, but not right now."

"I don't feel good about this. About leaving you."

Neither do I. Hate it, in fact. Not a chance I'll be selfish and ask him to stay.

From his insomnia and overworked brain and body, Tyron needs this break. Even if he can't admit that to himself. Going home and spending time with his family will do him good, and I hope his parents will see the struggle that I do and help him.

"Are you sure?"

"Of course." No.

"You promise to leave me a message and let me know when you get to Sammy's?"

Not trusting my voice, I nod.

When he studies me like this, I'm sure he can see into my soul. Worried he sees the truth of my feelings, I hug him tightly.

"Get through check-in and let me know when you're boarding." Before easing away, my mouth captures his. Our lips brush and tease. I want to kiss him forever. Certainly for longer than we can now. But we're in the middle of the airport, and who knows what type of assholes are around.

Reluctantly, I pull back fully, stepping out of his hold. "I best hurry and make this call. I'll speak to you later." I turn before he can stop me and before he sees the truth of how devastated I am.

Cell in hand, I'm out of the main exit. Chilly air greets me. It's not enough to cool my anger.

Choosing between the emotions battling for dominance, I know which one I'm going to settle on.

I hit Call as I walk away from the moving bodies, finding a secluded spot, and take a long, calming breath. I'm going to need it to get through this call while keeping my cool. There's no legit reason whatsoever Dad will have done this beyond spite. Plain and simple.

I turned down their invite to attend Thanksgiving, which won't have gone down well, but still. My father appears to have dropped to an all-time low with this one.

***

"Jesus." It tastes like something crawled inside my mouth, took a crap, then died. There may as well be glue in my eyes too. Finally, they blink open. Wincing at the brightness in my room, I slam my lids back closed.

But it's too late.

Pain pierces my head, and my stomach turns.

"Fuck." I stagger out of bed, tripping over something dumped on the floor, and collapse in front of the toilet bowl.

It's not pretty.

Retching until my stomach's empty and my

throat's sore, I fall back on my ass. Not even caring that I can't remember when I last cleaned the tile floor.

There's no burying last night. Not even my hangover can erase the spiral of self-pity I embraced after talking to my dad.

Well, talking implies some sort of conversation.

That's not what happened.

Tyron must be losing his shit too. Talk about me being a prize asshole.

It's enough to have me stripping off yesterday's clothes, clambering into the shower, hosing myself off, and brushing my teeth. I only gag a couple of times, so I'll call it a win.

"The fuck is my phone?" My voice seems loud in my empty bedroom. The whole house is actually empty, Bradley having left to visit one of his uncles yesterday. Thankfully before I staggered home from one of the local bars.

With a towel wrapped around my waist, I head back to the bathroom and check my pockets. No phone. Back in my room, I search my bed, under it, and my desk, but I can't find it.

Every movement hurts as I dress. But I'm not kidding about Tyron losing his shit.

Yesterday I was a chickenshit. Plain and simple.

After raging at my dad and him ceremoniously

putting the phone down on me, I waited until I was back in town and Tyron was safely in the air before I texted him, letting him know I'd gone back to my shared house rather than hassling Sammy. That I'd be fine, and for him to make sure he had a great Thanksgiving.

I turned my cell off after that. Who knew I could be such an asshole. But I was hurting. A gut-deep hurt from how low my dad had sunk. On top of that, there'd be no recovering from what I'd said to him. I haven't processed it yet.

Funnily, even drinking my weight in vodka didn't help.

Then there's the longing for Tyron, which makes me feel ridiculous.

What's worse, and something I will not share with anyone else, is I feel abandoned by Tyron leaving. Which is wrong and unfair and so not what happened. And I absolutely will not hold it against him.

Shit, I told him to go.

But with the open wound of my father's betrayal, my emotions will feel what they feel.

Oh, and I'm officially cut off.

Maybe I should have led with that.

When talking to Dad, my anger got the better of me. I didn't hold back, venom fueling my words when I told him my plans for when I leave college, where he can shove his job, and that he'll never control me again. Admittedly, me telling him to go and fuck himself is probably explanation enough for why he told me since I had it all worked out, I could pay my own college fees and living bills.

I didn't even get the satisfaction of rubbing my inheritance in my dad's face. He cut the call before I was able.

And now, like this house, I feel empty.

That doesn't mean I don't need to find my phone and apologize to Tyron for disappearing. Christ knows what his parents think.

No doubt Tyron's already told them how fucked-up my family is. Add in me worrying their son, hell, probably pissing him off, and I'll be lucky if they haven't warned him off me.

I drop my head forward and regret the movement, especially when I see the state of the kitchen.

Pancakes were a great idea at some point early this morning.

There's batter covering the surfaces. It can all be cleaned. The important thing is I turned the stove off. It's a relief I was able to function.

There are a few empty beer bottles and half a bottle of vodka. Just looking at it turns my stomach again. The glasses next to it—

"Oh fuck."

Three glasses.

Nausea threatens again, right along with the memory of who I ended up drinking with last night.

Payton isn't the issue. He's a decent guy who I've been friendly enough with at the club's social gatherings. It's Danny that's the problem.

In my defense, he wasn't being an egotistical dipshit last night. His housemates had headed home for Thanksgiving, something I sympathized with. And Payton, who I'd been drinking with, seemed to be enjoying his company.

Sure, I could have left and carried on drinking by myself, but it was my attempt at self-preservation that had me staying.

That ended up with both of them coming here after the bar kicked us out at closing. My place is the closest, apparently.

I have no idea when they left. Hell, or if they left.

It's silly for me to feel guilty about Danny being here, right? It's not like there was anything dodgy going on. Plus, he and Payton were totally into each other.

So why do I feel like I've done something wrong?

Knowing I can't ignore this, I head to the sitting area. Air whooshes out of me. It's gloriously empty and tidy.

Relieved, I renew my search for my phone.

After ten minutes of searching and my head throbbing, I have to stop.

Painkillers first. Maybe food, if I can handle it.

Perhaps I'll then think better.

The digital oven clock lets me know I'm going to be in deep shit. It's already midday.

It was something close to six this morning before I crawled to bed. That's not a euphemism, by the way. There's no dignified way of admitting that I crawled on my hands and knees up the stairs to bed.

Maybe once I'm feeling more human and have groveled enough that Tyron forgives me, I'll be able to laugh about it. Chuckle about waking up at one point with my head on the top step of the landing. Marvel at how I didn't tumble on down without breaking my neck.

I chug my coffee. Maybe not. Sharing that with Tyron will likely piss him off even more.

Laptop. The thought hits me as I'm cleaning up the batter.

I find it on my desk and power it up. The least I can do is email Tyron while I figure out what I've done with my phone.

I open the browser and direct myself to my email host.

All I can do at this point is apologize and let him know not to worry.

You never know; maybe he's taking all this in stride, and he's figured out I just need a breath. A breath being a gallon of vodka.

A knock on the door has me pausing. It hammers again, and my heart flips in my chest.

I sigh, sure I know who's at the door. It stands to reason Tyron sent Sammy to hunt me down. His parents live just an hour away, so it's not a major journey for him to get to me. And if Tyron's pissed, it means Sammy's going to be a pain in the ass.

All of which has warmth coursing through me. That they care enough to get to me is a hell of a thing.

I reach the door, my hope a tentative thing.

"Fuck, you're okay."

CHAPTER 21
TYRON

I DON'T KNOW WHETHER TO KISS THE SHIT OUT OF HIM or throttle him. Maybe I can do both.

"Tyron." Wide-eyed, Logan looks like shit. He's recently showered, his hair still damp. Coffee clings to his breath, the scent washing over me as I step into his space.

The vibration in my limbs from holding my muscles taut the whole journey makes me tremble. I've been worried sick, driving my parents to distraction too.

Not being able to get in touch with him, especially with everything that happened yesterday, proved to be too much. This man, who's still staring at me like I'm a hallucination, is everything.

Leaving yesterday was a mistake. As soon as I boarded, unease slithered through me. Not that I hadn't been worried when he said goodbye and left the airport.

It's not even about the days apart. Of course I can handle that. Truth is, I'm already mentally preparing for long-distance next year when we've finished college.

Instead, knowing he hurt cut deep. Logan being alone dealing with that is something I couldn't make peace with.

I cup his cheeks, battling with my anger that his phone's off. I'm here because I love him, and he matters. The rest I can grumble about later.

My mouth slants over his. I pour out my worry, my fear, my hurt, and my absolute love for him as I trace the seam of his lips with my tongue and own the kiss. Opening immediately, Logan groans against my mouth, letting me take it all. I drink down his whimper and shift one hand to the back of his head, holding him steady, needing to—

"And that's enough of a welcome. How about coming up for air so you can introduce us?"

Logan freezes, goes stock-still as I pull away. My gaze fixes on his rather than rolling at Pops's interruption.

"My dads are here."

"And his sister, who never needs to see him

making out like that again, thank you very much," Tammy sasses.

"My retinas are damaged. I'm going to need years of counseling, or fifty bucks should help save my innocence," Brody says.

"And my brother and sister."

"Oh shi—fu— I mean, okay, right."

Despite how pissed off I am, my lips twitch at his floundering. If we were by ourselves, I'd already be on my knees.

"Are you planning on keeping us on the doorstep?"

I hold Logan's hand and get him to take a couple of steps back, turning toward the door when I do so. "Pops," I say, "meet Logan." I squeeze Logan's hand. "Pops is the impatient, growly one."

"A family trait?"

I snort and look at Logan, whose cheeks are bright red.

"Uhm… I didn't mean—" he starts, but Dad cuts him off.

"You're absolutely right." Dad steps forward with a stretched hand, and Logan immediately shakes. "Good to meet you, Logan. I'm Jack, Tyron's less grumbly dad. We've heard a lot about you."

"That's the understatement of the year." My sister

smirks and pointedly ignores me, focusing on her phone.

"This here's my husband, Mac."

"Pleased to meet you, sir," Logan says, hand outstretched.

Pops, the asshole, studies his hand a beat. Dad's on the case, though, and prods his side. With a huff, Pops shakes Logan's hand, but I know he won't be doing any bullshit dick measuring. He was the one who taught me there were better ways to prove your worth.

"Detective Channing," Pops says.

"Pops, really? That's so lame." Brody comes to the rescue. He rolls his eyes and takes hold of Logan's hand, shaking it. "I'm sure you've already figured out I'm the handsome brother. But don't worry, you can just call me Brody."

Logan's chuckle is the best sound I've heard in twenty-four hours. It means he's okay. "I can see that."

"Hey." I wrap my arm around Logan's waist. "You don't want to play this game with me." I nip at his ear, earning me a collective groan from my family.

"I'm obviously Tammy, and have been kidnapped and dragged here, but it's good to meet you, especially as it's stopped Tyron from biting everyone's heads off."

Logan tenses in my arms. Tammy's words have brought everything back into focus.

"I'm so sorry." He looks at me. "I can't find my phone. I've been—"

A creak on the staircase has him cutting off. We both whip our gazes over.

"The fuck!"

CHAPTER 22
LOGAN

"Danny?" Shirtless, Danny looks worse than I did this morning. But what the fuck is he doing in my house? And coming from upstairs. "What a—"

Tyron moves. His step fast, his "What the fuck do you…" trailing off as he's in Danny's face, and somehow, Mac's there. Pushed past me. Hand on his son's shoulder, tugging him away.

"I don't—"

Tyron's gaze slams into me. The betrayal on his expression staggering, stealing my breath and punching the air from my lungs, even as I'm shaking my head.

"This isn't—"

"Whoa, I didn't—"

Tyron's "Shut the fuck up" has Danny clamping his mouth shut, but my boyfriend's focus doesn't shift from me. "I've been worrying all night. Dragged my fucking family out here, and you've been what, fu—"

"Tyron, enough." It's his pops. Mac looks at Jack, who shifts, still in the doorway.

"Okay, kids, let's take this outside."

I close my eyes in despair, only imagining what they're making of all this. What they think of me.

"Yeah, closing your eyes isn't going to make this go away." The venom in Tyron's voice has me snapping them open.

I shake my head. "I have no idea what he's doing here. Nothing—"

His snort snaps off my explanation. "So he didn't come here last night?"

I don't catch my wince.

"So yeah, he did."

"Technically, it was this morning."

Fucking hell. "Jesus, not helping, Danny."

Tyron's practically vibrating before me. I know this looks shit, especially on top of everything.

"Nothing happened." It sounds clichéd even to my own ears, but I need him to hear my words. That he's jumped to conclusions is a given. Even understandable. It's likely I'd do the same thing. But fuck. "I swear, Tyron."

"Maybe we should let this..." Mac seems to

struggle to land on the right word. "…gentleman," he settles on, "get his things and leave. Then you can find some privacy to talk this out."

"It's fine." With his hard gaze on mine, Tyron shakes his head. He's looking at me as if he doesn't even know me. "I can leave." I lose his eyes, and I can barely breathe.

Confused, frustrated, and hungover is a combination that makes everything seem pointless. Impossible.

He's too angry. Too sure what he's seeing means I've been unfaithful.

Tyron leaves, the door slamming shut behind him, and I'm left staring at the empty space he left behind. Aware I have two sets of eyes on me, one of them his pops's, I swallow hard.

I want to cry. Go and hide in bed. I can sort this out when my head's not hurting and Tyron's less angry, right?

"Everything okay?"

I jolt at the new voice. Looking disheveled, Payton peers down the staircase, straightening his glasses.

"Payton?"

In my periphery, I see Mac glance between us.

Fuck my life.

"Hey." His cheeks heat, and he waves awkwardly.

"I hope you don't mind us crashing. We took Bradley's room. I've already stripped the sheets." He continues down the stairs, Danny moving too and hitting the entry hall first. When Payton takes in the man at my side, uncertainty crosses his features. "Sorry if we're interrupting."

A humorless laugh tears out of me, and I shake my head. "You couldn't have come out of the room three minutes earlier?" Fuck, I sound like a bitter idiot. "Shit, sorry, Pay. Thanks for stripping the sheets." I'm so tempted to look at Mac, but the chicken in me is strong.

I already feel like a kid who's fucked up, and while I want to point and shout, "See, I didn't do anything. Fix this for me," I won't.

Tyron wasn't wrong a few nights ago when he said being a sort-of adult sucked. Okay, they weren't quite his words, but they're true.

Technically I'm an adult. I can vote, drink, fuck a man, and all that fun stuff. But being a kid hands-down is so much easier. Sure, I navigated bullshit at home, but Tyron's my future. I only sort of want his dad to put his son straight.

Again, I won't.

"Here." Payton passes Danny his shirt, and they do this honest-to-God sweet, coy smile thing.

Fucking Danny, not being an asshole two days in

a row? Maybe this is actually all a dream. A bad one, obviously.

"I hope you have a better day than yesterday," Payton says, graciously ignoring me snapping at him. "Let me know if you do want to come over for Thanksgiving, okay?"

"Yeah, sure. Thanks, Pay." Attempting a smile is futile. Instead, I open the door and watch them leave. The street outside is empty except for the two figures walking away. I have no idea where Tyron and his family are.

Keeping the door open, I hang on, letting the painted wood beneath my fingers ground me. "Do you know where he's gone?" I meet Mac's assessing gaze.

Those intense eyes have me swallowing. They remind me so much of his son's. His irises may be a different shade, their features nothing alike since Tyron is very much Jack's biological son, but Tyron wasn't wrong about him taking after his pops.

He tugs out his phone and puffs out his cheeks. As he fires off a text, he says, "Listen, you may want to give Tyron a little breathing room. I'm not going to lie"—he snaps his gaze back to me—"the kid was beside himself yesterday not being able to get in touch with you. Hell, we're here, aren't we?"

I nod, my lips parting to speak, but he waves me

off, saying, "I can see there's a whole lot that's happened here that Ty stormed away from before seeing. Admittedly, he gets that from me." He smirks, the gesture settling my pulse a little. "That son of mine loves fiercely, just like I do. It's the only thing that apparently gets us both going, so much so, all rational thought goes floating in the breeze."

Somehow, this man who looks so different from his son, but is clearly identical in every other way, pulls a small smile from me.

"He's going to be pissed he let his emotions lead him."

I nod. "He is, but I understand why he thought what he did. Reacted that way. I just hope he doesn't start second-guessing himself. The last thing he needs is more to keep him awake."

The chance of Tyron overthinking this and wondering what it means about his ability to join the FBI and rein himself in is a legit worry.

I shake my head. "He forgets he's human sometim—" The force of the stare aimed my way shuts me up. "What? Is something wrong?" I glance at his phone, worried he's received a text that's caused his gaze to zero in on me.

"Tyron's not sleeping?"

Shit. "Maybe that's something to discuss with Tyron."

Somehow his gaze narrows further. This is hands-down his cop stare, and hell if my bladder doesn't think it's a good idea to go and pee. "I'm asking you, Logan." When I don't answer, he sighs. "Listen, it's admirable you don't want to betray Tyron's confidence. I can see you care for him."

"I love him," I say, surprising the shit out of myself for speaking so plainly.

"As do I. I also know how insomnia can impact him."

Worry slams into me, and right or wrong, I ask, "He's suffered before?"

"Yeah. Hold on." He starts typing again and says to me, "How about you put a pot of coffee on? It's been one heck of a morning."

Guilt is a shit of a thing. Tyron uprooted his whole family because of me. Even more significantly, they came. My heart swells. It feels so full I'm not quite sure what to do with all these emotions zipping through me.

"Yeah, of course," I manage past the thickness in my throat. "The kitchen's this way." Mac follows me and tugs off his jacket as I put a fresh pot on. While it's brewing, I watch as he takes in the space. Thankfully I managed to clear the batter bomb. "Is he okay?"

Bobbing his head, Mac takes a seat. "They've

gone to Tyron's. Jack's gone to pick up lunch. Apparently, Brody's making it his mission to distract his brother."

The ugly head of sadness peeks up. "Tyron talks about you all nonstop. He says Brody's doing well in high school basketball."

A grin changes Mac's stoic expression in an instant. Jesus, with that smile, I don't think Tyron did his pops justice comparing him to Idris.

Before I can delve down the path of a comparable gorgeous man, Mac says, "Yeah, Brody's doing great. He just needs to work out how to make gaming a low priority and shift schoolwork a bit higher." Fondness wraps around every word.

Nothing about Mac screams hard-core pressure. I mean, he wants the best for his kids, but he doesn't seem like the sort of guy to drive Tyron to the point he doesn't feel able to stop or say no. Even that Tyron would have to be the best and ace every single thing he attempts in life.

"What's got you looking like you're trying to work out the Collatz conjecture?"

"Ha." His question catches me off guard. "How have you heard… never mind. Tyron." Mac's already nodding. Warmth for my boyfriend, who makes me feel as though happiness is possible, has me smiling.

"He does have a way about him."

"Was that difficult?" Question fills his eyes, so I clarify, "For Tyron, growing up with his level of intelligence?"

"Is this not something you've talked about?"

"Yes," I answer immediately. "I suppose I'm just curious about how things were from your perspective."

"Well, it was as amazing as it was challenging. Keeping him grounded and ensuring Tyron connected with kids his own age was our goal above everything. We've supported almost every decision he's made."

"Almost?"

That grin appears again. "Ask Tyron about ballet school."

The scent of coffee snags my attention. Seeing it's ready, I pour us both a cup and sit opposite him.

"So, insomnia?" I ask. Don't get me wrong, I'm more than aware I'm trying to keep Tyron's confidence while asking for details about his past.

We're all on the same team here, though, right? Team Tyron.

Hell, I already wear his name and will do so every game and as many days in between as necessary.

From Mac's quirked brow, I kind of figure I'm pushing it a little.

"Tyron can rationalize the merits of wearing a paper bag in the middle of a storm. He'd find accurate statistics to support it if necessary. Sure, he knows full well the damn thing's going to get sodden and fall apart, but when he's got his mind set on something, it can be a struggle to talk him around."

"Five hours a night?"

He bobs his head and picks up his coffee. "You got it. Five hours a night."

This is something I feel less wary of discussing. At least two conversations have been had in front of me when Tyron's defending his sleep schedule. It gives me a little more freedom.

This is all depending on whether Tyron gives me a chance to explain. Based on what Mac's shared, I'm feeling more confident and less miserable, so that's a start.

The coffee's too hot to drink, so I take my time and blow, trying to cool it down. It also gives me time to think. Most of what's going on in my head, my worry for Tyron, especially what he shared the other night, needs to be discussed with the man himself.

From this brief conversation with one of his dads, as well as how Tyron describes them, it's safe to say they love him fiercely. They also want the best for him.

I can't see a reason not to ask about Tyron's inability to say no. "Tyron takes on a lot," I settle on. Talking around the subject is as good a starting point as any. "He seems to be there for everyone."

"Tyron's a good friend. A great son." The pitch of his voice is different when he speaks. A little softer. Maybe even a little sad. "He loves without limits."

This I can attest to.

"And he doesn't give it lightly." Mac doesn't need any emphasis for his point to hit its mark.

And it does immediately.

Maybe I should be worried for my heart and the amount of hammering it's been doing against my chest wall since meeting Tyron. And the way it apparently swells or trips over itself, it's a wonder I'm still standing.

I speak through my thickening throat. "I know. I'm grateful for it. Most of the time I think I'm undeserving of it."

"Well, I don't know about that. I can't imagine my son choosing just anyone to give his heart to. I think we should give him some credit."

"You think that, even though he's hurting? Because of me?"

Just asking this question is alien. It also sends a shot of pain into my gut.

This here is the sort of conversation I only

dreamed of having with my own father. This sort of frank and open and honest discussion. One where there's respect and wisdom shared.

Mac is exactly the sort of dad Tyron deserves. My boyfriend having a happy childhood and experiencing such unconditional love even helps ease some of my own sting.

"Sometimes love hurts. It needs to on occasion. It helps to put what's on the line in sharp focus. Makes it clear just what we're fighting for. Neither of you in this situation has done anything wrong. You're both hurting, but for different reasons."

"He told you about what my dad did?"

Mac nods, his jaw clenching. There's no anger in his eyes, though. "I was fifteen when my dad kicked me out of home."

"Jesus. I'm sorry." I shake my head. "I can't imagine what that must have been like." Heat touches my cheeks. "And here I am, a grown man complaining about my dad canceling a ticket that I paid for on his credit card."

Reality is a bitter and embarrassing pill sometimes.

"It's not a competition, trying to figure out who has the worst hand. Who has the shittiest parents. Hell, ask Brody. When he's been grounded and we confiscate his cell, he'd swear on his Xbox that we're the worst parents in the world. That kid can paint a pretty picture of fiery hell." He chuckles. "I told you because I understand disappointment and hurt. Know what it's like to be let down by the people you should be able to trust most in the world. It's not fair, what your parents have done, and you have every right to be pissed and upset and apparently drink so much vodka that it's still seeping from your pores."

I side-eye the half-empty bottle of vodka that's still on the countertop. "My dad ended the call yesterday telling me he wouldn't be paying for next semester's tuition fees," I share.

"Fucking asshole."

I'm so surprised I bark out a laugh. "Yeah, he is."

"What did you tell him?"

"Everything except the inheritance. I didn't get the chance."

"I'm proud of you."

My heart hammers in my chest. He doesn't even know me, yet he's saying words I've always longed to hear from my own parents. "What, that I told him he's a controlling asshole and there wasn't a chance in hell I'd ever work for him?"

He shoots me a smile of understanding, no doubt seeing through my attempts to make light of a conversation with my dad that wrecked me.

"Tyron mentioned your grandfather and the inheritance, so you'll be okay?"

I nod. "Financially, yeah."

His lips tighten, once more understanding morphing on his features. "Emotionally, too, eventually." His cell pings, and he checks it while I drain my coffee.

There's still some thudding pain behind my eyes, but it's not as bad. Exhaustion bites at my heels, though.

"Are you going to be okay if I head to Ty's?" From his tone alone, I believe that if I said no, he'd have no hesitation in staying.

But I am, or at least will be okay. "I'm good. Thanks for sticking around." It's helped more than I expected.

He makes quick work of his coffee cup, rinsing it out and putting it on the drainer. When we reach the front door, he pauses. "What do you want me to tell Tyron about your unexpected guests?"

I don't miss his lips twitching, which I suppose is a good sign since he doesn't seem too worried. The problem is, it's not his heart on the line.

"If you can tell him I'll stop by at five and can convince him to answer the door, that would be great. Thanks."

With a smile, he pats my shoulder. "Good answer, Logan. And if he doesn't, I will. I'll see you soon."

"Thanks, sir."

"I think after all that, we can stick with Mac."

"Not Detective?"

He snorts. "It's easy to see why Tyron likes you. I think you're going to fit right in."

I watch him leave, wondering if he realizes how much those words mean and how I desperately want them to be true.

CHAPTER 23

TYRON

I'VE BEEN LOCKED IN MY ROOM FOR THE PAST HOUR.

Brody's tried his hardest to get me out of my head, but I had to escape before I lost my shit. The last thing I want to do is lash out at him.

It's not his fault that I packed up my whole family, practically forced them on the plane—which is a miracle in itself we were able to get tickets—and all for nothing.

The need to rationalize and make up possible reasons and excuses for Danny to be coming down-stairs half-naked nudges me. But I don't have it in me.

I can't. Not when a flash of anger rises as soon as I visualize him. Swiftly followed by a stab to my heart.

As soon as I'd switched flight mode off yesterday

and read Logan's message, I knew what he'd done—called his dad and hidden away.

No way could I let that stand. It's Thanksgiving. And this year, with Logan now in my life, I have so much to be thankful for.

Fuck. *Had.*

It took a couple of hours of unanswered calls, frantic conversations with my dads, and their increasingly worried glances for Dad to finally say that he'd book tickets for us all. This was after they argued with me about heading back by myself.

The bonus is they get to see Lexi.

And now here we are, and the unimaginable has happened.

It just doesn't make sense.

I slam my pillow over my face. "Fuck."

I hate this. Hate the drama. Hate that I can't think straight. Hate that a man I loathe—not only because he's an asshole but because of the shit he said to Dean last year—was at my boyfriend's house.

Just the memory of him hitting on Logan at the car wash has my pulse spiking again.

"Fuck." I throw the pillow across the room, not even wincing when it knocks something off my desk. I don't care enough to check what it is.

"Tyron." Dad taps on my door. Not waiting for

me to answer, he opens it, and the asshole in me wishes I'd locked it. "I've got you some lunch."

"I'm not hungry." Looks like I'm adding petulance to my growing list of traits. "Thanks," I add, attempting to at least rein myself in.

"Your pops will be here in a couple of minutes."

He's been with Logan all this time. I don't need to ask to know that. After I bolted and we made our way back here, Pops wasn't with us.

"Right." I sit up. "I'm sorry I dragged you all the way out here."

Dad shakes his head and perches on the end of my bed. "Nothing to be sorry for. We also get to see Lexi, so it's all worked out."

A humorless snort escapes me. "Not sure anything's worked out, other than me being a fool."

"Perhaps wait to have a conversation with Logan."

"Why the hell would I do that?"

"Don't you love him?"

"No" is on the tip of my tongue, but I can't lie. Instead, I keep my mouth shut. Petulance for the win.

When I keep quiet, Dad sighs and pats my leg. "Why don't you try to sleep, at least?"

"I'm not—" Dad quirking his brow shuts me up. "Fine, I'm tired, but there's no way I can sleep."

"Just try, okay. I know you didn't sleep well last

night." Narrowing his gaze at me, Dad studies me a little more closely. "How's sleep in general? And don't say fine."

It's amazingly hard not to sulk when being called out by one of my dads. Reverting to a teenager is so easy. I wonder if it'll be the same when I'm in my forties. I expect so, based on how Dad sometimes behaves when he's with Grandma Jo and Granddad Tom.

"I've been getting enough." I will not wince. The slightest twitch and Dad will be all over me.

Apparently, I don't do a good enough job. He furrows his brows. "Please tell me you're having more than five hours a night."

"I'm having more than five hours a night." When I don't have an early start at the gym. Or when I haven't missed out on studying.

"Tyron."

"Jesus, okay. Five to seven on average."

"But…"

"But mainly five."

Dad closes his eyes, and I expect he's counting to ten. Maybe even twenty if the depth of the lines between his brows is a measure. "Why do you feel you can't afford to get more sleep?"

"Life's busy."

"And why is that?"

Because I take on so much and don't like to let anyone down. I swallow hard, center myself, and square my shoulders. "I've been getting ahead in preparation for the season. Now we're in it, I'm not studying as much."

"Are you behind in any of your subjects?"

I snort. "Of course not."

"So, is dating a problem? Do you think you have enough time for it?"

"Of course it's not a problem," I say immediately. The thought of not being with Logan, not spending time with him, makes my heart ache. It's the thought of what I saw earlier that's a sucker punch, though. "I might not have to worry about that." Jesus, I'm miserable.

"Only might? So that means you're going to hear him out?"

I fall backward on my bed with a groan. "Adulting sucks."

Laughter fills the room as Dad pats my leg again. "It can suck, but it can also be amazing. And I think having a conversation with Logan is the smart move. But you not getting enough sleep is an issue."

I refuse to look at him, the cowardly custard that I am. He's thinking about when I was seventeen, and there was this whole intervention drama that took place. In fairness, I needed it. I'd been falling apart at the seams, not sleeping, and obsessively stud—

"Fucking hell." Those warning signs I thought of earlier smack me in the face.

Concern morphs Dad's features. "What have you just realized?"

I shake my head. "I just need time to process, okay? The past twenty-four hours have been a shitshow."

Understanding me completely, Dad squeezes my leg and stands. Rather than backing away, he steps closer and presses a kiss on my forehead. "I love you, Tyron." Angling away, he waits until we make eye contact. "You're loved unconditionally, and I'm sure your friends and Logan feel that way too. You don't have to be more. Whatever you give or do will always be good enough."

Unable to speak, I nod. My emotions can't take any more.

"Please try to sleep."

"Yeah, okay," I croak before Dad leaves me alone.

There's a phrase that legit pisses me off. One that makes me see red and gets my hackles up. It starts with "For a genius, you…" Because, however that sentence ends, it's always an insult. Or, in this case, a smack in the face when I'm saying it to myself.

For a genius, you missed all the signs of spiraling out of control spectacularly. Idiot.

Sleep. It's the only thing that's going to help right this second.

Getting under my covers, I close my eyes. If Logan was here, I'd fall asleep super fast. My stomach cramps. Sleep, and then I'll see if I have the energy to talk to him. Even if I don't like the outcome, at least I'll know either way.

"Why do you hate me?" I grapple with my brother, stopping the asshole from bouncing on my bed. I get him in a headlock and ruffle his hair.

"You stink. Get off me." Brody attempts to shove at me, and I won't admit it, but this kid is getting strong.

Releasing him, I pry my lids open and shoot him a "you're dead, asshole" look.

"Blame Pops. He said I had to wake you and make sure you showered as you're gross. He's right."

I sigh in defeat. "What time is it?"

The little shit shrugs. "Dunno."

"I find that hard to believe since your phone is wired to your hand."

"Uh-huh. It's how I can do this so easily." He flips

me off and jolts out of the way as I take a swipe at him. "You're getting slow in your old age, loser."

A step later, he's out of my room, and I realize I'm grinning.

I take stock.

Even though I woke abruptly, I feel fresher. There's a hollowness in my chest that remains, a pang of hurt. I exhale and push myself out of bed. My stomach growls. I haven't eaten anything all day. I couldn't face breakfast or the crappy snack food on the flight.

I sniff and grimace. Brody was right. I need to shower.

It doesn't take long to wash up and dress. I don't take my time with either, too hungry to drag my feet. Focus on my empty stomach helps me to hide away the ache when I think about Logan. So that's something.

As I collect my phone off my desk, my gaze catches the supplements I've been taking. Dad's right. I can't keep going like this. Logan's also been right on the mark about my insomnia. And these tablets are amplifying everything.

I throw them in the bin. Guarana may be herbal, and the supplements have helped me stay awake, giving me the energy needed to keep on top of every-thing, but the side effects are clear.

The thought of my racing heart when I lost it and overshared a few nights ago has me shaking my head. I should probably bitch slap myself too.

There are only so many times I can bury my head.

Go figure, right? Me. The master of facts. Choosing to ignore them when it suits.

Yep. For a genius….

Finding a better way to deal is going to have to be my priority. But first, food. Then I need to figure out what the hell I'm supposed to do about Logan.

Downstairs, there are voices. It reminds me my family is staying here, and I haven't checked the guys' rooms or changed the bedding. I already messaged them when I was at the airport, asking about taking over the house, their rooms included.

As predicted, no one had any issues. Well, Sammy did mention something about his sex drawer, but hell no am I going anywhere near it. The other three rooms will do just fine.

There's a meatball sub on the table. "Please tell me that's mine." I'm practically salivating.

"It is. Thought you'd be hungry."

"Thanks, Dad." He squeezes my shoulder as soon as I sit down. "Where's Tammy?"

"She's taken over Bentley's room." Dad sits opposite me, next to Pops. "We've already changed all the sheets."

I wince as I chew. Once I've swallowed, I say, "Sorry. I should have done that."

"No, you shouldn't have," Dad says pointedly. "It wasn't on you to prepare rooms for any of us."

I sigh and place my food on the plate. "I hear you." Reluctance tinges my words.

"Do you, though?" Pops asks.

It's hard knowing I can't juggle or achieve everything I want to. I like helping out. I get a buzz from stepping up and fixing problems or potential issues. Sure, I can get carried away and dive into things without considering the ramifications, but people also expect it from me.

Ask Ty. Ty'll do it. Ty, what's this mean? Ty will look out for his sister, his friend, his cousin's boyfriend's sister's dog. Okay, that last one never happened. It's not just other people putting it on my shoulders, though.

The responsibility rests on me.

I seek it out. Try to make life easier for people.

I don't like to see people I care for struggling or hurting, so if I can help take away a burden or stop it from happening, you're damn straight I'll do anything in my power to be there.

But something's got to give.

Before Logan, juggling was easier. Heck, I could

have set everything on fire and blindfolded myself, and I would have juggled away.

The pull of Logan, my desire to spend time with him, to make him happy and love him, it's made that balance pretty hellish.

I'm already singed. I can smell the burning with every late hour I'm still awake studying when I should be sleeping, wrapped in Logan's arms.

"Have you heard from him?" My stomach twists as I look at Pops.

"We had a good chat earlier."

"Did he seem okay? His dad…"

Pops's expression softens. "He's upset. I don't know what was said beyond his parents refusing to pay next semester's fees."

"Fucking assholes." Logan's father is a nasty piece of work. Realizing what I said, I scan the room, relieved Brody's not here. Don't get me wrong, that kid swears more than I do, but I wouldn't get away with cussing like that in front of him when my parents are here.

"He'll be okay. How are you?"

I pick at my food, no longer feeling hungry at the thought of Logan's pain. "Gutted," I admit. "Angry. Pissed. Confused."

Pops nods. "And willing to be calm enough to listen to what Logan has to say?"

There's no escaping Pops's stare. From that look alone, I'm sure he's got an opinion on the matter. He may even know something.

"Have you thought about what happened?" When I scrunch my brows, he clarifies, "Earlier, at Logan's house."

There's no amusement in my laugh. "How can I not have thought about it?"

"I mean, have you thought about Logan's reaction?"

"His reaction?" My brain ticks over, joining the dots that I know he's highlighting. Battling with the flash of anger threatening to take over when I visualize a shirtless Danny walking down the stairs, I redirect my memory to Logan.

His wide eyes before his brows furrowed. Confusion. His incomplete question. Me cutting him off.

There was guilt there, though. It's what stopped me from staying. That and having to get away before I did something I'd regret.

Pops's gaze doesn't waver. "There it is." He smiles. "And just in time too."

"Time, how?"

There's a knock on the door. My muscles lock up, my pulse quickening as I know exactly who's here.

"You want to talk here or in your room?"

"Seriously, Pops. There's interfering, and then there's plain old annoying meddling."

"Uh-huh. So, here or…?"

"I'll take him to my room. There's less chance of anyone snooping that way." I stand, shooting him a hard look. But with the way he's grinning at me, you'd think he can see my sweaty palms and hear the pounding of my heart.

I want to see Logan so badly my gut twists in anticipation. But what if something did happen? He has the power to pulverize my heart. Releasing a shaky breath, I open the door, revealing the man who makes me catch my breath every single time I see him.

His smile is tentative. Relief flushes his face when he sees me.

Before I can invite him in, he says, "There are nineteen types of smiles, but you have twenty. It's my favorite. You get this small dimple. And it's not wide and doesn't show teeth, but it's perfect and private, and every time you show it, I know it's because you're thinking about me. I don't ever want to lose the chance of seeing that smile again. Not ever." Pink infuses his cheeks, his eyes bright and a little teary, his voice emphatic.

"I would never intentionally do anything to hurt you. I absolutely would never betray you."

My heart's in my throat, reeling from the sweetness of his words. The passion and determination in his voice.

"I have twenty smiles?"

It's all I can manage, my heart clinging to those words.

"You have." His Adam's apple bobs, the swallow loud in the surprisingly quiet house. Either everyone is holding their breaths so they can listen, or they've shut themselves away to give me privacy.

My money's on the former.

"Let's go upstairs and talk." And fuck if his smile isn't radiant. Hope peers back at me, and the lightest twitch of my own mirrored feeling bubbles to life.

We head to my room in silence. Locking the door behind us, I side-eye him. Logan's staring at the mess next to my desk. It's different and out of place. My room is usually barracks tidy.

"Your bear." When he bends down, a stab of understanding slams into me.

"Fuck. Is it torn?"

He's smoothing out the paper, making quick work of checking it over. He lifts his head, our gazes locking. "No. It's okay. Just a little out of shape, but not broken."

There's no missing the meaning behind his words.

"That's a relief." I nod and take it from him. I place it back on my desk, next to the other three he's made me.

One for every game I've played so far.

Swallowing hard, I pick up the pillow that had caused the damage. "So, you called your dad." I sit at the head of my bed, needing some distance between us.

The hope in his eyes dims a little, but he shrugs and smiles. "I couldn't not. It was due, and at least now it's done."

"I'm sorry." God, I want to hold him close and kiss away his sadness. My fingers itch to touch him.

I sit on my hands.

"Me too." Tugging his bottom lip between his teeth, he gnaws while taking me in. He then sits on my desk chair, turning it to face me. "Will you let me explain what you saw? Hear me out?"

My "yes" comes easier than I expect.

From what he said downstairs, I already believe that nothing happened. But Danny was still there, and seeing him hurt like hell.

"I went straight to Keegan's Bar. It's where the rideshare dropped me. Dad said some shit that I will tell you about, but I don't have it in me right now. Is that okay?"

"Of course it is." I just wish I'd been there when

he made the call. That I wasn't stings. I feel like I let him down.

His smile is tentative but still makes my heart flip. "So yeah, the bar. I drank vodka. A lot of it. I was already a few glasses in when I saw Payton."

"Payton Anderson?"

"Yeah."

I don't have any classes with Payton, but I met him at one of the social events Logan asked me to attend with him. Logan seemed to like him and said he was a decent guy, so I semi-willingly engaged in a couple of conversations with him.

"We chatted, I offloaded, sobbed in my vodka about how much I missed you." His laugh is light and self-deprecating. I bottle it up anyway. "At some point, Danny turned up." I keep my expression in check, not wanting to put him off with my sneer. "He seemed different, not as cocky. He joined us. Apparently, his Thanksgiving plans fell through last minute. He and Payton got along, as in really well."

An inkling of where this story's going begins to form.

"They hooked up?"

"Yeah. At my place, apparently. I didn't even know they stayed over."

"How couldn't you know?"

He shifts uncomfortably, his cheeks pinking. "It

was probably close to six before I went to bed. I had to crawl up the stairs. May even have passed out on the way."

"You did what?" I clamp my mouth shut, back molars grinding to stop from shouting at him about how fucking irresponsible and dangerous that was.

"I know, I know. But I'm fine, and it all worked out."

"Really? This, what's happened, is 'all worked out?'"

A tired sigh passes his lips. My gaze is drawn to the sound and the movement.

"Them staying over, even though I didn't realize, meant they weren't driving or getting home while being drunk. It means they were welcome to stay. Sure, in hindsight, I wouldn't have drunk so much. I would have also preferred to go to bed at a decent hour and not have them both in my house. But Ty, I was sad and missing you and so fucking angry with my dad."

"You could have called me."

"I know, but you already do so much and worry about everyone, and you needed time to chill out and spend with your family. And now you're here, and I'm so happy you're here, and grateful. But I feel so guilty that you're not relaxing and having an amazing break."

I listen to his words and let them wash over me.

"I know Danny can be an asshole."

I snort. "And some."

His lips twitch. "But yesterday he wasn't. He was lonely and needed familiar faces."

"You're too nice."

He shrugs. "Maybe. But he's probably an asshole for a reason. It doesn't excuse his behavior in the past—"

"Or how he shit-stirred earlier."

"Well, no, but we can't always be as awesome as you now, can we?"

That he's teasing loosens some of my anger. I hear what he's saying, and assholes tend not to get that way by choice. Not that I'm interested in sharing a single word with Danny.

"I'm sorry you thought the worst of me."

Okay, that makes me feel like shit. I don't miss the tightness around his eyes either.

"I'm sorry, and you don't need to apologize." I rub a hand over my face. "I couldn't see past Danny. He was all up in your space, even when we were together, and with you being upset…." I taper off, as nothing I can say really justifies that I immediately expected the worst. "I do trust you."

I'm grateful he doesn't call me out.

"I do. I promise. I know my behavior sort of

contradicts that. I reacted badly. I was tired and stressed. I wasn't thinking straight. I was so worried when I couldn't get in touch with you. I kept going through scenarios. Everyone coming with me was really down to Dad. I was at the point of begging Pops to call any contacts he had, using his badge to get a cop to come and check your house."

"Oh shit, really?"

I nod. "Perhaps not my finest moment. I panicked."

"I'm sorry I cut you off yesterday and made myself uncontactable. It was a shitty thing to do. Forgive me?"

I'm off the bed and tugging him from the chair, wrapping him in my arms. "Will you forgive me?"

"Yes."

It's all I need to hear for relief to flood through me. It washes away the anger, the frustration, and the dread that has been lodged in my gut since yesterday.

I crush my mouth to his, lips slanting, tongues stroking as we kiss and touch and breathe each other in.

"I've missed you so bad." My words are spoken against his mouth, his cheek, his throat as I trail kisses along his skin.

"Missed you too," he says breathily. "When you walked away, I thought my heart ha—"

I cut off his words, not bearing to hear them.

I kiss him until we're breathless. I kiss him as we tear at each other's clothes. I kiss him until I groan against him, hands on each other's cocks, cum painted over us, and I'm whispering his name.

"I love you." We're dirty in the best way and breathing heavily.

Logan peers up from where he's resting his head on my chest. "I love you back. Do you think we can just stay here all night?"

From the crease between his brows, I figure he's remembered we're not alone.

"Our cum's going to get really crusty and is going to be a bitch to clean in the morning."

"I could always lick us clean." He bounces his brows, and I chuckle, aware my cock twitches, liking that idea. "I can't believe your whole family came here. I feel bad I ruined your holidays."

My loud snort has his eyes widening. "You serious? Don't feel bad about that. Pops was itching for a reason to get here to check out this guy of Lexi's. You offered the perfect excuse."

"Are you just saying that to make me feel better?"

"Nope. It was this, or Pops was about to run a background check. Dad had to talk him out of it."

Grinning widely, Logan draws circles on my chest. "Okay, that makes me feel a little better. Your pops is pretty awesome."

"He has his moments." My chest pumps up anyway, happy that whatever Pops and Logan talked about earlier has resulted in this.

"I suppose that means I need to get to know your dad better too."

"I'd like that." I seriously would.

My dads, my siblings are important. I love them and want Logan to feel the same way.

"You think we can sneak to the shower without anyone seeing us?"

I'm laughing before he's even finished. "You forget I grew up in a house of six. Everyone knows everything everyone is up to, and there's no entering a room without somebody asking you a gazillion questions."

"In that case, you go first and intercept."

I angle up and dot a kiss to his waiting lips. "Now that I can do."

CHAPTER 24

LOGAN

SATED AND TIRED BUT UNWILLING TO CLOSE MY EYES just yet, I snuggle up to Tyron. "You know, I didn't think it was possible."

"What's that?" My head's on his chest, and he's stroking my hair. This here is my favorite part of Thanksgiving so far.

Don't get me wrong, hanging out with his parents and all three of his siblings, plus Christian—Lexi and Christian showed up for a couple of hours to say hello—has been my best holiday ever.

There's been no stuffiness—other than our over-full bellies—and I have no shame in admitting I basked in the whole crazy chaos of the Channings. I absorbed it right up, and without fail, every time Tyron gave me that favorite smile I have a soft spot for, I was so unbelievably grateful he shared his family with me.

"Two whole days, and you haven't opened your laptop or a textbook once." While I'm teasing him, I glance up and catch his gaze. "I'm proud of you."

He studies me, those beautiful grays roaming my face. "I was thinking maybe we should find time and go over my planner."

"You mean it?"

"Yeah. I need balance."

I bob my head so fast, he chuckles.

To someone who doesn't know Tyron and understand his mind or his dedication—or how attached he is to his planner—they wouldn't get what a big deal this is. But this is huge. It probably means I can bring up something else that's been concerning me.

"What's on your mind?"

"I think looking at your planner is amazing. Thanks for asking me."

"Is there a but?"

"Not necessarily, more of a what about all the things you're asked to do or task yourself with that aren't on your planner?"

He frowns.

"If one of your friends needs help, for example, and it's something you can support them with, and it's not going to put you under pressure, that's one thing."

The way he searches my gaze, I expect he knows what I'm getting at. After a beat, he says, "You're thinking more of me doing deep dives and offering to do something—"

"When someone else could absolutely do it." Scooting up the bed, I settle my head on the pillow. He turns so we're face-to-face. "You're amazing and so generous and kind. I love you for it and don't want you to change."

"But… you want me to let others pick up the slack?"

"For a start. I would love you to know that everything isn't down to you. You don't have to do everything. No one is going to be upset if you spread the to-do list around a little, you know?"

He purses his lips and sighs. "I hear what you're saying, and I suppose it would help with that whole balance thing I'm aiming for." A wink follows, and I grin, relieved he's not upset and seems on board.

"It's okay to say no to people too. Even your friends."

Quirking his brow, Tyron trails his finger down my arm. "And my boyfriend?"

I smirk at his teasing tone. "Even me. Sometimes. But let's not make a habit of it."

He rolls me over, landing on top of me. A grunt escapes me at his solid, delicious body covering mine.

Before this can move to where I'm not sure I have the energy to keep up—for real, I'm stuffed with turkey, have already been stuffed with Tyron tonight, and I don't know if I have more in me—I say, "It's okay to make yourself a priority."

At my more serious tone, his smile drops. He lifts, taking his weight off me and holding himself up on his palms. He's listening intently, studying me in that beautiful, intense way he does.

"It's not selfish to put your own needs first every now and then. Especially over the next few months when you're under pressure and have so many commitments."

I don't like the worry that appears in his gaze. "Are you concerned I'm not going to have time for you?"

"No." I shake my head. "That's not it at all. I'm in this with you and am prepared to grab whatever time I can with you and do what I can to make your life easier. I'll also be selfish too and sneak you away so I can have you all to myself."

"If that's your version of selfish, I support this side of you." His smile's back and warmth fills me. It touches my toes and spreads to every cell, loving that I get to keep Tyron.

"There it is."

He tilts his head.

"My favorite smile."

Before I can offer him more sweet words, he takes my breath, capturing my mouth in a kiss. It's warm and gentle, not what I was expecting from the look in his gaze before he kissed me. This is even more perfect.

Our lips have only really just started exploring when he's pulling away. "Sleep."

While my cock gives a little twitch, somewhat valiantly, it's kind of on board with the need to crash too. "Sleep sounds good."

Climbing off me, Tyron settles on his side. He reaches over and switches off the bedside light, resting his palm on my chest.

In the darkness, warm and comfortable with Tyron's skin against mine, I relax. My breathing slows, as does my pulse.

"You know, when you came back to be with me, bringing your whole family, you've made it possible to see what a future with you could be like," I whisper after a few moments. "I don't know what's going to happen with my mom and dad."

Tyron presses a kiss to my head in silent support.

"I just… I love you so much, and I keep thinking about Grandpa and something he said to me just before he died, about family."

"What did he say?"

"Well, it was a quote he shared. Not his own words. It was 'blood does not family make. Those are relatives. Family are those with whom you share your good, bad, and ugly, and still love one another in the end. Those are the ones you select.' We knew he didn't have long left, and I think he was preparing me."

"I think your grandpa was a smart man. And if today hasn't confirmed it, you're absolutely my family." His lips find mine, just a tender peck, and it's all I need before I drift off to sleep, sure that Tyron and I are going to last the distance. A fact I'll happily prove every single day.

EPILOGUE
TYRON

"Are you about ready?"

"No. This freakin' tie." Frustrated, I undo the annoying strip of fabric yet again. After nine years of wearing the thing, I can do this in my sleep. Not today apparently.

Before I cuss, Logan's in my space and nudging me away from the mirror I've been glaring at for the past fifteen minutes. Immediately, I settle. I always do when Logan works his calming magic on me. While it still takes a lot to ruffle me, sometimes—especially in the middle of a hard case—I struggle to switch off and let go. It's just one of the reasons why I love him so damn much.

"You want to release that breath and I'll get this fixed up?" His smile is soft, patient as he waits for me to follow his instructions.

With a bob of my head, I exhale, using the opportunity to grip his hips and soak in his warmth.

Smiling as he redoes my tie, he searches my gaze rather than focusing on the movement of his fingers. "You're going to do great." Losing his eyes as he works the knot, positioning it just right, I absorb the moment with just the two of us. Today's going to be full-on, and while it's going to be a good day, I'm already counting down the hours until I can get Logan back into this expensive hotel room. "There, all done and looking unbelievably handsome."

Once he makes eye contact again, I tug him close, not willing to let him escape. "Thank you," I mumble, before pressing my mouth against his. Logan's mouth opens just a little as he kisses me back, the caress slow and sweet. All too soon he pulls away, his gaze lit with amusement and heat.

"Hold those for later. No chance we can be late."

He's right, but it doesn't make releasing his hips any easier. We've been apart for three weeks while I've been on assignment, and rather than head home to Boston, where we settled four years ago, we flew into DC last night on different flights—him from home and me from Cincinnati. At least tomorrow, we'll be heading home together.

"Fine." I'm totally not sulking, but with the smirk Logan shoots my way, he's silently calling out my petulance. "Dad texted me, saying he'll meet us in the foyer."

"Let's get a move on, then." Swiping his keys and phone, Logan reaches out for me. I go willingly, sliding my palm into his with practiced ease. He squeezes lightly and shoots me a playful wink. "I'm so proud of you."

Despite him telling me these words so many times I've lost count, heat hits my cheeks and emotion swells my chest. Hearing those words and the affection that comes with them will never get old. "Thanks." I roam his gaze, drinking him in. "I'm proud of you too." And I seriously am.

After finishing college, he did exactly what he set out to do. Joined FinCEN, which of course he's rocking. Last year he was promoted for the second time. Our professional successes made our relocation four years back possible—our request for the same district. It also means there are times we're able to actually work together, and hell if I don't love those assignments.

"I know you are, thank you," he says as he tugs me to the door. We head to the elevator. "But I'm not the man here getting special recognition." The elevator pings and we step into the empty cart. "You're the Special Agent receiving a U.S. Department of Justice

Award." Logan pushes his arm into mine, urging me to look at him. Immediately I do, my breath catching at the love directed at me. "So fucking proud."

There's not enough time to speak, let alone slam him against the wall and take his mouth like I want to. The annoying bell of the lift sounds, which means I have no choice but to do what I do best. Contain myself and be the ultimate professional.

Traits I still surprise myself with being the master of for sure. At home with Logan, or when we're visiting my family, are the only times I can let my filter go. Sure, I have friends in the Bureau who I shoot the shit with, but Logan is my person; there's no one who understands me more.

"There's your dads."

I follow Logan's gaze and see Pops and Dad, standing tall, focus already on us. Dad's practically vibrating with emotion, and he looks pretty handsome in a deep-navy suit. Pops is wearing his police dress uniform, his hand in Dad's, while he's beaming at me.

"Jesus," I mumble.

"Shh…" Logan nudges me as we make our way over. "They're just crazy proud, is all. We all are."

I know that, feel it, and am so unbelievably grateful for them all. What I'm not sure of is if I can handle the emotion of the day. Feeling wired messes with me.

"You know, two presidents kept alligators at the White House."

While my heart flips, my pulse slows. Angling toward Logan, I tilt my lips, gratitude surging to life. "There's a sculptured head of Darth Vader with the gargoyles on the northwest tower of Washington National Cathedral."

A broad, self-satisfied smile forms on Logan's lips, and he squeezes my hand once more before we're in front of my parents and being tugged into hugs.

It takes a few moments to get our small party moving and into the car organized for us, but we're on the way. Dad's already on a videocall with my siblings, and I'm giving them a goofy wave while they wish me good luck and tell me they're proud of me. We're all going to go to our folks' this Thanks-giving—a commitment we've all made. It's rare these days when we find the time to get together.

As I say goodbye, I peer at Logan, who's tucking his phone away. He sees me looking and smiles. "Group chat. The guys saying congrats again."

I bob my head, not needing clarification about who "the guys" are. Since leaving college, my team and I have remained tight. Despite being pulled across the country and in so many different professions, we still have each other's backs. Next year, we're going to a ten-year reunion. All our old household, and their respective partners, plus a few others on the team who we're still close with.

"I'll message them later," I say, having put my phone on silent before we left the hotel.

Logan bobs his head. "Mom also messaged, saying she was thinking of us and to have a nice time."

Genuinely surprised, I raise my brows.

Logan chuckles. "Yeah, that was my reaction too." His smile's sadder than I like it.

Not liking it one bit, I squeeze his thigh. "It was good of her to remember. That's something."

He purses his lips before releasing a calming breath. This here, Logan shaking things off, unfortunately is a common occurrence when it's to do with his parents. While I wish I could take his upset and frustration away, it's one thing I can't control. All I can do is keep being here for him.

That his mom has made an effort *is* a good thing. While I don't trust the woman not to hurt the man I love again, I trust Logan to know what he's doing and how to handle the tentative relationship he's rekindled with his mom. His dad, thankfully, is well out the picture. Funnily enough, we didn't get an invite to his wedding seven years ago—or the two others since—after Logan's mom kicked his dad to the curb.

"We're here," Pops says, drawing my attention to out the window.

I swallow hard and flex my neck, hearing Logan's soft chuckle beside me. I glance his way with an arched brow.

Brightness has returned to his eyes, happiness in their depths. "After everything you went through to earn this reward, *this* is what you're nervous about?"

His teasing hits the mark, and I relax my shoulders. The kidnapping case had made the headlines last year. The whole investigation had rattled everyone involved. Nailing the two perpetrators and knowing they were sentenced to a combined 800 years in prison went a long way to help me sleep at night.

The main reason, though, for nightmares to largely stay away is undoubtedly because of the man at my side. "I love you." I lean in and press my forehead against his, soaking in his steady breathing and his familiar scent.

Even close, I see the slight curve of his lips. I wait for his words. Wait for them to wash over me in a comforting hug, and even as my dads are exiting the car, I refuse to move until I hear them.

"I love you more. Fact." And just like always, he punctuates his "fact" with a tender kiss. It's all I need to smile, pull my shoulders back, and step out of the car with renewed purpose.

Having Logan's love is everything, and him at my side, me at his, is where I'll always want us to be.

THANK YOU SO MUCH FOR READING TY AND LOGAN'S story. I loved writing it so much. Next up is Leon's story in REGULAR, SMEGULAR! For updates, be sure to subscribe to my NEWSLETTER or join my FACEBOOK GROUP.

If you're enjoying my college basketball players, be sure to check out my pro basketball players in my ZONE DEFENSE SERIES—a whole series dedicated to the players falling for their best friends!

ACKNOWLEDGMENTS

As always, a huge shout out to my readers. It's always a struggle writing a new series, but you guys have been such fabulous cheerleaders, and after falling for Kieran, immediately demanded Ty's story. I hope I delivered.

My editing team are incredible—Liv, Keeley, and Donna. They push and prod and polish to perfection. It means any lasting errors are my own—ones I'll happily fix.

Thanks, CC, for keeping me organized. And Claire at BookSmith Design. You, lady, are beyond incredible. Thank you for knowing me so well.

A final thanks to my beautiful family. My folks, hubs, and kiddo keep me grounded and sane. I love you all.

ABOUT THE AUTHOR

I live and breathe all things book related. Usually with at least three books being read and two WiPs being written at the same time, life is merrily hectic. I tend to do nothing by halves, so I happily seek the craziness and busyness life offers.

Living on my small property in Queensland with my human family as well as my animal family of cows, chooks, sheep, and dogs, I really do appreciate the beauty of the world around me and am a believer that love truly is love.

To check for updates head to my website:
https://beccaseymour.com
Join my mailing list:
https://landing.mailerlite.com/webforms/landing/r9f0i4
Plus, join my Facebook group:
www.facebook.com/groups/rommancewithbeccalouisa/